YOU'VE GOT TAIL

Peculiar Mysteries Book One

RENEE GEORGE

Barkside of the Moon Press

You've Got Tail

Peculiar Mysteries Book 1

Copyright © Renee George 2015

All rights reserved. No part of this publication may be reproduced, stored in a retrieval system, or transmitted, in any form or by any means, without the prior permission in writing of the copyright holder.

Any trademarks, service marks, product names or named features are assumed to be the property of their respective owners, and are used only for reference. There is no implied endorsement from the author of this work.

This is a work of fiction. All characters and storylines in this book are inspired only by the author's imagination. The characters are based solely in fiction and are in no relation inspired by anyone bearing the same name or names. Any similarities to real persons, situations, or incidents is purely coincidental.

Cover Art: Renee George

Second Print Edition 07 Sept 2018

ISBN-13: 978-1-947177-23-9

ISBN-10: 1-947177-23-0

Welcome to Peculiar

Sunny Haddock, an animal-loving vegetarian psychic, is stoked to leave California behind to start a new life in the Ozark town of Peculiar with her best friend Chavvah Trimmel. She ups the moving date when Chav goes missing and high tails it to the small town.

When the gorgeous Babel Trimmel, Chav's younger brother, (along with the sheriff, the mayor, and some other nice folk) suggests Sunny haul her U-haul and butt back out of town, she's undeterred. Her psychic abilities might be out-of-whack, and blood makes her faint, but she's not a quitter. Besides, she's not about to go anywhere until she finds out what happened to Chavvah.

But Sunny has more to deal with than unfriendly townsfolk...like disturbing killer visions and the dog-like animal no one else sees that seems to be stalking her every move. To make matters worse, she is finding Babel to be more irresistible than crack on a donut.

Kidnapping, murder, romance, and a town full of people hiding the truth will keep Sunny Haddock busy as she tries to unravel the strange happenings in Peculiar, Missouri.

NOTE FROM AUTHOR ABOUT PECULIAR, MISSOURI

Dear Reader,

I'm a proud Missourian. I've lived here most my life. While I know there is an actual Peculiar, Missouri (my son played several basketball tournaments at Raymore-Peculiar High School), my own version of Peculiar and all things related to the town in my book are strictly works of fiction. I've taken artistic license with the town and its true geographical location to suit my story's purposes. But do note, the Peculiar Mysteries are an homage to my love of my home state.

Hugs,
Renee

Acknowledgements

This book has been a long time coming, and it's seen many, many incarnations over the years as I developed the storyline. Thank all that is good and chocolate that I had BFFs holding my hands, reading, helping me to revise and revise during the process. So in that light, I must praise Robbin Clubb, Michele Bardsley, and Dakota Cassidy for always having my back and believing in my ability to tell an entertaining story. This book might have seen the light of day without you all, but it wouldn't be nearly as good.

I have to thank my husband as well, for putting up with all my many moods (think *Three Faces of Eve*, people! I don't think another living soul could put up with my crazy for twenty-five years like he has.

I need to also mention Renee's Rebels and The Wolf Pack for continuing to support my work, read it, promote it, and love it. You all are ROCK STARS!

Finally, I need to thank my editor Kelli Collins, who painstakingly combed through this manuscript and called me out when I needed it. You, lady, are awesome.

*For my sister, Robbin
Thank you for everything.*

CHAPTER ONE

SOME PEOPLE JUMP into the deep end of the pool feet first, some head first, but I've always been a traditional belly-flopper. Splashy, messy, and usually painful. Which still didn't explain why I was sitting on the floor of a closed diner, nursing my bruised butt, not to mention my pride, and staring woefully at a naked unconscious man in the middle of Peculiar, Missouri.

My parents are crazy from way back. Maybe that's where I get it from. Seriously, who names a child Ambrosia Sunshine? Two hippies, that's who. They told me when I was old enough to resent the flower child name that they'd thought it was cool at the time, but I personally believe it was the result of one too many 'shrooms. As it is, I've been forced to sit through many painful renditions of "You Are My Sunshine." If I had a dead body for every time I was teased, well, let's just say I'd get an express pass to the electric chair. Although, if

I got a sympathetic judge, he'd probably consider my lifetime served.

Maybe my parents' experimentation with drugs is what had made me psychic. (No, I didn't say psychotic. I said *psychic*.) On the other hand, it could also explain why I'm so bad at it.

My ability allows me glimpses, more like screenshots, of the past, present, and future. But, clearly, the visions have *not* been helpful over the years. And the side effects, sheesh. Most of the time I feel a little dizzy when they hit, but every once in a while it's as if someone has taken a sledgehammer to the inside of my skull. Usually, I can feel one coming on; otherwise driving might be an issue. If only they made medic-alert bracelets for my type of ailment. It certainly hasn't been a gift.

That's why my friendship with Chavvah Trimmel is so important. We'd met at the community college in San Diego. She thought my name was weird and awesome all rolled up into a spring roll. After finding out her family's propensity for strange biblical names, I thought it was a bit of the pot calling the kettle rusty. Chavvah, or Chav, as she likes to be called, was my first best friend. And when she's around me, my psychic mojo kicks up twenty notches. It's as if I can tap into some kind of mystic hotline whenever she's near.

As a matter of fact, the last time I'd gotten a clear vision had been in my dining room back in California. Chav, who'd been renting my spare bedroom at the time, had just turned down the heat on the spaghetti sauce, and I was setting the table. We were having an "I finally dumped the cheating bastard" celebratory dinner. Did I mention I'm a bad psychic? So I hadn't a clue what I was walking in on when I caught my boyfriend of three years having sex with the skank waitress from the coffee shop. On my couch, no less. Jerk. I took his spare key and kicked his ass (and the couch) to the curb.

At dinner that night, when the vision hit me, I'd hit the ground, along with some clattering dishes. I saw a present moment of Chav's parents huddled together, debating whether to call her about her missing brother. Talk about being the bearer of bad news. I didn't blame her for not believing me at first, or the stunned look she gave me when she called her parents, and it turned out to be true. Her brother Judah had dropped off the map.

Chav flew back to Missouri the next day. After a year of searching for him, the local police had pretty much given up on Judah, but by that time, Chav had forgotten about the ocean and fallen in love with the little town of Peculiar. Hell, from her letters and phone calls, I'd kind of fallen in love with the place as well. She'd bought a restaurant in the rural town, a real fixer-upper, for the two of us to run. A fifty-fifty partner split.

I wasn't supposed to leave California for another two weeks, and Chav had said she needed to talk to me "in person" before I made the trip, but the text I'd gotten from her had sent me packing in a hurry.

All it said was: *Sunny. I need u.*

After that, every call I'd made to Chav went straight to voice mail. Without any real plan, I jumped into my gas-guzzling Toyota 4X4, which I had purchased explicitly for the move. One thousand six hundred and sixty-two point four miles later, as I drove over a swinging bridge (the only way in and out, I soon discovered) into the quaint little town, my whole body heaved a sigh of relief. I felt strangely wonderful. It was as if someone unzipped my off-the-rack skin and fitted me with a tailored Sunny suit.

The town looked very similar to Mayberry from *The Andy Griffith Show*. Dirt streets, old fashioned shops and houses, white picket fences, and lots of Chevy and Ford pickup trucks. I was a little nervous when my GPS said, "You have arrived," right outside a two-story yellow building on the corner of Third Street and Main.

My heart pounded as I stood outside our restaurant for the first time. I'd always expected some kind of fanfare. Chav waiting to usher me into our future. She'd even named the restaurant for me. Sunny's Outlook. I'd blame allergies for my eyes watering at that moment, but I knew it was a mixture of happiness and sadness all rolled into one big bundle. This was *our* place. Mine and Chav's. And she'd done it up spectacularly.

I smiled at the brightly colored lettering. All the letters except the big O in Outlook were blue. The O was not an O at all, but a bright orange sun. If it was possible to feel both warm and cold at the same time, I accomplished it.

Where was Chav? I knew in my bones something was wrong, but the nearly two years we'd spent apart had dulled my psychic ability toward her, so once again I had become inept with crazy flashes that didn't amount to much of anything.

I jiggled the door handle. It wasn't locked, so being

the smart, city-savvy girl I am, I decided to let myself in. After all, I owned half the joint, so I wasn't trespassing.

Darkness enclosed the front room except a few areas illuminated by sunlight filtering into the two small windows near the ceiling. They were surrounded by open wooden shutters. Where were the large storefront windows? This place was more dive bar than restaurant. Strange decor choice but my concern for Chav kept me from imagining a complete makeover. I couldn't find a light switch around the door. I should have just gone back out to the truck for a flashlight, but I thought I saw a panel on the wall across the room, and frankly, it was sheer laziness that moved me forward.

I managed to maneuver around the counter, open the panel, and flicked several of the switches at once. The lights came on and when I stepped back to admire my new home lit up—it didn't look half bad; hardwood floors, cute little tables with black-and-white gingham cloth, and a couple of booths with the same checkered design on the benches.

And that's when it happened. My heel caught on something large, and I fell ass-backward to the ground. It didn't take more than a nanosecond to see that I'd tripped over a naked man passed out cold on the floor.

After a startled yelp, heart palpitations, and worry that he'd wake up at any moment and kill me, I reached over and touched him. Just his arm, mind you. He didn't move, but his skin felt warm, and his chest raised and lowered, so I didn't bother to check for a pulse.

Instead, I found myself staring...for several minutes.

(Come on. He was naked and lying on his back. Who wouldn't stare?) Dark-brown hair populated his broad chest and led to a happy trail that, well, if the circumstances had been different would have made me very happy indeed. He had thickly muscled thighs and arms, and his face, except for the scruffy five o'clock shadow, looked as if it had been chiseled by Michelangelo. Imagine a better-looking Wolverine (Hugh Jackman's version), but much younger and with a burly lumberjack vibe, and coarse, medium-length walnut-brown hair.

I chewed my lower lip as I took my time pondering the situation—in other words, I wasn't ready to stop staring at the naked man. His hair was near the same hue of brown as my own, when it wasn't dyed blonde, which was never. And mine was shorter with a better haircut. I sighed with regret. I already missed my stylist Serg.

Taking a deep breath, I counted backward from ten to pull myself out of the hormonal frenzy going on in my head. The man was hotter than a habanero, but I wasn't looking for a date. I smelled a pungent sweet scent I hadn't noticed before, but frankly I was surprised any of my senses still worked. It was whiskey. Some kind of blended version, if I had to guess.

Great. Just perfect. Burly Hugh looked more and more like a drunk who had crawled into the diner to sleep off a bender.

I found an empty spray bottle by the sink and filled it with water. Positioning myself on the opposite side of the checkout counter (just in case I needed to make a run for it), I leaned over the top and proceeded to spritz the unconscious man. The mist must have been too fine, because other than the rise and fall of his chest, he still didn't move.

Crawling farther up onto the counter, I stretched my arms over the other side, hovering just inches from his face. I pumped the trigger hard three or four times, then screamed and dropped the bottle when his hand shot up and grabbed my wrist. The Neanderthal yanked me completely over the top and onto his naked self. He growled— honest to goodness, I wouldn't lie about such a thing. He growled. The noise started in his chest. I know, because I could feel it in mine, which was now crushed against him.

Why hadn't I just left and called the police? It would have been the easy thing to do—the smart thing. His arms were squeezed tight around me, and I became acutely aware of his Mr. Happy pressing against the skin of my thigh.

His eyelids cracked a peep, then he narrowed his gaze. "Who are you?"

"I..." I should be the one asking the damn questions, but the only ones coming to mind were completely inappropriate. Like, where did he work out? How good looking were his parents to create such a fine specimen of man? And did he have a girlfriend?

There was a moment, a very weak moment on my part, where I began to lower my face to his, our lips only centimeters apart.

What the hell am I doing? Where was my head? He could be a serial killer, a rapist, or someone *really* bad, like an Amway salesman. I turned my head away from his.

"Could you let me up, please?"

He squeezed me tighter. "Are you going to answer me?"

Finally, I gulped and squeaked out, "Sunny Haddock."

His left eyebrow rose. "Sunny Haddock?"

"Uh, that would be me. Yes." I'd been in town less than an hour and I was already famous. Well, my name was on the side of the building. "And you would be?"

"Babel Trimmel."

"Chav's baby brother?" I'd heard stories about him, but I'd imagined him to be terminally twelve. The age he'd been when Chav had left Missouri for the West Coast.

"Chavvie made a big mistake. She shouldn't have asked you out here."

Talk about judging someone before you get the know them. Barely through introductions and he already wanted me out. I've made a bad first impression before, but what the fuck? What didn't he like about me? Although maybe it wasn't about like. Because, by the rise of his hoo-ha against my leg, I could swear he liked me a little.

An unfamiliar flutter twittered in my stomach. It'd been awhile since I'd been so physically attracted to anyone. Babel's nostrils flared with a slight huff. His brows narrowed. His eyes dark with purpose. I felt like Little Red Riding Hood, and Babel filled the role of the

Big Bad Wolf intent on eating my goody basket. Oh, if only.

Pull yourself together, Sunny. But it was really hard, along with his arms, his chest, his abs, his...

Holding me tighter, his arms locked around me. He stroked my back with his firm hands. I trembled, fighting back a deep moan. "Please let me up, Babel," I said again.

He froze for a second then relaxed. He unlocked his arms from around me and smiled. "Call me Babe. Everybody does."

To say I scrambled off his body would be a bit of an overstatement. The trembling had left my arms and knees weak, but I managed, albeit slowly. "I don't know you well enough to call you Babe. Sorry." I couldn't keep my eyes off his semi-erect package.

"Could you put some clothes on? I'm feeling a little..."

He propped up on an elbow like a *Playgirl* centerfold and grinned. "Overdressed?"

What an egomaniac! "No. Sheesh." Okay, so maybe I felt a tad overdressed, even in my pink spaghetti-strap shirt dress with black short-shorts and sandals. It was hot in Missouri. Sticky hot. And besides, I'd put in more hours than I care to count at the gym to counterbalance my donut habit, so I deserved to wear those shorts. My exercise routine wasn't all about the donuts. Over two years of no sex, since the dickhead had cheated, and while I'm no sex maniac, that's a long time for someone who had been getting it on the reg.

The "no sex" could also explain why I had such a

visceral reaction to this guy. No doubt the man was a hunka-hunka. "Could you quit posing on the floor?" I wagged my finger toward his poker. "And for the love of daisies, put some clothes on before that thing puts out someone's eye."

He had the courtesy to look the tiniest bit embarrassed. "Nothing personal. It's a purely physical reaction."

"I'm sure you say that to all the girls."

"Sorry, I just meant, well, I'm a guy. You brush against the junk, it goes stiff."

"And here I thought I was special." This line of conversation bordered on hurting my feelings. I know I'm not a beauty queen, but neither am I Medusa. "You can shut up now."

Color rose to his cheeks—those nice fuzzy, chiseled, scruffy, manly cheeks, so perfectly bookending his Roman nose and gorgeous bow lips. And damn it to hell, his teeth were friggin' perfect! He pulled himself up by grabbing the counter, and holy schmoly, the man was tall. If I had to guess, he bordered on 6'5". I'm pretty sure I hated him for being so beautifully handsome.

"I only meant to say…"

I almost offered to buy him a shovel, but he managed to dig his own hole quite deep without any help from me. "I've got it already, jeesh. Not interested, physical reaction, yadda, yadda, yadda. No need to explain yourself further. Besides, I'm not looking for a boyfriend, so doesn't matter. And even if I were, it certainly wouldn't be my best friend's baby brother.

We cool?" I didn't wait for him to answer. I waved him off. "Great. Excellent. Awesome even. Now, put on some damn clothes." Why-oh-why was I attracted to crazy?

"Perhaps you could find me a diaper."

Guess he didn't like the "baby" comment. Oh well. Sucks to be him.

He covered himself with his hands. Thank God. However, it didn't stop me from checking out the rest of his body. *Ay Chihuahua!* Damn, it kind of sucked to be me.

I knew from Chay that Babel had moved back to Kansas City where their parents lived after he'd taken a year off from university to look for their brother Judah. What was he still doing here? A horrible thought entered my head. "If you're here, does that mean..."

His face suddenly sobered. "I don't know. Mom and Dad haven't been able to get ahold of her for the last couple of days, so they sent me down to check in. I got here yesterday."

"She texted me a couple of days ago. I haven't been able to get ahold of her since then." I lifted a hand to comfort him, but his nakedness stopped me from breaching the distance. "Babel, we're going to find her." Even if I had to turn over every stump and stone in this backward-ass town.

"Call me Babe. Everyone does."

That was the second time he'd said that to me, but I couldn't call him Babe. No way, no how. Too intimate. Especially since I'd seen him in his birthday suit. "I don't think so."

He chuckled, low and sexy, and everything went right south of my navel. "Sunny,

I'm afraid I've, err...lost my clothes."

"You've got to be kidding me." How did a person go about losing all their damn clothes? "Fine. I'll stay on one side of the counter. You stay on the other. Kapeesh?"

"I understand," he said with a practiced tolerance. It made me wonder who he'd gotten so much practice with.

He hadn't turned around yet, and part of me felt really sad about it. I'm sure he had a killer butt to go with his killer bod. I was all about the teeth and ass. But there were no complaints about the whole frontal part of him either, so...

"Good. Should I call someone for you? Or do you want to call someone? A girlfriend? Anyone who can bring you some clothes?" Subtle. Not.

"The phone's not working here even if I could call someone."

I noticed he'd didn't say "no girlfriend." Much to my annoyance, I cared. And why was the phone turned off? "Don't you have a cell phone that works?"

He moved his hands, indicating his lack of attire. "No pockets."

In the immortal words of Homer Simpson, *Doh*! I snuck another quick glance at his dangly bits, even more annoyed with myself for not having better self-control. "Great. Fantastic." I waved my hand again and purposefully looked away. I had a cell phone out in my truck, and was just about to tell him I'd go get it when he stepped out from behind the counter, still full Monty. "Hey! Keep the mammoth covered."

"Flattering. But there's nothing prehistoric about it." He cocked his eyebrow and smirked.

Bastard.

"Look here, darling." He pointed to his "junk" as he'd called it and said, "This here is what you call a penis. It's connected to the bladder and the bladder is full. Turn your head if you want, sweetheart, but I'm heading to the john."

"Lovely. And I'm not your darling." I made a show of rolling my eyes and turning away. "I'm going to get my cell phone. I expect you to be standing behind the counter by the time I get back." Now, for the sake of posterity—well, at least for the sake of his posterior—I glanced back as he headed left to the bathroom. Of course, it was sort of hard to notice his ass when I saw the— "Blood..." I whispered.

A pain pierced my temple as my knees buckled beneath me. I dropped to the ground. My peripheral vision narrowed to black. The pounding of blood racing through my arteries swelled loudly in my ears. It was out of beat with my heart.

The thumping of blood stopped, my eyesight began to clear, and I was in Babel's arms.

"Sunny? You okay?" I heard his voice as a muffled echo.

No, I wanted to tell him. I wasn't okay. But my mouth didn't work. A vision came over me. I could sense it like death come knocking. Then I was no longer in Babel's arms. I was a ghost. A spectator.

13

I was...in a shabby apartment with furniture dating back to the seventies? Had I traveled to the past? It wasn't unheard of for me, but it couldn't be relevant for something in my life now since I hadn't been born until 1974. Or could it? Great. The powers that be were giving me a psychic reading on my lost Crissy doll. Useless.

I heard a muffled cry, maybe a scream from beyond the front door. I passed through and down the stairs. The noise grew louder. Animalistic growls and snarls. Fear tightened in my stomach.

It's not real, I reminded myself several times as the feral sounds made me shiver.

I couldn't see any creature, but it certainly sounded like someone was getting voraciously attacked. And the room—it looked familiar. Two windows high up on the far wall spilled moonlight across the floor to...the counter? This was the restaurant. The noise continued, loud, animalistic, with grunting, groaning, and a masculine "ah!" Oh. Oh no.

If I'd really been there, I'd have run, but the vision took me closer to the scene of the crime. On the floor, behind the counter, a gorgeous woman with long dark hair, golden eyes, and even in the bad lighting, a body I'd give my right tit for, straddled the very naked and very sexy Babel Trimmel. I wanted to gouge out my eyes. Where was a hot poker salesman when you needed him?

The woman threw her head back and laughed. "You were fantastic, Babe. As always."

He smiled, his eyes rolling back a little. Coming up on his elbows, he leaned his left shoulder forward and looked behind. "You've got to do something about those fingernails."

"Just marking my territory."

Holy smack, the blood on the floor had happened during sexcapades? Yikes.

"I'm not your territory, Sheila."

The woman, Sheila apparently, picked up a bottle of Canadian Mist from the floor beside them, took a swig, then dumped some of the amber liquid down his large chest. No wonder the place reeked.

Babel shook his head and gave her thigh a light slap. "It's time to go, Sheila. I've got to get the place cleaned up."

"You sure you don't want to move here?" She licked his nipple. "I've sure missed you."

He sighed. The sigh sounded like it'd been one that he'd perfected over and over for this very argument. "It's not this town or you. I've got a real life out there.*" He said "there" as though he was talking about an alien planet. "I'm going to find my sister, then get back to it."*

"And what if you don't find her?" Sheila asked. "You never found Judah."

Babel's eyes narrowed. "Not an option," he said. Then added, "I'm finding her, and after, getting the heck out of this town. It's brought nothing but bad luck for my family."

"Sorry," she said, as if she wasn't sorry, an evil smile playing on her lips. Okay, so maybe more mischievous than evil, but it was my vision, I could use whatever adjectives I liked. "But you know that answer pisses me off."

Before he could blink, she whacked him super hard across the temple with the bottle of blended whiskey, and Babel was out like a light.

"Bastard," Sheila muttered. Which I understood, because it had been my sentiment exactly.

She dressed quickly, gathered up Babel's clothes, and walked into the kitchen area. It was small, but nice. I hadn't had a chance to see it yet, so it was like my very own psychic tour. She opened the walk-in freezer and chucked the jeans, boots, socks, and T-shirt inside. No underwear. Huh. I'd file that nugget away for later.

My vision stopped with her slamming the front door, and suddenly I was back, looking up from the floor at the towering and still very naked Babel. "Ow." My head, my back, my butt—everything hurt. "Did you drop me?"

"What the hell just happened?" He looked a little freaked out.

I got up on my elbows and rubbed the back of my skull. "Did you drop me on the ground?"

"You were having a seizure or something. I laid you on the floor." He was definitely freaked. "If I'd had a phone I'd have called for the doc, but..."

"I'm fine now. You can stop worrying." I moved my feet off the chair Babel had propped them up on.

"I'm sorry. I'm squeamish about blood."

Which wasn't a complete lie. Blood tended to bring on funky psychic mojo that left me drained and pained. Although, I'll admit, these visions had been much stronger than normal. Apparently, Chavvah wasn't the only Trimmel who put my psychic stuff on speed dial.

"I'm getting that about you." At least he sounded less upset.

I closed my eyes. "Why would you let someone do that to your back?"

"That's a story for another day, darlin'."

Yeah, I knew the story. Not so sure I wanted the

blow-by-blow again. I felt his arms go under me, and I opened my eyes, staring into the deep abyss of his gorgeous, Midwest baby blues.

I let him carry me upstairs to the apartment. I'm not a small woman, but he held me like I weighed next to nothing, which made me think kindlier of him. With my arms around his shoulders, I could smell an unidentifiable musk and spice to his skin. He sat me down on a couch—the scent went from musky to musty—then he went into another room. I heard water running in the sink. More than a whisper of regret passed through me. I barely knew the man and I missed being in his arms. I looked around the living room.

This was the seventies place where my vision had started. The retro decorum lacked any sophistication that could've made the space sensational. I knew this had been where Judah lived when he'd been in town. He'd rented this building before his disappearance, and Chav had used our stake to purchase it during her search for him. His vanishing had hit her hard.

Chav told me once that she hadn't agreed with her oldest brother's "lifestyle choice," but she respected him. I'd asked her what she meant, but she had shaken her head, unwilling to elaborate. I knew it wasn't as simple as him being gay or anything like that, because Chav, like myself, was socially liberal. Hell, she'd have started her own PFLAG (Parents, Families, and Friends of Lesbians and Gays) in Peculiar if that had been the case. No. There was something else she hadn't approved of.

I heard the water turn off in the kitchen. Babel

returned and proceeded to wipe my face and neck with a cool cloth.

"There now, all better." For a second, he sounded like my father. Which totally squicked me, considering the hard-core fantasies I had about him. He put the washcloth in my hand and patted my shoulder. "I'm going to jump in the shower real quick. I'll be back in a few."

Part of me wanted to watch him walk away strictly for the view, but since that part seemed to have done gone and lost its damn mind, I waited until I heard water running before looking in his direction.

He'd left the bathroom door open. Perv.

I couldn't believe it, less than an hour in a new town and I'd witnessed a *Red Shoe Diary* moment, and the star was lathering up less than ten feet away. I would've been downright disgusted by the whole morning if I hadn't been so preoccupied with thoughts of slippery suds sliding along his perfectly formed pecs. (Now I understand how bad porn gets started. Bow chick-a bow-wow.)

I will not go stare at the naked man. I repeated this mantra in my head over and over as I ran down the stairs to the kitchen.

Grabbing his clothes from the freezer, I contemplated where they'd been and how they got there as I carried them back upstairs. They were cold and held the scent of sweat, but at least he'd have something to put on so he could go away. I placed them on the couch, and dear Lord, it was a really ugly couch. It would be the first piece of furniture to go when Chav and I started fixing the place up. And with that thought, I went downstairs to wait for him.

Fifteen minutes later, the light flickered on in the stairwell. Babel's arms and face glistened with dewy goodness as he walked down the steps. He rubbed a tea towel, barely big enough to dry a fish's butt, against his loose mane of wet hair. His blue T-shirt clung to his chest. Water soaking through the fabric made spots the color of midnight.

He must have felt me staring, because he dropped his arm to his side and looked at me. "Where'd you find my clothes?"

"The freezer." I wrapped my knuckle on the counter. "Guess you can go home now."

"Guess so." He shrugged as he stretched his body to tuck in his shirt. "But we should probably talk."

"I'm in no mood." *For talk.* Damn, he was super-fine.

"Well, you kind of need to get in the mood." He shook his hair out, droplets spraying out around him. It began to feel like a bad (or really good, depending on who you asked) shampoo commercial. "There's been a mistake. My sister should've never invited you out here, Sunny."

"You've said that already, but unfortunately for you, my name's on the property, same as hers, all legal and binding. I'm staying. Period. End of discussion. Besides, I'm not going anywhere until I find Chav."

Babel chewed his lower lip and narrowed his eyes at me. "I don't think you understand the situation."

"Oh, I think I do. You don't like me. Fine. I get that."

"It's a might more complicated than that." He scratched at his five o'clock shadow.

I resisted the temptation to offer him a hand. "Why do you care, anyway? Don't you have a *real* life you want to get back to? You seem awfully concerned for a guy who isn't even sticking around."

"And what makes you think that?" Babel asked.

"Uh..." Fair question. I couldn't exactly tell him that I'd heard him tell his cuh-razy lover in a vision. "Well, you didn't exactly stick around after the search was called off for Judah."

A pained expression crossed his face. I instantly regretted being such an ass. It was a low blow, and petty even.

"I stayed for as long as I could stand it." He shook his head. "I'm not meant for this place, Sunny. And neither are you."

Another twinge. "It doesn't matter." We would find Chavvah, then he would be gone. "Have you heard anything? Are the police searching for her?"

"No and yes. I haven't heard from Chavvie, but Sheriff Taylor isn't giving up." He flicked his thumbnail against his ring fingernail. "Not yet, anyways."

"She'll show up, Babel. I just know it." But I didn't know it. In my heart, I believed she was alive, and not because of any vision. "She's my best friend. I'd feel it if she was gone. Now, go on back to wherever you're staying..." Oh, crap. Maybe he'd been staying here. "You do have another place to stay don't you?"

Babel nodded once. "I've been staying at Chavvie's cabin down by the lake."

"Good," I whispered. I'd want to check out her place later for clues to what happened. "It's been a long drive for me, and I need a nap so I can figure out what I have to do next to find her."

He shook his head as if he was having an argument with himself. "I'll be back in a couple of hours with some cleaning supplies and get the floor behind the counter scrubbed."

I didn't want to talk anymore. I wanted to get my bags out of the truck. I'd hassle with unpacking the U-Haul later, but the bags were a must. I needed something personal, something of mine in this place. I held out my hand. "That's a nice offer. I can manage. Thanks."

Babel took my hand, and gave me a tight-lipped smile. "You don't handle blood very well. After I clean it up, maybe we can compare notes about Chavvie."

I nodded, afraid that if I spoke the dams would open and I wouldn't be able to stop the tears. Then I heard a voice like a whisper in my ear.

Save her.

Babel let go of my hand. "I'll be back." The way he said it sounded more like a threat than a promise. As he walked out the front door, he added, "You've got an audience."

CHAPTER TWO

AFTER A LITTLE exploring, I'd found a brick in the kitchen to prop the front door open. I needed the fresh air almost as much as the place did. Outside and across the street, a small crowd of about ten men and women gathered under the awning of the Johnson's General Store. They kept looking over my way and talking amongst themselves. Babel relaxed against the hood of the Toyota. "Looks like you've given them something to talk about."

Apparently, I was quite the buzz about town. Hell, if they'd pulled out barbecue grills, we'd have had a regular block party going on. For a second, I thought they might be the welcome wagon, but no one held pies or baskets of goodies, so...Probably not.

Bravely, I smiled, showing lots of teeth, and waved.

This action must've startled them because they all looked away at once. Well, if they were going for inconspicuous, they were failing miserably.

"Hello," I said loudly, sounding more in command than I felt, and more foolish than brave, I walked across the street to join them. After all, we were going to be neighbors, and they might as well meet me face-to-face. "I'm Sunny. Sunny Haddock." I pointed to the sign over the diner. "The Sunny in Sunny's Outlook. Chavvah Trimmel's partner." Just in case they missed the connection. They were looking at me as though I'd just beamed down from the mothership after creating crop circles. Maybe it was the clothes. "I'm from California," I explained.

"I've got a brother in California," a young woman with brown hair and warm brown eyes said.

"Oh, whereabouts?" Finally someone brave enough to make small talk, and I wasn't going to let the opportunity go by.

She gave me a funny look. "Just outside the town. He's got a few acres of land up there."

Up there? "Up around Pismo Beach? Or closer to Oxnard?"

"No, just outside California." She looked as confused as I felt. "You know, the county seat of Moniteau. Where are you from again?"

"California. Lakeside. It's in San Diego County."

"Oh." She grinned, and it was nice. Friendly even. "My brother lives in California,

Missouri. My fault." She held out her hand. "I'm Ruth. Ruth Thompson."

I laughed, and she chuckled, throaty and real. I liked her. She seemed sassy. Taking her hand, I shook it

23

firmly, placing my left hand over the top. "It's so nice to meet you, Ruth."

"My husband Ed and I own Doe Run Automotive at the end of town. Once you get settled in, come on down for some coffee and pie." She garnered several harsh stares and mutters from the others after her generous offer. "Oh, shut up, y'all. I'm allowed to invite someone for pie if I want to."

While they hadn't said anything out loud, I knew exactly where she was coming from. Two men sporting long white beards, and desperately in need of grooming tips, stepped forward next. They had milky blue eyes and wide mouths and looked identical.

Both wore overalls covering their rounded bellies. "I'm Delbert Johnson," one of them said, then nodded toward the other. "This is my brother Elbert. We own the general store."

Delbert and Elbert; that explained the similarities. They had to be twins. "Nice to meet you, neighbor." I smiled, and despite their crotchety demeanors, they smiled back.

Nice white teeth. Unexpected really. Then one by one, the rest introduced themselves. "Elton Brown, I own the used furniture shop up the way."

A brunette with a severe bun went next. "Becky Baker, I have a bakery just down the block. I know, I'm a baker who married a Baker." She grinned at her own joke. "Life's funny like that sometimes."

"Blondina Messer. Blonde Bear Cafe." The largish woman, with big platinum blonde hair, bright blue eye shadow, and a tan that would make George Hamilton jealous, pointed up the road. "You can see the sign from here, sugar."

There was Tammy Tolliver, the local seamstress, and Neville Lutjen, owner of the C Bar and mayor of Peculiar, and finally, Robbin Clubb, who owned the used bookstore in town. It was like the whole damn Chamber of Commerce had shown up. Definitely a tight community.

"Well, it's really nice to meet each of you," I finally said after the introductions wound to a halt.

Ruth placed a slender hand on my shoulder. "Have you heard from Chavvie? I've been really worried."

Dizziness hit me, then *a flash of trees, the wind brushing against me, and the feeling of sheer freedom as I leaped over a small brook.* I jerked my shoulder away from Ruth's touch.

She frowned. "You okay?"

"Sorry, I...no, I mean, yes, I'm okay. But no, I haven't heard from Chav, not for almost a week now."

Ruth's eyes softened, sadness brimming on the surface. "She's a good friend. If you hear anything, you let me know."

"Of course."

"You think you'll be opening the diner up soon?" Delbert asked. "What are you planning on serving? Some of that fancy West Coast cuisine. We've been hoping to find out, but Chav's been pretty tight-lipped."

"I'm not sure. She and I have talked about adding a vegetarian menu," I mumbled, feeling stupid for talking about the diner. What if I couldn't find her? No, I wouldn't let myself go there. I would find Chav.

"Vegetarian? That some kind of newfangled religion?" Elbert asked.

"No, just regular food, but without meat products."

Delbert started chuckling, and I realized Elbert had been teasing me. Delbert nudged his brother with an elbow. "Good one, El." Ah. Country humor. Interesting.

Mayor Lutjen cleared his throat, and the brothers stopped laughing. While Neville Lutjen's appearance was that of a good ol' boy—short-cropped chestnut hair, jeans, cowboy boots, button-down shirt with pockets—his brown eyes were sharp with intelligence.

I was hot and tired, and I didn't want to talk to these people anymore. At least not now. I needed a bed, or anywhere soft to lie down and relax my brain for a minute. I rubbed my arms as goose bumps formed, causing the little hairs to stand on end. With the temperature ninety-plus degrees, it wasn't from the cold.

Suddenly, a medium-sized dog, with reddish-brown fur and large ears that stood alert, appeared from I don't know where and circled the mayor. Its left ear, snow white in contrast to the rest of the beast, moved forward and back, its lips curling into a snarl.

"Is that your dog?"

Mayor Lutjen looked around. "What dog?"

"That one." I pointed to where the animal had been just seconds before, but it had disappeared. "Uh, well, the one that was just in front of you." Glancing around, I silently asked for someone to confirm what I'd seen.

"I didn't see no dog." Elton Brown shrugged.

Withholding a heavy sigh, I dropped my shoulder in

concession. "All right, fine. No dog." The low droning buzz was getting worse in my ears.

"Ms. Haddock." Neville smiled, wide and charming. "Sunny," he said, using my first name to soften his next statement. "I'm afraid everyone has to get back to work. Town doesn't run on its own."

"Oh, yeah, completely," I said. A truck-load of boys raced down the street, the wheels kicking up dust. Wolf calls ensued. "Nice," I muttered.

There were four of them, two boys up front, two in the truck bed, and they couldn't have been much older than seventeen or eighteen.

"Damn pups," I heard Delbert mumble before he went back into his store. I wondered if that was a local gang or something, or if "pups" was an Ozark euphemism for rowdy teenagers.

One of the boys in the back of the truck smiled at me. I won't call it a wolfish grin, because it was friendlier than that, and without thinking, I smiled back. He jumped out of the moving vehicle with catlike grace.

Too stunned to move, I watched as he coolly sauntered up the street toward me. His hair was cut short. It was brown with bleached-blond spots. He wore a sleeveless T-shirt, blue jeans, and sneakers. His arms were covered in tattoos, and his face glinted with piercings in his ears, nose, eyebrows, and lower lip.

Tall and lanky, the kid was a walking billboard for angst and rebellion. As he approached, his smile became more confident—that is until he tripped over his own feet and landed in a push-up position at mine. He looked up and blushed.

I held out my hand and pulled him up. "Are you okay?"

"Yeah," he said, his voice two octaves lower than I thought it would be considering his age. He dusted his hands on his jeans. The smile was back. "You are one hot mamma. New in town?"

As pick-up lines go, this one was pretty amateurish. I fought hard not to laugh at him, didn't want to crush his self-esteem so early in life. "Yes, I'm new. Sunny. And you'd be?"

"Jo Jo, but you can call me Jo Jo."

I couldn't help myself any longer. I laughed.

He put his hands on his hips, like he wasn't quite sure what to do with them, and I noticed the black polish on his fingernails. "Something funny?"

I pulled myself together. "Not a thing."

Babel pulled up in a small compact car. I laughed at the sight. He must have had it parked close by because I hadn't been distracted by the townies long enough for him to have gone very far. His head in the small driver window looked like someone had zoomed it in. I nearly laughed again.

"This boy bothering you, Ms. Haddock?"

The way he said my name carried the weight of possession that metaphysically drew me to him. I actually started a step toward him before I stopped myself. Closing my eyes, I took a few deep breaths to shake off the feeling.

"What?" I asked, trying to get a grip.

"Is the kid bothering you?"

"Uh." The only person bothering me was Babel—the

hot-and-bothered kind of bothering. "Nope. Not bothering me. Not at all. Everything is fine and dandy even. I'm totally cool with Jo Jo." Sheesh, I sounded like a moron.

"All right then." He raised a questioning brow. "I've got to run a few errands, but I'll be back later this afternoon."

"Okay," I said, a stupid grin plastered on my stupid face as Babel drove off down the street. Gah! How embarrassing.

Heat rose to my cheeks as I felt Jo Jo's stare. "That was interesting," the boy said.

"Why, I have no idea what you're talking about." Glancing at my U-Haul, I nodded at Jo Jo. "How'd you like to make fifty dollars, kid?"

"What do you got in mind?" He wiggled his eyebrows and smiled.

"Nothing like that." Holy crap. "I need help unloading my stuff is all."

"Oh." He laughed. His teeth were small and narrow, but perfect. I'd noticed that I hadn't met anyone with poor oral hygiene. I'd have to find out who the local dentist was, because with his skill he could make a fortune in Hollywood.

"So? You in?"

"Sure." He sniffed. "My pa's been on me to earn some extra cash."

"Excellent. Meet me outside the restaurant in a couple of hours." I still needed a power nap, and besides, when Babel came back, it would be nice to have Jo Jo there as a buffer.

In my rush to get out of the street and away from people, I'd nearly forgotten to get my stuff from the truck. Nearly. I grabbed my suitcase and my necessities bag, the one women carry that contains all the pertinent items they might need in any given situation—makeup, hair spray, brush, toothbrush, rubber bands, small flashlight, tampons, matches, Mentholatum, chocolate, and clean underwear. My mother didn't teach me a whole hell of a lot, but she taught me to always be prepared in case of an accident.

Mom. If she could only see me now. You see, the hippie commune where I was raised was a neo-pagan colony in Northern California. I never bought into the Druidic worship-mother-earth, commune-with-nature bullshit they peddled, but my parents, well, they were true believers. The only thing I wanted as a teenager was to get the hell out and be part of the real world, where your parents didn't run around naked or practice polyamory. When I turned eighteen, I hitched a ride to San Diego and never looked back.

After I closed the door to the diner behind me and crossed the room to the counter, I heard the dog snarl and growl before I saw him. The reddish dog with the white ear stood in the center of the room, its ears back. He looked really unhappy and territorial. "It's okay, fella. I'm not going to hurt you," I said, trying to keep the terror out of my voice.

Its ears popped forward, and I swear it looked confused. The dog whined then lay on the floor.

"Good doggy. Good boy." I backed away and took the opportunity to crawl up on the display counter—a defensible position if the dog attacked. The animal put a paw over his muzzle, and if he'd been human, I'd have sworn he shook his head.

My phone was in my necessities bag, near the door, but even if I could get to it without having my throat ripped out, who would I call? I had no one nearby on speed dial. And like an idiot, I hadn't asked Babel for his phone number to add to my contacts. I took a few deep, cleansing breaths to calm myself. Babel had said he'd be back in a couple of hours. Jo Jo was coming as well. I could wait.

After the first thirty minutes, my ass was so sore I couldn't hold still any longer. I shifted to my knees and lay on my stomach. The dog tilted his head, giving me the once over. "Quit looking at me."

He blinked, but turned away.

"How'd you get in here, anyway?" Like I really expected the creature to answer. "I wish you'd leave the same way."

He didn't look at me, but he whined again.

"I'm sorry." I felt a little ashamed. After all, he hadn't done anything to make me think he'd eat me, but..."Look, it's not you. It's me. I'm afraid of dogs. I had a really bad experience when I was a kid." I didn't know why I was sharing with the animal, but I continued. "A community dog chased me up a tree and got hold of my pants, along with my ankle. It hurt really bad, let me tell you." I had the scar on my ankle to prove it. "Anyways, I'd had to take off my jeans to get loose from it, and Moonbell, a boy I had a serious crush on, saw me in my underwear. It was really traumatic."

Moonbell. I hadn't thought about him in years. What a putz he'd turned out to be. His parents were hippies as well, hence the stupid name. I let him take my virginity when we were sixteen. Under a freaking cherry tree, no less. I thought I loved him and he loved me, but it turned out he didn't love me enough to leave the community. We'd planned for our escape, and the night I left, he backed out. Total mamma's boy.

I bet Babel was a mamma's boy. He just looked like one. Okay, so maybe I was projecting a little—giving him some faults so I wouldn't feel so attracted to him.

Like that would work. Not.

Yawning, I put my head down. Between driving and arriving, I was worn out. I decided it would be okay to rest my eyes. Not sleep, because that would just be reckless and stupid, but resting my eyes would be okay. If the dog even twitched, I'd hear him, at least that's what I told myself, and I was too tired to fight the logic.

I woke with a yelp as the front door closed.

Adrenaline surged as I bolted up on the counter. Babel held up a hand. "Hey. I'm back as promised."

I fell off the counter, landing on my ass once again, and looked around for the dog.

"Where is he?"

Babel raised a brow. "Who?"

"The dog. The stupid dog that's been holding me hostage for—" I looked at my watch, "—nearly two hours. Wow, I can't believe I've been asleep that long."

"A dog held you hostage?" Babel set down the bucket of cleaning supplies he'd been carrying. "Did he put a gun to your head?"

"Smart-ass." I stood up and dusted my butt. "If you didn't see him go out the front door when you came in, then there's got to be some other way in and out."

"I didn't see a dog coming or going. Are you sure you didn't dream it?"

The fear had passed, and now that free thought could function in my brain once more, all I could think about was how damn sexy Babel looked. He'd brushed his wild hair, and if he hadn't been such a mountain man, I'd have bet money he used product. His face was freshly shaven, and he smelled really nice.

Damn him.

"No, I didn't dream it." I chewed on the inside of my cheek. "Maybe you could just look around, make sure nothing can get back in."

He grunted. "Okay."

While he checked the place out, I spent my time thinking about Chav, and wishing I could get a sense or a vibe about what had happened to her. It wasn't my fault that every once in a while important thoughts were interrupted with visions (and not the psychic kind) of Babel naked. Again. Shaking my head, I tried to put him out of my mind. I didn't need the complication or the heartache.

"Did you find anything?" I yelled when he'd disappeared into the kitchen.

Babel reappeared in the front. "Nothing." He wiped his hands on his jeans. "If the dog made it in or out without using the door, then I'm not sure how he did it."

I sighed. Heavily. "Damn."

"Sunny," he said, friendly but wary. "I don't know why Chav invited you to this town, or why she thought, well, that you'd be a good fit for Peculiar. But you're not."

Seriously? I was beginning to develop a complex. "In time, when we find Chav, I'll fit in just fine." After all, if they'd accepted Chavvah, who, for all intents, was an outsider, why wouldn't they accept me? I really liked this place. It felt comfortable, and I never feel comfortable anywhere.

"No. No, you won't." He rubbed his eyebrows. "The townsfolk are all the same.

You're different."

"Different makes the world go 'round. At least that's what my father used to say."

"In this case, your father would be wrong."

"So, what? Are you all aliens or something?" I asked, trying to lighten the ever-increasing oppression filling the room.

"Or something." He didn't even smile.

"Don't tell me you all have some kind of Jonestown, crazy-Waco thing going on here. Because if ATF guys start showing up in full-on weapons and gear, I might consider leaving." I flinched as soon as I said it. Growing up the way I did, I had to hear the same kind of jibes about our community. But I was just super tired of him trying to get rid of me. "Other than that, you and the town are just going to have to get used to the idea of having me around."

His so-serious face didn't even twitch. "I'm afraid

you can't stay. I'll buy you out of your share of the diner if that's what it takes."

I huffed my frustration. "Fine, you can buy it back." Yeah, when cows quack and ducks moo.

"Yeah? You'd do that?"

The relief on his face pissed me off. "Sure. Two million dollars and the place is all yours."

"But you only paid two-hundred grand," Babel said incredulously.

"Yes. Well, the economy is bad, haven't you heard? And besides, I think I should get extra for all the pain and suffering."

"So, you're not going to sell it back to me. Is that what you're saying?"

Ding, ding, ding. We have a winner. "That's what I'm saying. I'm staying. You'll just have to deal with it."

His voice became growly and gruff and super sexy. "This town can be dangerous for outsiders." And super annoying.

I looked up at him sharply. I could take his words as a threat, but also as a warning. "Do you know what happened to Chav? Is that what you're trying to tell me?"

His blue eyes swirled with intensity. I never knew such a cool color could burn with such heat. "This isn't about Chavvie or Judah. This is about you."

There was a menace about Babel, one that brought goose bumps to the surface of my skin.

The front door cracked open, and what looked to be about a size-twelve tennis shoe shoved through the opening. It was soon followed by the rest of Jo Jo. He wiped a red paisley handkerchief across his sweaty forehead and shoved it in his back pocket. It was my turn to be relieved.

"Hey, Sunny." He acknowledged me first, then Babel. "Babe."

Babel tsked in disapproval. It made me think less of him. Beautiful body or not, he wasn't on my top-ten list of favorite people at the moment.

"Hi, Jo Jo." I jerked my thumb at Babel. "Ignore him." Big talk, coming from me. I hadn't been able to ignore the man since I met him.

Jo Jo smiled, wide and friendly. I was glad that at least one person in this weird little town was happy to see me. "Are you ready to work?"

"Sure thing." His eyes never left me. Secretly, I was thrilled that he seemed intent on freezing Babel out. "Where do you want me to start first?"

I rummaged the keys to the U-Haul out of my purse and tossed them at Jo Jo. The kid caught them like a natural-born ball player. "Bring in all the stuff you can carry and

I'll help with the larger items."

"I'll help with the stuff he can't manage," Babel said.

I wasn't quite sure what to make of his offer, considering just seconds earlier he was trying to get me to leave town, but I nodded. "Good enough."

Babel took off his flannel shirt and tied the sleeves around his waist. Under, he had a tight, faded blue tank. His biceps, triceps, and all the rest of the muscles in his arms bulged as he filled the mop bucket in the sink. My legs, especially my thighs, felt like the inside of a jelly donut. He rolled his head sideways and dropped his gaze on me.

I could barely meet his eyes. Jerking my thumb to the door, I said. "I'm going out for a bit." I needed distance from Babel Trimmel before I did something regrettable. Or pornographic.

When Jo Jo came in with his first armful, I said to both of them, "I'm stepping out for a minute or two. You cool with that?"

Jo Jo shrugged. "Where do you want me to put your stuff?"

"Upstairs. What you can manage, anyhow."

"Good 'nuff." And he took the stairs by two, bounding up, making me anxious about my lamp, along with a small circular table and a toaster he carried.

I fought back a sigh. "You okay with me getting out for a while?" I asked Babel, since he hadn't responded the first time.

"Yep," he answered noncommittally as he scrubbed at the stain behind the counter.

"Good 'nuff," I said, mimicking Jo Jo.

CHAPTER THREE

*A*S I WALKED down Main Street, I drew expected stares. Apparently, not everyone in town had come to meet me under the awning of Johnson's General Store. I tried to stay positive, smiling, waving at a few. Most of them just darted their eyes away as if I had a second head. I decided it was the way I dressed that kept me from fitting in. I'd have to rummage through my luggage for more conservative clothes.

Because they'd totally fall in love with me if I looked like a townie. Right? A girl could dream.

A black and white police car pulled up next to me before I'd walked less than a block, and that's when I met Sheriff Taylor and his wife, Jean. I looked around, fully expecting Aunt Bea and Opie to show up any minute.

"Hello, hello. Welcome to Peculiar." Jean's hair was pulled back in a loose bun, neatly held together by a dozen bobby pins I could see when she turned her head. Her hair shone in the sunlight, glittering with strands of silver. She looked middle-aged, except for the eyes. The skin around them was flawless, apart from the slight darkness that made her look as if she hadn't slept the night before or the night before that. She glanced around at my truck and open U-Haul. "Is there something we can help you with?"

At last, friendlies. "No, thank you. Babel and Jo Jo have it under control, but I appreciate the offer."

Sheriff Taylor, a short and stocky man, cocked his eyebrow at me. "Uhm, I think there's been a mistake, darlin'."

The use of "darlin'" (no "g") was said in such a way that it didn't sound condescending. I figured it was just the way people must talk in the Ozarks.

Besides, I hadn't introduced myself, and maybe it was his way of asking who I was.

"Sunny." I held out my hand. "Sunny Haddock. And there's no mistake."

Jean gave me the eye. It was the same look my geometry professor used to give me when I wasn't getting a concept, but he thought I really should. Pure disappointment.

Sheriff Taylor stepped toward me, which made me nervous, so I took a step back toward the diner.

"Young lady," he said in an official way. "This isn't a town you want to live in."

"Oh, yes, I do." What was wrong with these people? I was feeling less than welcome for certain, and frankly, I'd had enough. "Look, even if my best friend hadn't gone missing less than a week ago, this diner is half mine. In other words, I own a small piece of this town. The other half belongs to Chav, the only person who has a chance in hell of getting me to go anywhere. You know, I didn't expect a lot when I made plans with her to come here." Maybe a small parade, some confetti, the local marching band, and some banners..."But, I didn't expect animosity. And just what are you doing to find Chavvah? Maybe you should be more concerned about what's happened to her and less about running me out of town because I'm certainly not going *anywhere* until I see for myself that Chav's okay."

He cocked his head sideways, sizing me up. For a minute there, I had a vision (again, not a psychic vision) of the sheriff pushing me against his vehicle, handcuffing me, and hauling my ass to jail. I resisted the urge to run back and jump into the Toyota and head for the hills. Instead, I pulled my shoulders back, held my chin high. Perfect position if someone wanted to knock me out.

The sheriff shrugged and tilted his head toward the shop. "I don't think you'll be staying too long."

"And you would know this how?"

"Call it a hunch, darlin'." He tipped his official sheriff's hat. "Keep your tail tucked and your head low."

That was the oddest send-off I'd ever heard. "Uh, whatever."

Jean smiled a tolerant smile and patted my hand. "He just means stay safe, sugar. Oh, and..." she leaned in close and whispered, "...peaches and cream."

All right, an even stranger colloquialism. "Uh, back at ya."

"I mean to say, your fanny's showing, dear. Just thought you should know."

Embarrassing, most definitely. Note to self: Booty shorts may not be appropriate attire for the Ozarks.

Under Jean's reproachful stare, I pulled them down in the back. She smiled again. It was sort of freaking me out.

I didn't move or stop holding my breath until Jean and the sheriff pulled away.

The buzzing in my ears had settled into a dull hum. Maybe the change in air pressure was causing it, and there would be a short adjustment period before it went away.

As I walked down the street, I passed an antique shop, a quilt shop, and a leather and tack store, before pausing outside of Blonde Bear Cafe. I should have asked Babel if he wanted lunch. Not a date or anything, just a bite to eat.

Man, I would have liked to take a bite out of him. He'd be a seven-course meal complete with dessert. Thinking about the way he would taste almost made me forget how irritated I was with him. Thinking about how Chav might feel about me crushing on her baby bro reminded me how irritated I was at myself.

The dog, the one with the white ear, appeared next to me while I contemplated how filling Babel would be for lunch. Cold fear knotted my stomach, stripping the lust-filled thoughts from my mind. Outwardly I kept calm. The beast hadn't done anything threatening yet.

Yet being the operative word. It lay down in front of me, and I felt a push inside my head.

Judah.

"Judah?" I said. The dog looked up perceptively, and if it hadn't been of the four-legged variety, I'd have said it seemed shocked. Did this dog know something about Chav's brother? Maybe this was his dog? "Did you belong to Judah?" It blinked its eyes once at me.

"Better question, are you planning on making a meal out of me?" I tried to put humor in my voice when I said it, but I was serious as hell.

It blinked twice, and I hoped like crazy once was yes and twice was no. Maybe I should have established some kind of baseline.

The door to the cafe opened. Blondina Messer was holding the door. The dining room smelled of grilled onions, hamburgers, and fries. All the stuff you'd expect in a country restaurant.

My stomach turned a little. I'm a vegetarian. I don't eat meat. It's not a personal choice, more like a necessity. Now, don't get the impression that I'm a health freak, I'm not. I'm all about Sticky Buns and Otis Spunkmeyer Chocolate Chip Muffins and glazed donuts. (Just thinking about those tasty carbs makes me salivate. Pavlov's dog has nothing on me.) But for as long as I can remember, meat of any kind has made me physically and psychically ill. I throw up, I have visions of blood pouring from the poor creatures' wounds, and more often than I like, I pass out. So, vegetarian.

Blondina clucked her tongue. "Well, come on in.

YOU'VE GOT TAIL

Unless you plan on just standing around all day gathering flies."

Stunned, I stuttered, "Uh, yes. To the coming in, not the gathering flies part."

She laughed, and it was deep and loud, like a man's burly laugh. It shook her all over. Even her bleached-blonde hairdo trembled. "Then come on," she said.

I looked down at the dog, who was blocking my way and wasn't moving, so I stepped around him and into the cafe. Blondina sat me at a table and brought over a menu. "What'd you like to start with, honey?"

I'd never been darlin'-ed, sugared, or honeyed so much in my entire life. Not even by people who knew me well enough to call me darling, sugar, or honey. Funny enough, it didn't really bother me. It felt downright homey. "I guess I'll start with coffee?" I made it a question.

"Good choice, Sunny. Cream or sugar?"

"Just black. Thanks." I was rewarded with a smile. Her teeth were overly large for her mouth, but again, perfectly white and cavity free, at least superficially.

When the waitress, not Blondina, brought over the coffee, she gave me a sweet smile that beamed "how can I serve you?" She had golden-brown hair, nearly coppery, with a Marilyn Monroe figure. Ample, but with curves in all the right places. Her name tag read Selena.

When I took the coffee, our fingers brushed. I caught a glimpse of her curled up in a bed with pink ruffles, crying, as she clung to a picture of a pimply faced boy.

I nearly dropped the coffee. That had been a clearly

focused vision. Much like the one I'd had with Babel earlier. Something that only happened when Chav was around. I should've kept my mouth shut, but I had to know if it was real. "Do you have a boyfriend?"

"Why, yes." She smiled brightly.

"Does he have a bad case of acne?"

Her smile dimmed. "He's growing out of it."

Oh shit. Real! Should I warn her? My brain screamed, "Nooooo!" But my scorned lady parts said, "Definitely."

"Be careful of that one. He's likely to break your heart."

"That's not a nice thing to say." Selena frowned. "You don't know Bobby so shut your pie-hole."

I was glad I already had my coffee, or it might have come with an extra shot of spit. Talk about winning and influencing people. I should have listened to my brain. "Sorry, I didn't mean to upset you."

Curtly, she asked, "Can I get you anything else?"

Okay, so she didn't like me either. What else was new? I shook my head, but before she could get away completely, I asked about my new stalker. "Do you know who that dog outside belongs to?"

Selena looked in the general direction of the door. "What dog would that be, hon?"

"He was lying down in front of the door just a minute ago. Reddish-brown fur, sharp nose, kind of skinny. White ear?" The description didn't seem to register with her, or if it did, she was careful to keep her face blank. "I think he might have belonged to Judah Trimmel, but I can't be certain."

A momentary expression of surprise crossed her face, then it was gone. "I don't believe I know of a dog like that around here." Huh.

I had my coffee along with a chef salad with no ham, ignoring the wary glances from the other customers. A potent gamey scent wafted through the restaurant. It reminded me of the milk shed we had at the commune where I grew up. All damp and musty and animal. The smell disappeared as quickly as it had presented. No one else in the diner noticed. Or if they did, they didn't react.

I'd already opened my mouth and offended the waitress, so I kept quiet about the odor. It wasn't worth the extra bad ju-ju. After I finished eating, I paid for lunch, left a nice tip for Selena (it was the least I could do after opening my big, fat mouth), thanked Blondina for inviting me in, and headed out.

A very tall woman in tight blue jeans, low-heeled boots, and a fitted red blouse nearly ran me over on the sidewalk. I looked at her face and recognized her instantly. *Sheila of the Canadian Mist.* An image of her perfect naked body straddling Babel popped into my head. It was something I didn't think a thousand hot showers could wash away. It made me wish someone would develop a mind-bleaching pill. They could sell the shit out of something like that.

"Pardon," I said, more polite than I felt.

She stopped and sniffed me as if I was wearing some sort of exotic perfume. Her expression became hostile. "Look where you're going next time, bitch."

I could have said the same to her, but the menace in

her demeanor promised violence, and I was a pacifist for the most part. At least when it looked like I had no chance of winning. I waited until she'd gone into Blonde Bear Cafe before I continued my walk.

On the right, I passed the courthouse. It was big, three stories, but nothing flashy about it. It was constructed from white stone and brick, giving it that official feeling. I wondered if Neville Lutjen worked out of the building, or if the mayor's office was located elsewhere. On down toward the end of Main Street, I saw Doe Run Automotive. Ruth Thompson's place. She'd been nice and friendly, and, right at this moment, nice and friendly was worth a visit.

She came out of the garage in greasy overalls, wiping at a smudge on her cheek. I liked that she had a hand in the business, more than just a glorified receptionist.

"Hey Ruth," I said cheerfully.

"Sunny!" She smiled that flawless smile of hers, and I felt warm inside. I hadn't been mistaken about her.

"I was out walking and thought I'd take you up on your offer of pie and coffee." The Cobb salad from lunch hadn't filled me up, and the thought of pie made my stomach rumble.

Ruth beamed. "Well come on around back. My house is just on the other side of the shop."

I followed her around the path leading to a small two-story house. It was painted pink with light blue trim. I fought off a giggle. Her yard was neat, freshly mowed, with a row of purple irises and yellow daffodils painting the walkway to her stoop. She stripped off the overalls and hung them on the porch before going inside. I stayed close behind.

The kitchen was small, utilitarian but tidy, like everything about Ruth, except her appearance. "You have a lovely home."

"Thank you." She blushed as if she wasn't used to compliments. Her large brown eyes looked around her modest kitchen as if she hadn't seen it all before. "It'll do." Ruth started the coffee and dug a pie out of the refrigerator. "Apple okay?"

"Sounds great." I stared out the picturesque window. It had a great view of a well tended garden. The dog I'd been seeing walked across the yard, turning its head once toward me before strolling out of view. "Hmm."

"What was that?" Ruth asked, taking the cover off the pie tin.

"Did Judah Trimmel have a dog?"

I probably shouldn't have asked the question as she was slicing downward on the pie because she jumped then stood frozen as a small amount of blood welled up on her left thumb.

I passed out.

When I came around, Ruth hovered over me pressing a cold cloth to my head. A bandage covered the cut. "Land sakes, girl. You damned near gave me a heart attack. Are you all right?"

"Fine. Sorry. Blood. It makes me woozy," I managed to say. Though not to this degree. There was definitely something about the fresh country air that was upping the ante on my blood-to-fainting ratio. I sat up, then pulled myself back into a chair with Ruth's help.

47

"Heavens to Betsy. It wasn't more than a little scratch." She put the bandaged hand in front of my face. I closed my eyes and turned away, afraid she might want to show me.

I opened them back up again when she said, "You want cream or sugar?"

"Black's fine. Thank you."

She placed two pieces of pie and two mugs of coffee on the table and sat opposite of me. "Judah wouldn't have had a dog."

I frowned. "Are you certain?"

"Positive, honey." She chuckled. "Why'd you ask?"

How could I answer? Because the dog told me so. Yeah, that didn't sound loopy or unstable at all. So, I lied. "I thought I'd smelled a dog in the apartment above the diner."

"Oh." She glanced up at the ceiling but didn't elaborate.

"Did you know him well?"

"Who?" she asked, meeting my gaze. "Oh, you mean Judah. Of course." A deep sadness turned down the corners of her brown eyes. "He was a good man."

Was? Not is? I guess she'd given up on him along with everyone else. I wouldn't be giving up on Chav. "What about his sister?"

"I haven't known her for as long as Judah, but I like her all the same." She leaned forward. "I'm really worried about Chavvie. And Babe."

I guess no one but me had a problem calling him Babe. "So you know them all pretty well?"

"Oh, heavens no. Judah, sure. He'd been here for

eight years before..." She shook her head. "Nice man. Lonely. But nice. He'd just got tired of living out there." She made "out there" sound like a dirty word. "Wanted to be among his own—" Ruth faltered as if searching for the appropriate word. "Well, let's just say he was a kindred spirit. He'd really settled in," she continued. "But two years ago, he just up and vanished. After a couple of weeks, when he hadn't shown up, the sheriff called his family in Kansas City. That's when Babe and Chavvie came. Such a sweet girl. I was pleased as punch when she decided to stay."

"Do you have any idea where she could be?"

"I'm afraid not, Sunny." Her long eyelashes closed and opened in a slow blink. "Babe. That poor boy. He was frantic about finding out what happened to his brother, then time took the fight out of him. And now this with his sister. He's got to be devastated."

Babel had only come to Peculiar to find his brother and now to find his sister. I could understand why he didn't want to be here. I had my own worries concerning Chav, but this town held nothing but loss for him. It would be hard for me to stay in a place where I kept losing people I loved.

I wanted to take back every mean thing I'd thought about Babel. He was grieving, and I hadn't noticed. "Have you heard any rumors about Chav or Judah? Anything that could explain why one or both of them vanished?" Or did disappearing off the planet happen all the time around this place?

Ruth looked stricken for a moment, but she pulled herself together quick. "There are always rumors, Sunny.

Usually half-truths and innuendo. You can't take stock in such tales."

My gaze traveled past Ruth to the hall outside the kitchen while I thought about Ruth's aversion to straight answers. A flicker of movement caught my eye, startling me. I spilled the coffee I'd brought to my lips when I saw what looked like the back half of a deer disappear around the corner.

"What? I..." I felt silly when a small boy with buff-colored hair and holding some antlers came running into the kitchen. He flung himself onto Ruth.

"Mom!" He couldn't have been more than five or six years old. He rubbed his face against Ruth's and she smiled, her expression relieved. In his carefree way, the way most children are, he didn't notice I was there —until he noticed. The boy stood stock still, his brown eyes, so much like his mother's and stared at me.

Absently, Ruth touched his cheek. "Linus, this is my new friend, Sunny." She'd said "new friend" with a hint of caution. I wasn't sure if it was meant for me or Linus.

"Hi, Linus." I held out my hand, he took it in a firm grasp. As firm as his small hands would allow. "Nice to meet you."

"Nice to meet you, Sunny," he said shyly. His tone was an octave high for a boy, but his face was soft and bright like a cherub, and it seemed fitting he should have the voice of an angel.

"Linus is my baby." Pride filled her face.

"Mom, I'm not a baby anymore."

I suppressed a grin thinking he'd probably said that

line more often than Ruth cared to hear it. "How many children do you have?"

"Nine," she said, suddenly looking tired.

"Holy cow. You don't look old enough to have had eight children."

She grinned at that. "I've been telling myself that for years. But sure enough, eight kids all the same. Tyler and Taylor, the oldest boys, are twins. First and only set, thank the powers that be. Not an easy birth, let me tell you. Next was our oldest girl, Dakota. Ed and I had a whale of a fight over that name. Then Michele, Emma Ray, Butch—well, Leroy, but we've always called him Butch—then Thomas, Lisa Ann, and last but certainly not least, Linus." Ruth hugged her son for emphasis. The boy beamed his pleasure through a toothy smile. "Go play," she said to Linus and gave him a slight smack on the butt as he exited the kitchen.

"He's adorable." I was still trying to get my head around nine kids. The woman didn't look nearly as worn out as she should have. "Incredible, five boys and three girls."

"Yep, and two grandkids."

"No freaking way. You must have started when you were twelve." I realized after I'd said it that I wasn't being very PC. So, I amended my statement. "I only mean that you look way too young to be a grandmother."

"It's okay, Sunny. No offense taken. I did start young, as you say. I was seventeen when I married Ed. He was just so handsome, he took my breath away. By the time I was eighteen, Tyler and Taylor had been born. Tyler's been married two years now. And funny enough, his wife Darla had twins recently. Girls, mind you, but still." Ruth looked wistful and happy as she thought of her grandbabies.

"So, Tyler married when he was…" I let the question hang.

"Eighteen. Just like his father."

That made the boys twenty, which put Ruth at thirty-eight.

"Wow." Again. Her figure was tight and compact, not like you'd expect with a woman who'd squeezed out a bunch of kids. And her face was smooth, not a wrinkle in sight. I mean, I was a little younger than Ruth, only by a couple of years, and I was already getting small lines at the corners of my eyes. "So, Taylor didn't marry?"

"No," she smiled again. "Taylor and Tyler are identical twins, but no two boys could be more different. Taylor's left-handed, Tyler's right; Taylor is rowdy and loud, Tyler's gentle and quiet. Taylor is carefree while Tyler is serious about everything. I'll tell you this, I'm proud of both of those boys, really I am, but Tyler was definitely easier." Ruth chuckled. "Over the years, I've learned that being a mother means being adaptable. Every one of my children is different from each other, and what works for one doesn't necessarily work for any of the others."

Mommy wisdom. Interesting. I nodded my agreement. Mostly because there wasn't much I could say or add. I'd never been a parent, and until you are one, you just don't know. At least that's what I'd been told.

Ruth got up and opened a cabinet. She pulled down a photo album and flipped through the pages, pointing out her children through different ages and stages. I nodded, smiled, and fawned when appropriate. All her boys, along with her oldest daughter, Dakota, had their father's buff-colored hair, while the rest of the girls had their mother's tawny-brown locks. I was a little surprised to see that Ed, her husband, had the same large brown eyes that Ruth had, and each of the children had inherited that particular trait.

The next page was a wedding photo. Tyler's wedding. The picture included the whole party. Taylor stood next to the groom, then Leroy, and though I had no idea who he was, the third man in the groomsmen line looked familiar. Loosely kempt, medium-brown hair, except for a shock of white on the right side, square, chiseled jaw, compact build. I pointed. "Who's that?"

"Judah." She sighed as if the name pained her. "I think if Tyler hadn't felt obliged to name Taylor his best man, he would have asked Judah. They were great friends."

"Were? Did something happen between them?"

My question made Ruth pause for a moment. Then she said, "No, just, well he's gone now is all."

There was more she'd left unsaid, but I didn't push. "He looks a lot like Babel."

"No." Ruth shook her head. "Babel looks a lot like Judah. Judah was older by twelve years."

"How old would he be now?"

"He'd be thirty-four, give or take a few months."

"Oh." Inside I kicked myself hard. Judah being thirty-four put Babel at twenty-three now. I'd been literally lusting after my best friend's *baby* brother. I'd never asked her how old he was, but Chav was thirty-five, so that made Babel an "oops" baby. He'd just seemed more mature, the scruff on his face giving him the appearance of a man who'd done more living.

I stroked my finger over the picture of Judah. I felt buzzy again, right before a vision of Judah standing in this kitchen, holding Ruth, his lips pressed to hers. She'd pushed him away, surprise written all over her expression, and slapped him hard across the face. As I took my finger off the picture, the vision went away. The glimpse of Ruth's past left me embarrassed. It wasn't any of my business.

Ruth scooted her chair, bringing me back to the present. "Sunny, I like you. I really do." I could feel a "but" coming. "So it pains me to say this. You need to leave town. I'm sorry Chavvie's missing, but this isn't a place you want to live."

My lips tightened against my teeth. Not her, too. "Ruth, I'm staying. I don't know why everyone wants me to leave, but...Do you believe in destiny?"

She seemed to consider the word for a moment, then slowly nodded her head once.

"Maybe."

"When Chav first suggested I come out here, I thought she was nuts. I'm a California girl, the sun, the beach, all of it, but even then I was attracted to this place. Before I'd even laid eyes on Peculiar, I knew I wanted to be here. That I needed to be here."

She turned her head sideways to really look at me. It reminded me of the small beagle that used to run around the compound where I grew up. It would cock its head toward its shoulder and stare at you curiously. A little unnerving.

"I will tell you this if you're determined to stay. Lock your doors tomorrow night.

Lock your windows. Lock everything."

"What's going on with this town? I know there's something you're not telling me."

"I don't like to lie, Sunny. I almost never do. So, don't ask questions about things I can't tell you."

"Fine. Can you at least tell me what's going on tomorrow night?" She didn't answer.

"Is there a storm coming in or something?"

"Something like that," she said. "Sunny, if you were a smart woman, you'd get out of town."

I liked to consider myself a smart woman, and while my head told me to heed Ruth's warning and run like the wind, my heart had already decided to put down roots.

I'd left Ruth's feeling wholly unsettled. When I got back to the diner, Neville Lutjen and Babel were arguing. They both got quiet as they saw me approach. "Hello again,

Mayor Lutjen."

"Hello, Sunny," he said with the full force of his charm. When he smiled, it made his face look young and handsome, even under the beard and mustache. I could see why he'd been elected to office. He gave the appearance of confidence and competence. Add in charisma, and probably money, and Neville was the epitome of a politician. "Nice day." He tipped his head to me.

Through clenched teeth, Babel said, "Thanks for stopping by, Neville."

"We'll continue this discussion later, Babe. Bet on it." He tipped his head again to me. "Ma'am."

"What was that about?" I asked when the mayor was out of earshot.

Babel shook his head. "You're coming to town has stirred up a hornet's nest, Sunny. Folks around here aren't happy with Chav or me."

The "folks" would just have to get over it, I nearly said aloud. With all the warnings to leave, I had a healthy sense of alarm, but I was more concerned for Chavvah. She'd stayed in Peculiar because of her determination to find out what happened to her brother, and if I had gone missing, she would have been just as dogged. It is the kind of person Chav is and has always been at her very core. So, there was no way in hell I was going to let the local yokels run me out of town until I found her safe and sound.

Before I could say as much, JoJo came barreling out the door. "Oh, hey, Sunny. Everything's in. You had a lot of junk in that trailer."

I didn't take offense to the use of "junk" to describe the only personal items I brought with me from California. Most of it *was* junk, but it had sentimental value. "Are you trying to renegotiate your salary?"

He blushed, and again it made him seem impossibly young. "Nothing like that." JoJo grinned sheepishly.

I dug into my purse and pulled out two twenties and a ten. I handed the money to Jo Jo, which he eagerly accepted. "My keys?"

"On the counter inside." He stuffed the money into his front pocket. "You need any more help, you just let me know."

I liked Jo Jo. It seemed he was the only one in town who actually wanted me to stay.

"Thanks. I might take you up on that."

"Get on home, boy. Your pa's probably fretting," Babel said.

"Doubt that." Jo Jo grimaced and rolled his eyes. "I'm going." He took off toward the south end of town, practically skipping as he went.

I went inside, Babel following close behind. I could sense his presence, even without turning back to look. "What an odd name. Jo Jo. What's it short for?"

"Jolon. His father owns a small piece of property just outside of town. Good kid for the most part. Gives his dad a lot of grief. It's got to be hard being a single parent."

"Where's Jo Jo's mother?" I turned around and found myself toe to toe, and nose to chest, with Babel. His nearness made my lungs tighten.

He shrugged. "She ran off, or so some say, when the boy was only eight."

This close to Babel, I found it hard to think. His wide masculine shoulders made me swoon. His lower lip stuck out just the tiniest bit in a too-cute-to-not-kiss way. Ack! I had to look somewhere else, but when I tried, my gaze immediately went to his abs and hips.

Definitely not better. Not if I wanted to string sentences together coherently. I chose his eyes as my final target. His blue eyes were the color of cold, but they warmed me up from the inside out. I held his gaze, gulped, then managed to say, "And his dad never remarried?"

"No. I don't think Brady Walker has ever given up on the idea that she might return one day."

"Wow, that's sad." And romantic. In a tragic and lonely way.

"Yep." Babel stroked his hand down my arm. A simple touch that left me squirming on the inside.

Why was he touching me?

His mouth, slightly fuller on top than bottom, relaxed into a soft pout. I wanted to feel the softness of his lips pressed against mine. My heartbeat quickened, and my palms went cold and clammy. I could warm them on his skin if I could just make my arms move. He dipped his head toward mine, slow and careful. I wanted him so badly, it frightened me.

He sniffed my hair, a long drag of air. "You smell... Like home." He traced the skin of my lower jaw. "You shouldn't, but you do."

My knees were pudding under his weighted gaze. There were so many reasons why jumping on Babel couldn't happen. Shouldn't happen. First, he was much younger than me. Second, he was my best friend's brother. And third, finding Chav was my number one priority, not finding a boyfriend. And in spite of those obstacles, I felt strongly attracted to him, desperately attracted to him. The kind of desperation that made me stupid and impulsive, and made me forget my best friend was probably in serious trouble.

I had to stop whatever was going to happen. I had to stay on track with the reason I'd come early in the first place. "Does that happen a lot around here? People just up and disappearing?"

Babel looked stricken. He stepped back. His kissable lips pressed into a thin line.

"I'm sorry, Babel." And I *was* sorry, for more reasons than just one. My brain said I'd done the right thing, while the more primal parts of me cussed like a sailor on shore leave.

He narrowed his eyes at me. "What are you getting at?"

"I don't know." Shrugging, I looked away from him to stare at the small window above the door. "What you said about Jo Jo's mom, and..." I had no idea where I was going with this line of thought. So, I changed the subject. "I met Ruth Thompson today.

She told me a little about Judah—"

"She should mind her own damn business." His voice combined anger and hurt all rolled into one painful package.

"She didn't say much. I swear."

He sniffed. "What did she say exactly?"

"Only that Judah had been a good man and a good friend. I got the impression that she missed him."

This seemed to surprise Babel. "I didn't know they were close."

I didn't tell him I'd seen Judah kiss her in a vision, and even without that vision, her voice had betrayed how much she'd felt for him. So instead, I said, "He was best friends with her son Tyler."

He grunted. "Hmm. Tyler's always given me the impression he didn't like Judah much."

Strange, but okay. At least Babel didn't look angry with me anymore. "What do you think happened to your brother?" My voice held an edge. "And do you think it has anything to do with Chav?"

I watched him tug his lower lip between his teeth. My body reacted to the gesture. It seemed to be reacting a lot around Babel. The impulse to take that lower lip between my own teeth ran through me like a double shot of espresso. I clenched my fists, digging my fingernails into my palms, trying to force out the feeling. I didn't understand my reaction to him. Sure, he was yummy goodness in a hard-body package, but the lure was more primal.

"I don't know," he finally said. "Neither Judah nor Chavvah would have disappeared without a word to anyone. It's not in their natures. They are somewhere out there, maybe together, maybe not, but I have to hope. Right?"

He referred to his brother in present tense. He believed Judah was alive, that both his siblings were in trouble, but not in a no-turning-back kind of way. I touched his hand, a gesture of compassion, and in that moment, I saw him sitting alone by a fire in a large living room. He looked much younger, less seasoned. He couldn't have been much older than fourteen or fifteen in the vision.

Judah walked up behind him. "Don't be mad, bro."

Babel turned to him. "I just don't understand why you want to leave."

"I can't make it work out here. Not like Mom and Dad." Judah ran his hand through his loose curls, tucking the white patch behind his ear. "I don't want to integrate. I want to be what I am. What *we* are. Without always stressing and hiding."

A young Babel had pivoted away from his brother, unable or unwilling to respond. Tears formed in his deep-blue eyes, and I staggered back, breaking the small thread linking me to Babel's past.

"What *we* are," I mumbled.

"What?" Babel asked.

I realized he had a hold on my upper arms, keeping me upright. "What?" I said back as the fog cleared from my head.

"You going to pass out again?"

"No." At least I didn't think so. But something else nagged at me hard. I'd had several visions in one day. All very clear. Bizarre, but exhilarating at the same time.

I hugged my upper arms. I would find Chav. I believed it now more than ever. I was exactly where I was meant to be. The shift in frequency of my ability since I'd arrived was all the proof I needed. I would find Chav, even if I had to turn over every rock and expose every skeleton in this town.

CHAPTER FOUR

*M*IDDLE OF THE night, I woke up sticky with perspiration. I couldn't believe how unbearably hot Missouri nights were. California got hot, it was California after all, but Missouri added an intense humidity that could only be called sweltering. I felt like I'd melted into the bed. I'd left the windows closed at Babel's urging. Something about "critters" crawling into open spaces at night, and after the whole dog incident, I believed it. But the ceiling fan didn't work, and I couldn't take the heat one minute longer.

Sliding the window up, I vowed to bring central air-conditioning to this backwoods town.

A gut-wrenching scream pierced through the sound of crickets and tree frogs.

Quickly, I slid the window back down and did the heebie-jeebie dance. It had sounded like a child being tortured if I could even imagine such a thing. Horrified,

I was nearly too immobilized to act. Then I thought about Ruth's little boy, and I didn't think I could live with myself if I did nothing and some poor kid got hurt out there.

I peeked out the window, hoping someone else had heard and gone to investigate. But nope, the street looked pretty damn deserted from what I could see. I'd read that mothers have a predisposition to instantly waking upon hearing a crying child. Where were all the freaking mothers?

I knew I should go check to see if someone was hurt —after all, it was the civic-minded thing to do—but I was scared. What if something big and bad waited in the darkness, perched and ready to kill the next unsuspecting victim who crossed its path?

I mean, I'd begun to feel a bit like an unsuspecting victim. Not a great feeling.

While my head was trying to talk myself out of investigating, my body had other ideas, and before I knew it, I was completely dressed. I think my head was the smarter of the two. Not wanting to be completely TSTL (too stupid to live), I called the sheriff.

"What'd it sound like again, Ms. Haddock?"

I sighed, rolling my eyes. I mimicked the noise once more. This was the third time he'd asked, and with the muffled grunts of laughter in the background, I was pretty damn sure he'd put me on speakerphone.

The bastard.

"Sheriff Taylor, are you going to investigate or not?"

"Not."

"What? Someone could be really injured or worse."

"Doubt that. What you heard there, little lady, was what we like to call in these parts, a barn owl. Nothing more than that. And while the sound they make is gawdawful, we don't usually have anybody die over it."

The whole barn-owl scenario sounded convenient but much better than my theory of a child-murdering psychopath. For a moment, I missed the ex-asshole. Sure, he was a lying, cheating whore of a man, but at least he'd been present. At least I hadn't been alone to face potential critters crawling through my windows and barn owls mimicking children being tortured by whack-job killers. Even if I hadn't been psychic, I think my Spidey senses would have been tingling about this place.

Being that I was hot and not a complete chicken-butt, I cracked the window open again.

When I turned around, I wasn't alone. "You again," I muttered to the mystery mutt who'd started to become a fixture in my life. "How'd you get in here?"

He cocked his head sideways at me, and his eyes were alight with intelligence. It pawed toward the door. I huffed, hands moving to my hips, and stared at it. I'd stopped being afraid of the animal after the whole restaurant appearance. After all, if it had wanted to attack me, it would've done it already. No, this dog wanted something from me, and with great determination, it kept tracking me down.

"What's the matter, boy? Is Timmy trapped in the well? Is Johnny pinned under a tractor? Did the cow kick Mary Lou in the head?"

The dog growled, obviously not a *Lassie* fan. A

growing push inside my head, like earlier, blossomed, giving me a slight headache. I knew what the dog wanted; it wanted me to follow it out the door. Crap. I'd always had a way with sensing basic emotions and needs from animals: anger, fear, hunger, joy, but this...

"No freaking way." I shook my head. "I'm not going anywhere tonight, so just get that thought out of your head. Or better yet, get it out of mine."

It growled again. Anger replaced any residual fear, and I growled back. Since when did I start taking orders from dogs? Ex-boyfriend included. "You do know what happened to Old Yeller, right?"

The animal whined, placing his nose under his forepaw. Great, I'd hurt its furry feelings.

The push came again. *Chavvah*. The word came across as a barely audible whisper. The dog began to paw at the door once again.

"Fine," I sighed. It was dumb to think a dog might hold some clue as to my friend's whereabouts, but I wouldn't forgive myself if I didn't at least try. "This better be freaking worth it, or I'll be adding dog stew to the menu."

Thirty minutes later I was dressed and walking through town in the middle of the night. Dim-witted dog was leading me to my doom. I felt it in my bones. "Ow!" And my big toe was most likely broke after tripping on a concrete step outside one of the storefronts. Peculiar was lucky no one had sued them for piss-poor lighting.

Darkness and nature noises filled the small town—in San Diego, even at 2:00 a.m., you had cars driving up and down the streets, twenty-four-hour convenience stations, and people out and about. After three blocks, really not as far as it sounds, the dog stopped and shifted its ears forward. We were just to the left of the courthouse, with its wide-open lawn of well-manicured grass and precisely placed silver maples and oaks.

I could hear something, but whatever, or whoever it was, was too far away. There were two options at this point—go back or go forward.

Pigheadedness moved me forward.

A couple of dark blobs stood on the other side of the front steps of the courthouse (again, not well lit). I kept my distance and hid behind a nearby tree, not wanting to alarm any potential psychopaths. Besides, the dog had gotten low to the ground and stopped, so I assumed he'd taken me where he wanted me.

A voice rose above the other. "I don't give a shit. I'm through. This is over here and now, got it? No more."

I should have freaking known. *Sheila*. I couldn't get away from this chick.

The other person kept his side of the conversation quiet and hard to hear. Was she talking to Babel? A hint of jealousy ran through me at the thought. I wanted to get closer, but my legs felt cemented in place.

"Don't you dare threaten me. I can bring a whole can of whoop ass down on you." Sheila again, lots of bravado. Although, the way she'd smacked Babel in the head with such force, I didn't doubt her ability to do damage.

My calves were getting sore, so I leaned forward to

adjust and chipped the tiniest piece of bark from the tree.

"What was that?" Sheila snarled. "Who's there?"

A sinking feeling started in my chest and ended just below my belly button. Surely she couldn't have heard the bark chip fall from thirty feet away?

Before I could think of my next move, the crazy bitch was in front of me, yanking me off the ground and pinning me against the trunk. Her brown eyes looked nearly black in the dark, and she had a maniacal quality I usually liked to avoid in people.

Sheila held me with her forearm against my chest and with her free hand she pinched my cheeks together, giving me fish lips.

Unflattering, but effective. I debated for half a second on whether to fight back or try to diffuse the situation. Since I'm a lousy fighter, I went for the latter.

"You're really strong for a woman." (Not easy to say with fish lips, let me tell you.)

"What. The. Fuck. Are you. Doing. Out. Here?" She pinched hard with each punctuated word. My poor cheeks were going to be sore for a week.

"I wawws woiwing uhn..." (You try talking with fish lips.)

She cocked her head sideways. "What?"

I pointed to her fingers then gently pried them from my face.

"There." I rubbed my cheeks. "I said, I was on a stroll with my dog. Hot night and all. AC's broke. Needed some air. Stopped to tie my shoe. That's it. Honest." Well, not completely honest, but close enough, really. And where was the damn dog? Dumb creature got me into this situation then bolted at the nearest sign of trouble. So much for man's best friend.

Sheila rubbed her hand through thick, shiny brown hair. Then she gazed down at my shoes. I thanked all that was right with the world (which didn't feel like much, by the way) that I'd worn my tennis shoes and not my sandals.

She grunted, digging her fingernails into my arm. "Take my advice, little girl. Next time you feel like walking at night, take a stroll around your living room. You never know what might be out in the dark just waiting to eat you." She snapped her teeth. Really effective.

Feeling good and warned, I scraped my back against the tree trying to get some running room. "Uh…Thanks for the advice."

Before she let me go, an image of her and Judah seriously making out flashed in my head. "Jeezus."

"What?"

She'd finally unlatched herself from me, and I didn't want to give her an excuse to "bring a whole can of whoop ass" down on me, so I said, "Nothing."

But come on! This chick definitely liked to keep it in the family. Babel and Judah. And what about Judah? First, I'd seen him kissing Ruth, now Sheila. What a man-whore. I mean, I liked Ruth, but she was a married woman with a gazillion kids. And Sheila, well, she obviously got around. Curiosity got the better of sense, and I decided to risk an ass kicking.

"I didn't mean to interrupt you and…"

She glared. I could swear her eyes flashed with some unholy light. "None ya."

"I just mean, it sounded pretty serious."

Her brow narrowed, and she pursed her lips. "What exactly did you hear, Sunny Haddock?"

Uh-oh. Crazy knew my name. "Not much. It just sounded like you were breaking up with someone." Which it had. "But I couldn't hear a whole lot." Which I hadn't. "But I don't mean to pry." Which I really did.

There was something innately fascinating about Sheila. Sort of like a ten-car pile-up on the freeway. It's hard not to slow down and take a good long look no matter how disturbing you might think it is.

She turned on her heel and walked off into the night with the parting words of, "Go home, Sunny Haddock."

I got the distinct feeling she didn't mean the diner. When I got back to Sunny's Outlook, I allowed the tension to leave my body and breathed a sigh of relief.

The light came on, and I saw Babel standing near the switch. "You okay?"

To say I nearly jumped out of my skin was an understatement. "How did you get in here?" I'd locked the door when I left; at least, I was pretty certain. He held up a ring of keys. "I have an extra set."

"Why?"

Babel arched a brow. He took a step toward me, holding out the keys. He jangled them in the air like a dangling carrot. "Chavvie gave them to me."

"I don't know that I like you having a copy."

"I just thought..."

Before I knew what had happened, he was inches from me. I felt woozy and just a little breathless.

"You thought wrong."

His fingers laced with the metal keys traced a path down my bare arm. "I don't think so."

Before turning to a complete pile of slush, I stepped back, just out of his reach. Babel made a lot of assumptions about our level of intimacy, and I planned to set him straight. "Hold up, fella. You're definitely cute. I'm not going to lie and say I don't find you attractive." It's hard to fake "no chemistry" when it's thick in the air. "But not only are you a decade younger than me," which I could get past under different circumstances, "but you're also Chav's brother." Which I couldn't get past. You just don't do your friend's exes or siblings. It's like an unwritten code. "Beyond that, there is nothing between us." My heart sank as I said it.

Babel pulled on all my emotional and physical strings. Maybe because we both loved Chav and our mutual concern pushed all the right buttons in me. My reaction to Babel reminded me of the first time I met Chav, only without all the pining and puddling. After meeting the tall brunette, I'd instantly wanted to be her friend. To be close to her. Chav had told me once that our friendship was yin and yang. A perfect balance. I think the reason Babel freaked me out so much was that I felt the same intense connection to him that I did with Chav, only more pervy.

"I think you know that's not true, Sunny."

I was angry. More than maybe I should've been.

Suddenly, I realized why. "Were you just over at the courthouse with Sheila?"

He looked genuinely confused. "Sheila? When?"

"Never mind." It hadn't been Babel with her out there in the darkness. Inside—and childishly, I might add—I did a happy dance.

Babel leaned forward and breathed in deeply. His lip curled in a snarl. "Did she hurt you, Sunny?" He sniffed at my cheeks where she'd pinched me; then he inhaled the area on my arm that she'd grabbed. A rumble drew from his throat.

"I...no."

Anger brimmed his words as he lifted my chin. "Your cheeks, they're red and slightly bruised. I know Sheila had something to do with it. I can smell her on you. Tell me."

"It's nothing. Really." Smell her? What the heck? "I think I just surprised her is all."

"I'll talk to her." His thumb brushed my cheek. A flash of vision haunted me. Babel and Sheila had bonded over the mutual loss of his brother. And even though nothing had gone on between Babel and me, inexplicably, I felt like the other woman. It made me ashamed.

"She's not a bad person. I'm sure." What a stupid thing to say! She *was* bad. Horrible even. But if Babel and I got involved there would be drama, drama, drama between me and the nut job long after he was gone. I didn't want it or need it. "Stay out of it. I can handle myself."

His lips relaxed into a half smile, turning me back into slush. "Of course you can."

My knees buckled for a second. Crap. Why did he have to be so sexy? "Babel," I said firmly, trying to sound in more control than I felt. "Is there a purpose to tonight's visit? Other than the initial scaring the bejeezus out of me?"

"Sheriff called. Said you were nervous about a barn owl. He thought I could come over and *reassure* you."

The way he said "reassure" made it sound like a naughty, naughty word. I'm almost positive when the sheriff had said it, he hadn't made it sound that way at all. "Consider me reassured. Anything else?"

"Do you want me to stay?"

Yes. "No."

"I could sleep on the couch. It might make you feel safer, what with all the dogs and owls creeping around you."

Okay. "No."

"You sure?"

No. "Yes." I was a woman of many contradictions. My brain had apparently joined forces with my libido, but at least my mouth hadn't betrayed me.

He shrugged. "Suit yourself."

"You can take the couch." Traitorous mouth! "Just for tonight, though. And don't be getting any ideas," I added. After all, I was in control. Right? Babel winked. "Got it. No ideas."

CHAPTER FIVE

THE NEXT MORNING, I jumped out of bed, ran a comb through my hair, brushed my teeth, and pinched my cheeks for color before casually strolling into the living room.

Unfortunately, it had all been for naught. The spare blankets I'd given Babel were folded neatly on the side of the couch, and he was gone. No note, no nothing. Which shouldn't have pissed me off, but it did. How come he hadn't stuck around? I felt like a one-night stand without all the hot, sexy fun that comes before the shame and regret.

Ruth stopped over and invited me to go to Lake Ozarks. She enticed me with the promise of name-brand outlet malls. I'm weak. What can I say? Besides, I needed a distraction. We went in her car, and during the drive, I found out that the only access road in or out of Peculiar was the long one-lane bridge I'd come in on. I enjoyed being a passenger. The country was beautiful and lush and green, something San Diego lacked, especially during water shortages. I hadn't really paid attention when I'd driven in—more focused on the destination than the journey.

After we'd finished shopping, (and hell yes, we shopped! I found some really cute things for the restaurant at an antique mall), Ruth said, "Are you sure I can't talk you into getting a hotel room for the night, Sunny?"

"Don't you have to get home?" After all, Ruth did have a dozen kids.

She shrugged. "Sometimes it's nice to get away."

I could see that. Hell, if I had that many ankle biters I'd want to run away. But damn, I'd already run away from home once before, and I wasn't looking to go anywhere else at the moment. "I have some stuff I need to do in the restaurant today. Plus, I want to go through Chav's things and see if I can get a clue to where she is. You don't mind, do you?"

Ruth tensed, pursed her lips, and wiggled them. She minded. "Please, Sunny. You don't want to go back to Peculiar. Not tonight anyway."

"I had a good time today, Ruth." In other words, she was killing my buzz. She didn't respond.

I'd had it up to my eyeballs. "Do people really want me gone that badly?"

"There's good reason for not wanting you around." Ruth wouldn't look at me. "You're not one of us."

Great. There was some kind of hillbilly club that required membership I wasn't privy to. "I could be 'one of you' if you guys would just stop treating me like I'm a boil on your asses."

Ruth cracked a smile. "I can't explain it. Not in a way to make you understand. So, no offense, hon, but you will *never* be one of us."

That hurt. I'd come to expect the rest of Peculiar to try to drive me out of town. But I hadn't thought Ruth would break out a torch and pitchfork. The rest of the ride home was in total awkward silence.

Ruth dropped me off at the diner, and I was beginning to think maybe we couldn't be friends so much. Especially if she was going to keep joining in the rousing chorus of "get the hell out of town."

When Sheriff Taylor pulled up in his Crown Vic, I wasn't really surprised. The bell dinged on the door as he walked in. I smiled to myself. I'd bought the bell at one of those country-chic stores, and the noise confirmed I'd managed to put it up right.

"Nice," he said.

"So, how are you planning on running me out of town today?"

His mouth quirked up in one corner. "You're a funny gal."

"Most *gals* are, don't you know?"

"Seriously, though, Ms. Haddock."

Who wasn't being serious? I certainly was. Jumbo-sized serious. "What now?" I whined.

"There's a big storm coming in tonight. Talk of tornadoes and such. They can come on mighty quickly and without warning. So best to stay in and lock your doors and windows."

"Huh?"

"You know." He whistled and twirled his finger around in the air. "Tornadoes."

Tornadoes? I'd heard of tornadoes in the Midwest but hadn't given them a second thought when I'd moved out here. But I was a Cali girl. I'd suffered tremors and the threat of earthquakes. Surely I could take on big, swirling, monstrous funnel clouds of death.

Oh my God! What was I thinking?

Funnel clouds of death.

Great. Like there wasn't enough shit already. "Hmm. So, like out of nowhere. Bang!

I could be in Kansas sitting on top of some old batty chick wearing red slippers?"

He nodded somberly. "Yep."

"Well, screw me blue."

"I'm a married man, Ms. Haddock."

To say I was shocked wouldn't do my reaction justice. "I..."

The corner of his mouth quirked again. These country folk could deadpan humor with the best of them. "So you'll stay in tonight?"

"Uh, yeah. I can manage that."

He looked so damned relieved, I got a warm-fuzzy. Someone in this town cared about my well-being. Then another thought struck me. "If a tornado hits, where do I go? What do I do?" Crap! I didn't have a basement or anything. There was a crawlspace, but how many other things would I be sharing it with? Spiders? Snakes? What other godforsaken creepy-crawlies?

He seemed to chew on his response for a moment before he answered. "Well, if you hear the sirens, just head on over to the courthouse. It has an underground shelter for folks without basements."

"Okay, I can get there." But could I get there fast enough? I wondered just how quick adrenaline would carry me if a violent wind chased after me.

"I'm not saying it's going to happen." He shrugged. "Just in case, though, stay in."

"Cool. Got it. Fantastic. Thanks for the warning," I mumbled, not thankful at all. The threat of bad weather seemed like one more way for this town to try to get rid of me. If I woke up in Kansas in the morning with my place on top of some wayward witch, I was going to be pissed.

Sheriff Taylor patted me on the shoulder, and my eyes rolled back. A large banded raccoon hissed, eyes flashing as it leaped into the air on the attack.

I shrieked, stumbling back. When my ass bumped against the counter, and no actual animal landed on my head, I peeked out from behind my sheltering arm. The sheriff was staring at me as if I was crazy. He acted like he hadn't ever seen a woman scared witless by a vision. Imagine that.

"I'm fine." I waved my hand. "I thought I saw a bee." Lame, but whatever.

"O-kee. Well..." He dragged out the "well" like a man who recognized crazy. "I'll see you tomorrow."

I didn't know what was wrong with me. I mean, psychic shit happens, but not on a daily basis, and not over and over with crap that didn't make any sense to me. Not to be self-aggrandizing, but my visions were *usually* about me. Not generally helpful, but not so puzzling either.

After the sheriff left, and Babel entered. It was like a rotating friggin' door. I sighed and tried really hard to leave out the lusty shudder. It should be illegal for a man to look that savagely good.

"What do you want?" I meant to say hello, really, but that's what came out instead.

He scratched his chin, his face full of apprehension. Or maybe annoyance. Or maybe he was just constipated. "I guess you've been told about the storm?"

I guessed he needed more fiber in his diet. "Yeah, yeah, swirling winds of doom. I got the message."

"Good. Just making sure."

He licked his lips, and my knees knocked. I scolded them profusely then wondered how horrible it would be if I used Babel for courage-building boinking?

As if he could read my mind, he arched a brow and grinned.

"Uh-uh." Shaking my head, I absently dusted the already-clean counter. My body may have wanted the quick roll, but my common sense knew better. "Did you need something?"

He moved closer, and I could smell his cologne. Eau de Hubba-Hubba. "I think it's clean." His voice had deepened an octave—his tone like aural sex—and my stomach went tight.

His wild, shoulder-length, thick, thick hair made me want to grab a fistful and yell, "Say my name, bitch!" I resisted the urge and focused on scrubbing harder, but I couldn't deny myself a sneak peek at his crystal-blue pools most people would call his eyes. And there it was, that spark, that leap, that…electricity. "It's clean when I say it's clean. I'd hate for someone to get skewered by a dirty piece of counter during the coming storm."

My skin shivered with excitement when he turned me in his arms and pressed his lips hard against mine. I tried not to respond.

Impossible.

I melted into the kiss, my fingers tangling in his soft mane. So much softer than I could have imagined. Mental note: Ask the man taking liberties with me what conditioner he uses.

Every joint in my body felt as if it had come unhinged and I grasped at him to keep tucked in tight to his wide, muscular chest. All thought drained from my head as his hands kneaded my back. By the time his lips left mine, I felt all wonky and loose. "What the heck was that for?"

"Keep yourself safe tonight," he murmured, reluctantly releasing me from his embrace.

The bell sounded again, and like boxers ending a round, we moved quickly apart. Neville Lutjen, mayor extraordinaire and total cockblocker, walked into my little establishment. Jeezus. I hope I got this much traffic when we actually opened.

"Nice day, Ms. Haddock," he said, giving a nod of acknowledgment to Babel, who nodded back. Even though it was a Friday, Neville wore what appeared to be his Sunday best—tan slacks, blue blazer, light cream-colored shirt, with a blue and brown striped tie. "Just stopped by to check in."

Isolated with the two men, I noticed a similar raw chemistry. Even if Neville was a bit older, he didn't look as though he'd wasted a moment of his youth, or that he couldn't still hold his own with anyone half his age.

"Hi, Mayor Lutjen."

I smiled. Babel snarled. Lutjen grinned.

I grabbed a broom from the corner and started sweeping, and let me tell you, I don't even like cleaning. That's how desperate I felt. If the testosterone got any thicker, I'd be growing a full beard soon.

The mayor's bright-green eyes twinkled, easy laugh lines creasing the outer edges. "Like I said, I'm just checking to see if you're settling in okay." His voice had a lyrical quality. Charming, very charming. I didn't trust charming men. "I like to converse with the new business owners." His gaze traveled to my breasts. "See if there's anything I can do to help you adjust."

I had the feeling he could "adjust" me just fine if I had been interested, but all I could think about was the possessive press of Babel's lips on mine. The memory made me smile. I stared at Neville. "Oh, it's all good." Other than the fact that my best friend was missing, and no one seemed to care. Oh, and everyone seemed to want me out. Other than that, perfect. Although, I couldn't help but feel a little warmer toward the town's leader for offering to help. Even if his offer had slightly lecherous overtones.

"You know, I could use some help getting a certificate of occupancy and whatever other permits I need." Chavvah and I had talked about that several weeks earlier. She'd said she'd been having trouble getting the permits. Maybe Neville's weird need to suddenly "help" could come in handy. "I'd like to get the business open within the next month or so, once Chav turns up. Have you heard anything about where she might be?"

Inadvertently, I looked over at Babel. He was staring at Neville. His face unreadable.

Hmm.

"No." He cleared his throat. "I barely know Chavvah. Why would I have heard anything?"

"Oh, I just meant with you being the mayor and all, you might get notes or something from the Sherriff's department."

"It doesn't work that way, Ms. Haddock." His sour face turned to an instantly bright and sincere-appearing smile. *Politicians. Ick.* "I'm sure she'll show up. And, I'll let Sheila Murphy know that you'll be in sometime in the next week. She's my assistant, and can help you get the paperwork started."

No! Not Sheila. Well, at least the mayor thought I'd be around another week. How refreshing. I gave Neville a small yet triumphant smile, then turned a glare toward Babel to say, "hah!" But immediately softened, my mind and oh so many lower things in my body going back to the kiss.

Neville sniffed the air. Something I'd noticed more than one citizen of this fair town had a habit of doing. His smile became slightly lurid, much to my discomfort. Babel's lip curled into a snarl again. Territorial much? Both men exchanged heated glances, and I thought I was going to have to start snapping my fingers to break the tension.

"Hello?" Startled, they turned their interest to me. "Thank you both for coming to check on my welfare. Mucho appreciated. But I've got some hatches to batten down and all that good stuff. So, unless you want to help..."

Neville cleared his throat. "I have a few appointments this afternoon, or I surely would, Ms. Haddock. I'm half-tempted to cancel, but it wouldn't be good business." He certainly knew how to sound sincere—a good politician, if not a bit indolent.

"I'll stay," Babel said tersely.

I wasn't sure how good an idea that'd be, but I didn't argue considering I wasn't quite sure what battening entailed.

In short time, we'd gotten all the safety precautions taken care of with the exception of the windows above the door.

I breathed a heavy sigh and tried to find something high enough to stand on so I could reach the upper window on the wall. The shutters would need closing, just in case. I moved a chair over, got up on it, and reached for the latch.

Heat radiated from Babel's body as he came up behind me and put his hands on my hips. "Sunny." His voice was a hoarse whisper.

"Don't." I pushed away from his grip, my body turning awkwardly, and I fell from the chair.

Babel caught me in his arms, of course. Not that I wasn't grateful, but come on! The only thing missing was the Barry White background music. He dipped his face toward mine. I fought the urge to meet his lips as he drew nearer. Not easy, let me tell you. He smelled so damn good.

"What are you wearing?"

He looked surprised. "A flannel shirt and jeans?"

"Not your clothes, dummy. That cologne." I sniffed his neck—musk and...some kind of earthy herb like cumin and basil. It made me feel both hungry and horny.

Babel groaned softly, gooseflesh rising on his skin when I sniffed him again. His eyes rolled up, and he spoke through gritted teeth. "Please, stop." Then he focused in on me with fierce determination. "Or don't stop. Choose one or the other, Sunny."

A dog barked. I turned slightly and could see the reddish-brown mutt crouched in the corner. I wet my lips and met Babel's gaze. "Put me down."

He obliged, watching me curiously as I walked to the dog. "It's okay, boy," I called soothingly, reaching out to pet his fur. He whined. "No, no. It's okay."

"Sunny?"

"Shh," I told Babel, without looking back at him. "You'll scare him off."

"Scare who—"

I crouched next to the dog and stroked...

"—off?"

Nothing but air.

I jerked my chin in a confused tuck. Helplessly, I looked back to Babel, who watched me curiously.

"Don't you see him? The dog. He's right..."

I glanced back to the corner. The dog was gone. Disappeared. Vamoosed. Fucking hell.

"He was there." I pointed. "Right there. You saw him, right? I'm not crazy." Truth be told, I was feeling a little crazy.

"I didn't see anything." His tone was light, gentle. It really pissed me off.

"I'm not crazy!" I reiterated, less and less certain. I mean, holy crap, I'd been chasing a hallucination around for two freaking days. "Come on. Skinny dog, reddish brown, about yea high?" I gestured to right above my knee. "Surly disposition?" His eyebrows shifted upward, and he paled. "I swear I didn't see any dog."

"But?"

Babel's expression told me there had to be a but. There was always a but. "But..." he said reluctantly. "Have you ever seen a coyote before?"

Coyote? "Uhm, maybe. I dunno. I might have seen one on television or something like that. I can't really remember." It couldn't have been a coyote. How could I be having a delusion about an animal I couldn't have identified if it walked up and bit me? A tingling sensation started in my lips. No. Not again.

"Sunny?"

"I feel..." Before I could finish, the world went black.

Chavvah was sitting at a counter. She was in a living room, but not the one above the diner. This one was modern, with black furniture and steel and glass accessories. It lacked the warmness of Chav. She was reading a journal and jotting numbers down on a piece of paper. She looked up, an expression of horror on her face. The fear in her voice chilled me to the bone when she said, "It can't be. They killed him. They really killed him."

When I came to, Babel was holding me in his arms and carrying me up the stairs.

"You should really go see a doctor." He stroked my hair, perspiration causing it to cling to my neck.

Great, passing out was beginning to become my M.O. around Babel. The vision had made one thing clear. Babel and Chav's older brother was no longer missing. He was dead. I don't think Chavvah would have been that emotional about someone else, but then again, I hadn't seen her in two years.

I wanted to wrap my arms around Babel and comfort him, but I wouldn't be able to explain to him why I felt he needed it. Not in a way that wouldn't earn me a trip to the funny farm.

Now more than ever, I had to find Chav. She'd discovered something horrible and terrible, and that something had caused her disappearance.

I gazed at Babel, barely able to meet her eyes. "I'm fine, this happens all the time," I said unconvincingly. "How long was I out?"

"Just a little while. I was going to call Doc Smith if you hadn't come to by the time I got you to bed."

"Trying to get me in bed, huh?" I smirked. Yes, I was flirting. It was hard not to while being held in his fantastically strong arms, and besides, he was grieving, even if he didn't know it. I could afford to be kind.

He growled, a low rumble emanating from his chest. "Don't tease, Sunny. I'm not a strong man." His mouth quirked in a half-smile, but his blue eyes were deadly serious.

"Got it. Don't tease the mountain man." I patted his shoulder. "Okay, big fella. You can put me down."

"You sure?"

"Don't I look sure?"

My foot hit the landing wrong when he lowered me. I fell sideways with a "Yikes!" Babel caught me and yanked me close to his chest. As my fingers slipped inside the buttons of his flannel, a much softer "yikes" came out.

What was I doing?

Babel chose that moment to claim my lips.

The next thought: *Why wasn't I doing*?

His tongue swept across mine, his mouth incredibly warm. I felt my knees give way beneath me, but Babel kept me upright. What harm could a little quicky bring? After all, the man had just lost his brother. Besides, he was young. Too young to be considered a serious suitor. Right? Just a little bit of fun. It could be a whole no-strings-attached kind of affair.

I leaned my head back. "I'm not looking for a relationship."

"You want to talk about this now?"

"Look, I think you're a nice guy and all." Translation: Damn sexy mutha-friggin' hot! "But I'm not emotionally available right now for, you know, more than something...Physical." Translation: I want to boff you raw and have you leave before the lights go out.

His chewed his lower lip. His eyes narrowed. Then he shrugged. "No."

"Yay!" I said with the expectation that he'd jump at a casual fling. Then followed with a, "What?"

He pushed me against the wall. Leaning forward, he grabbed my thigh with his big, meaty hand and pulled it up onto his hip. "I don't want you *no strings attached*. I want you, Sunny, in a way that makes me ache like I've never felt before. I know it's wrong. It has to be. But I don't care. I don't fucking care." He pressed his entire body tightly against mine and claimed my mouth with his once again.

Have mercy! The way he kissed me made me think he wanted to enter my body through my tonsils. I vibrated against him as he ripped my shirt over my head. "Pink bra must go," he said.

With one little click of his fingers, the bra snapped open, releasing the girls for his eager hands. I moaned as he lifted me off the floor. Instinctively, I wrapped my legs around his waist, grinding my sex against the growing bulge in his jeans. He tore away from the kiss, his mouth nibbling and nipping the skin along my jaw and neck until his lips found my right nipple. He worked the nub between his teeth, his tongue laving it until it stood tight and erect before he moved to my left side and gave it the same attention. I fisted his hair with both my hands, moaning as I ground myself against him. Wet heat blossomed between my thighs. Goddamn! I was going to have an orgasm without ever taking off my pants.

His hand cleverly rubbed over the middle seam of my jeans, finding just the right pressure to make me groan and tremble with pleasure. "Oh, hot damn. Hot damn," I murmured, grabbing his flannel shirt and yanking the front apart. Plastic buttons hit the hardwood floors. I'd always wanted to do that, and damn if it wasn't as sexy as I thought it would be.

"I think you need to be punished for that," he said playfully.

My eyes widened. "Bring it on."

He threw me over his shoulder and gave my ass a slap.

Kicking and giggling, I let Babel carry me through the apartment to the bedroom. He tossed me easily onto the bed. I landed with an unflattering bounce, but it didn't matter at all. He stripped the damaged shirt off first, giving me the full-on benefit of his wide chest and ripped abs.

I whistled low and soft, "There ought to be a law."

He snarled, not mean-like, but oh-so-mind-blowingly-hot. "There is."

I laughed. Until his pants dropped to the floor, along with my jaw. Soft, he was big—hard, he was super-sized. And yes, I'd seen it the day before, but not in this context.

The context where he was planning on inserting it into me. "Holy schmoly."

"It gets better." He grinned.

"As long as it doesn't get bigger." As it was, I wasn't sure if it was going to feel really, really good. Or really, really bad. "Don't break me. I may need my shit at some later date."

He retrieved his wallet from his pants and pulled out a condom. Funny enough, it didn't bother me that he carried them around. I was actually glad the gorgeous slut practiced safe sex! I swallowed hard as he rolled the condom down the length of his shaft. It didn't quite reach the base. I swallowed hard again.

"I'll be gentle." His low voice caused my belly button to feel like someone had tied a string to it from the inside and tugged. I was so wet and ready, gentle or otherwise.

He crawled up the bed with the confidence of a predator stalking its prey. His shoulder-length hair falling forward, giving him that primal something-something that made my thighs quiver with anticipation. He started at my ankles, tenderly licking and nipping, making the nerves in my body raw with excitement.

The farther up he went, the more my legs spread to accommodate his wide shoulders until his tongue met my...

"Ah," I grunted as his mouth found the sweet spot. His hands reached up to my breasts, caressing and tweaking. The simultaneous stimulation made my back bow, raising my body to meet his every manipulation.

My sex slick with heat, my throat thick and heavy with desire, I muttered, "I want you in me."

Babel growled his own eagerness as he raised his body over mine. He entered me slowly, inch by languid inch.

"Oh, God," he rasped. "You're so tight. I don't want to hurt you."

It felt too good and we'd gone too far to stop. I raised my hips to meet his, taking him all the way in. A moan fell from my lips unbidden. I could feel the pressure mounting inside me as his thick shaft slid deep and withdrew in a slow, easy rhythm.

He arched his back, taking my nipple into his mouth again, teasing it with his tongue. My hips thrust upward, driving him deeper inside me.

Babel's growls and moans only heightened my excitement. His rhythm quickened. I rocked my lower body, meeting every hard thrust with the same enthusiasm. The musky scent of his skin added to the wild feeling growing inside me like a ticking time bomb. A burning rapture of ecstasy exploded through my body. I cried out, the intensity overwhelming all my senses.

Suddenly, I was on the street outside the restaurant. A large dog—again with reddish-brown fur, but not the one I'd been hallucinating—jumped on top me, its lips pulled back in a snarl as it growled and bared its teeth.

Screaming, I scrambled backward, its hot breath licking at my skin. I shut my eyes tight, waiting for it to tear into me.

The bite came, the teeth digging into the flesh of my shoulder. Searing pain ripped through me.

I screamed again, and didn't stop until the vision ended and I was back in the bedroom, Babel shaking me as he shouted my name.

"Stop. I'm okay. I'm fine." I was panting, breathless with fear. I was anything but fine. When he released my shoulders, I could feel the tears burning my eyes. I brought my hands up to cover them. "Oh, God. It was horrible."

"Sunny, what happened?"

"I don't know why. I don't know when," I managed through the shock. "But I'm going to be attacked soon."

CHAPTER SIX

"**LET ME GET** this straight," Babel said for the sixth time. "You think you're psychic?"

"I don't think I'm anything." I was beginning to feel a little bit like Bruce Banner. He was making me angry, and he wasn't going to like it if I got angry. "I *know* I'm a psychic."

He made a "pah" noise. (Irritating.) Then shook his head. "Prove it."

If it were possible at the moment, I would have turned green and started busting muscles out everywhere. "What about your clothes? How did I know that your clothes were in the walk-in freezer?"

"You could have stumbled on them when you were looking around."

"Okay, I didn't want to go here, but I *know* that skank Sheila made those scratch marks down your back." Which, come to think, were remarkably healed for just one day.

He had the good sense to look embarrassed. "Lucky guess?"

Hands on my hips, I harrumphed. "Fine! How about the fact that she cold-cocked you with a bottle of cheap whiskey after you finished doing the nasty!"

His eyes widened then narrowed. "You talked to Sheila. Easy explanation."

I blamed Babel completely for what came next. He'd left me no choice. "I saw your brother...You were much younger."

Babel sat down on the bed, eyeing me wearily, the rawness of his pain nearly forcing me to stop. But I had to make him believe.

"He didn't want to...integrate."

Babel's serious face grew hard. He grabbed my arms and pulled me close. He stared accusingly. "What do you know of integrating?"

"Nothing." I consciously slowed down my breathing to belie the panic. "I only know what I see. He said something to you. Something about being what you are."

"Stop, please, stop." Babel could no longer look at me. "How? How can you know this?"

"I'm sorry. I didn't mean to see your past. I can't control the visions. If I could, I'd use them to find Chav. But they don't work like that. They take me back, and they take me forward, but they don't always make sense, and I can't see things just because I want to. This curse of mine...I feel fucking useless. Chav knew. She understood and helped me. I wish I could control it, but I can't. But the important thing is that my visions are always true. That's why I know I'm going to be attacked by an animal. Right out in front of the diner."

Babel stood suddenly and grabbed my arms, his expression fierce as he kissed me. "It'll be dark soon, Sunny. Lock your doors. Double-check your windows. Don't go outside. Whatever you do. Don't. Go. Outside."

I think I'd seen this scene in a horror movie. It was the one that occurred right before the hapless female who, moments after having sex, is hacked into tiny pieces of gore.

"I have to go now." He kissed my cheek, tenderly, carefully. "Be safe."

Before I could ask him what the hell was going on in this town, he took off out of the apartment.

"Great." I sighed. "I'm going to be attacked by a vicious animal, and he leaves me alone."

I sighed again but did what he told me. I went downstairs, locked the door, made sure the windows were all locked down, then went back up to my apartment to wait out the coming storm.

Three hours later, around eight-thirty in the evening, I watched through the cracked shutters in my bedroom as the sun dipped below the horizon and the moon came up in the east. The sky, clear of clouds, made me wonder what kind of storms they had in Missouri. It looked like a beautiful night out.

Suddenly, howls and yaps sounded in the distance, making me shiver. I rubbed my arms, trying to ward off the feeling of foreboding. While the defiant part of me had been determined to stay in Peculiar, the chicken-butt side of me wanted to jump into my truck and head for the sunny coast of California.

I checked out the window again.

What I saw frightened me as much as the howls.

Deer, opossums, raccoons, and all sorts of wildlife skirted the street, running as if their lives depended on it. I read about animals acting weird when a storm was brewing, but what the hell kind of weather would make them all to run through the middle of a human-populated town?

Not watching was impossible. I hadn't experienced this much craziness since the night a friend drunk-dialed me at four in the morning to ask me if she could date my cheating ex. (Totally breaking girl code—Thou shall not date thy friend's ex ever.) I never forgave her.

A fawn ran out from between the general store and the antique place right into the stampede. My heart thumped in my chest as it wove itself into the fray. I thought about Ruth's little boy, running around his house with his father's antlers clutched to his head.

My anxiety upped a notch.

Biting my fingernails, I watched it stumble and couldn't hold back a gasp. This was worse than when Bambi's mother got shot.

A raccoon whacked the fawn in the side, sending the creature tumbling to the ground outside in front of my building.

It was horrible! Even the squirrels were running it over. Its little mouth opened as if to scream.

I couldn't watch anymore. I know I'd been warned to stay inside, and the logical part of my brain told me the move was TSTL, but I had to do something to help the poor baby animal.

I hit the stairs running and nearly tumbled myself. Sliding across the restaurant floor, I grabbed the keys off the hook near the door and unlocked the deadbolt. The noise outside had grown to a roar. Keeping myself pinned against the building, I waited for a small break then dashed out into the road and grabbed the fawn's leg.

The damned thing kicked the shit out of me with its back legs as I pulled it to safety around my 4X4 truck. As soon as I had it cleared of the chaos, it jumped up on all fours and bounded off down the street without a glance at me.

No *thank you*, no *sorry about the bruised ribs,* no *nothing*. Ungrateful beast!

I turned to get back into the store, but I'd done something wrong when I'd unlocked it from the inside. Somehow, it had stayed locked on the outside. I heard a roar, not just the roar of the multitude of animals, but a real, honest-to-goodness roar.

A large black bear stood on its hind legs, then dropped into a gallop, coming up the street my way. I fumbled for the keys in my pocket, dropped them once, and panic had me shaking so bad I couldn't get the right one into the damn hole!

Why couldn't I have just left Bambi alone? After all, it was nature that only the strong survive.

Dropping my keys, again, I bent to retrieve them.

Then it happened. It felt like a giant tree branch whacked me hard across my back, hammering me to the concrete sidewalk. I rolled over with a groan, and a dog or dog-like animal, maybe a coyote like Babel had mentioned, with the darkest brown eyes jumped onto my chest.

It was the vision. It was coming true. Right fucking now!

I screamed as it snarled and snapped, ready to make me a Sunny-snack. Throwing my elbow up, I managed to knock it off me once, but the damn thing was quick and vicious. It twisted its body and was back on me in less than a second. I screamed again as its warm breath panted across my skin.

I wrenched sideways, the animal's maw barely missing my neck as it sank its teeth into my left shoulder. The adrenaline rush of being attacked dulled the searing pain a little as I used my right hand to punch at its head and body with everything I had. It twisted and pulled at my shoulder. My left arm began to tingle with the first signs of numbness. So much better than the pain, but scarier.

I screamed again.

Its neck pressed against my face and I bit it until I felt my teeth break through the skin under the fur. It yelped, releasing me, pain flooding back into the damaged arm. I kicked it in the side as hard as I could, and it caught my jeans by the cuff and started to drag me. I kicked the animal in the jaw, but the coyote wasn't going to let go twice. It pulled me out into the street.

With my useless arm bloody and dragging behind me now, I started feeling lightheaded.

No, no, no. This was not the time to pass out. Not now.

If I lost consciousness, there would be no coming back. I used my good hand to undo my pants, desperately trying to get them off. I finally got them unzipped and down around my thighs, but I couldn't get them down my legs.

I screamed in frustration, my heart beating a mile a minute, my brain trying to come up with an exit solution.

My saving came in the form of another coyote.

It was nearly twice as large as the one attacking me, and it barreled into the brown-eyed devil with a ferocity I'd never seen. It grabbed the smaller one by the back of the neck and shook it before casting it aside. The smaller coyote yelped and whined, but the bigger one held its ground, standing between me and death.

My hero, I thought. Then another thought came to me. The animal probably saved me so I could be its next meal. I scootched backward to the storefront, grabbing my keys where'd they'd fallen. The large coyote turned its face to me.

Blue eyes.

It raised its upper lip, baring sharp white teeth.

The better to eat you with, my dear.

But instead of attacking, it took off down the street after the rest of the animals.

In severe pain, lightheaded, and completely panicked, I ran to the passenger door of my truck, hitting the unlock button on the keychain. Thank heavens for remote-control locks! I pulled the door open and crawled into the driver's seat.

I managed to get the key into the ignition, though I was shaking so bad, I don't know how. The truck started, and I had one thought in my head. If Peculiar didn't want me, well, who cares, I didn't want Peculiar anymore, either. So there!

I was going back to California, and I wasn't going to waste a moment of time getting there. Then I noticed the blood. Lots and lots of blood. Oh boy. "You cannot pass out, Sunny," I said firmly. "You will not pass out. Hold it together, girl."

Normally, I didn't talk to myself. Not aloud, anyways. But I so needed a pep talk. "We'll go to the nearest hospital. You'll be fine." I had lost feeling in my left hand. "Stop thinking about it. Just drive."

And that's exactly what I did. I put the truck in gear and peeled out of my parking spot. I'd forgotten Ruth had told me the one-lane bridge was the only way in or out of the small town. I headed for the west side, dodging creatures big and small, and found there wasn't an exit. I did a U-turn and head back the other way.

Fishtailing out of town, the pain in my arm intensified, and I wished like hell the whole damn thing would go numb, that *I* could just go numb.

I saw the bridge up ahead, signaling freedom. I'd be out of this insane town and, after a visit to the emergency room, out of this horrible state.

No such luck.

A large gray wolf jumped in front of my headlights

and stopped. I slammed on the brakes and cut the wheels. The 4Runner hit the ditch with a jarring *wham*! The air bag deployed, smacking me hard in the chest and face. For a second I saw pretty colors, then as had become my habit, everything faded to black.

CHAPTER SEVEN

SMOKE? **I SNIFFED** the air again before opening my eyes. Yep. Smoke.

I turned my head and blinked. Steam rose in front of me. I heard the hiss of water hitting something hot. I tried to sit up, but the pain in my shoulder kept me down.

Groaning, I rubbed my eyes. A man, at least I was pretty sure it was a man, sat across the steam from me. His face and body, what I could see, was painted with thick paint in red, black, and yellow. His hair, a tangle of long, silvery-gray dreadlocks, spilled over his shoulders. He chanted softly, rocking gently, as he poured another ladle of water over a pit.

I touched my wounded shoulder. A thick dressing covered it entirely, smelling of herbs and earth. I gazed wearily at the man covered in leather and fur. Then I noticed the room I was in. It was hand-sewn leather held up with thick saplings.

Huh. It appeared I'd been rescued and tended to by a Rastafarian-Native American. I wondered where he hid his good shit because weed and peyote both sounded like they couldn't hurt at this point.

"You were badly injured," he said, raising his eyes to me. They were the clearest gray I'd ever seen. His voice held a slight drawl, as though he was from farther south than Missouri.

"Yes." To avoid impoliteness, I added, "Thanks for helping me out." I managed to get up on an elbow, and the fur covering me slipped down.

Naked. I was naked! I nearly undid all his good work on my shoulder trying to yank the fur up around my breasts.

He didn't seem in the least fazed. "I sent word to town after I transported you here. Ruth brought you a fresh set of clothes. Yours were shredded pretty badly. They had to be removed so I could make sure you didn't have any more injuries."

I appreciated the clinical way he spoke about treating me. He was an old guy after all, probably like an elder or something. My modesty should be the least of my concern. "Who are you? And where is Babel? If you sent back word to town, how come Ruth came and Babel didn't? Why am I fooling myself? So we'd had a one-afternoon stand. No commitments. Hell, I'd even told him as much by word and deed. Plus, I'd told him about my abilities, which I'm sure he thought means I'm insane." Suddenly, I stopped talking and stared at the old guy. "Did I just say that out loud?"

He nodded. His mouth formed a small smile,

flashing white teeth. Very white. Like the rest of the townsfolk. "I'm the town's shaman."

A shaman? "So, do I just call you Shaman? Like, is that your name?" Maybe I had misunderstood.

"Shaman is my title. Name's Billy Bob Smith. You can call me Billy Bob."

I snorted. "Shaman Billy Bob?" I laughed and wished I hadn't. It made my shoulder hurt worse. "Seriously. Billy Bob?"

He sighed. Heavily. I couldn't blame him. I was sort of being an ass.

"I'm sorry. That was very rude of me."

"It's okay."

"So, Billy Bob." I tried to hold back the smirk when I said his name again. "Is this your teepee or something? Do you live here?" Seemed like awfully small living quarters.

"No. My house is just up the hill. This is a sweat lodge. It helps purge your body, giving you the ability to heal quicker."

"Again. Seriously?"

"Seriously." He poured more water over the pit.

The steam actually felt really good, comforting. Like a wet hug. I didn't really believe the whole "purging" theory, but I was alive, and as long as I didn't move around too much, I didn't feel all that bad.

"Sooo...Billy Bob." I giggled. I couldn't help it.

He sighed again. "Yes, Sunny."

Well, of course, he knew my name. He'd obviously talked to Ruth and who knew who else from the town. "How bad's my shoulder?"

"The muscle was torn to the bone, but you didn't have any nerve or tendon damage."

"You sound like a doctor."

"I am. Medical school in Columbia and a three-year internship in general medicine at the VA hospital."

I giggled again. I felt a little...high. "What did you give me?" I smiled.

"I put a Demerol patch on your back to help you manage the pain when you woke.

It's a two-day patch, so you should be good for another day."

"I've been here a day?"

"And night. You were pretty out of it." He stood and had to stoop to keep from hitting his head on the top of the tent. If possible, he was taller than Babel.

Babel. Had I asked about Babel? Where was he?

"I found you in the ditch yesterday morning. You had me worried for a while."

"Let me get this straight. Your official title then is Doctor Shaman Billy Bob?" I sniggered again.

Billy Bob shook his head. Obviously, he needed his own Demerol patch to appreciate me. "Rest now, Sunny. Sleep. Sleep will help you heal."

He left the tent after putting a few hot stones into the pit and adding more water. His advice seemed good, sound even. I took it.

I felt the lick of a rough tongue on my shoulder, and I reached out, filling my hands with warm, thick fur. My eyes fluttered open. I stared into the eyes of the big beast that had saved my life. Its blue eyes were intense and almost human in the way they expressed worry. The beast licked my injured shoulder again.

"I'm all right," I said. I wasn't feeling any pain. I stroked the beautiful fur, so much softer against my fingertips than I imagined. The animal that had attacked me, the fur was coarse and cool to touch, but not this one. He—yes, it was a he—was luxurious to touch.

Having him so close felt like home—felt safe. He nudged me over with his muzzle until I made room for him to snuggle down next to me. He lay his head on my stomach, and together we slept.

When I woke up again, I wondered if the blue-eyed coyote had been dream or vision, or maybe a little of both. All I knew for sure was that a part of me that I didn't understand felt a painful loss at his absence.

Shaman Billy Bob was back. I'd sensed him hovering before I even opened my eyes.

"I'm alive," I said.

"I had no doubt." I could hear the amusement in his voice.

"How long was I out this time?"

"Six hours."

Jeezus. "I can't believe I'm still tired."

"It's the pain meds." He reached down, his hands firm and unlined, that of a younger man.

The patch tugged at the skin on my shoulder as he peeled it off.

"That a good idea?" I wasn't in much pain, but I wondered how I'd feel when the good ju-ju wore off.

"You're healing well. Better than expected. I think

we can switch you over to something less...potent. Like ibuprofen."

I sighed, closing my eyes. "Spoilsport."

A rustling at the edge of the blanket made me open them back up. The white-eared dog, which I now knew was probably a coyote, or at least a figment of a coyote, rested at my feet. "Oh, you again. Go away. You're not real." There was a big part of me disappointed it wasn't my blue-eyed boy.

The shaman gazed at me curiously.

I shook my head. "Don't mind me." I nodded to the patch he held. "Good drugs," I said by way of excuse.

He walked around the edge of my blanket, and I jumped when he stepped through

Fido. He knelt down beside me and felt my head. "No fever."

"Is that your professional opinion?"

"You're funny." He didn't smile, those spectacular gray eyes of his gazing wearily at me. "Do you see the spirit?"

"Huh?" Maybe we were both nut-jobs. "You see it too?"

He shook his head. "No."

Great! I'd just admitted to a perfect stranger I saw things. Shaman Billy Bob was a tricky sucker.

"I don't see it either." Hah! Two could play this game.

He basically ignored me. "Chavvah told me you were powerful. That you can see a spirit is powerful earth magic. I have felt its presence since I brought you here."

"Uh, sure. Okay." Chavvah had talked to him about me. Why? What did this old man know about me? About her?

"Tell me about the spirit," he said.

"Tell me about Chav. Were you friends with her?" I chewed my lip, contemplating the ramifications of telling Billy Bob what I knew. I wanted tit for tat. He had been close enough to Chav that she told him about me. Maybe he knew something that could help me find her.

I glanced at the ghost or whatever it was. It moved its head onto my leg. He didn't have any weight to him, which made sense. He *isn't* real, I reminded myself. "Dog-like animal, reddish-brown fur, white ear..." It looked up at me. "Green-blue eyes."

"I see." He sat cross-legged on the ground beside me. "Judah."

I snapped my gaze to Billy Bob. "You mean...he's really dead." I'd known, but I hadn't known for sure. I would have to tell Babel. Oh, God. I didn't know if I could.

Rubbing my arms, I fought to ward off the chill forming inside me.

"I'm afraid so." His lips were pursed in thought. "The white ear. It's most likely him."

Great. I was having a whole Haley Joel Osment, I-see-dead-people moment. Though in my case, it was dead animals.

"This means something, Sunny."

"Ya think?" I still didn't get it. I'd seen Judah in my visions as a man. "Why does his...er...spirit look like a dog? Please don't tell me when we die we become animals." If that were true, after death, I'd probably come to on the ethereal plane as a platypus or something.

"I'm going to tell you something, and I want you to listen, really listen, and take it in."

His voice was so serious and somber, I simply nodded.

"Judah was a *therianthrope* of the *Canis latrans* variety, known to humans as a coyote."

I searched the databases in my head, trying to grasp ahold of anything resembling sense. "Therianthrope? Thrope. Like lycanthrope? Like werewolves?" It couldn't be that.

Billy Bob cleared his throat and said stiffly, "There's only one lycan in this area. The rest are all therian."

"Oh sure." I'd spent my entire life having people laugh at me in disbelief when they found out I was psychic, so I should've been less skeptic, but come on! Being psychic is way more feasible than being able to turn into an animal. "So...Judah's a werecoyote and..." I was trying. Really, really trying.

Demerol high or no Demerol high, there weren't enough pharmaceutical drugs in all the world to convince me that shapeshifters were real, and frankly, the topic was starting to scare me. "And his ghost, in coyote form, is haunting me. I get it. No problem. I think I'm feeling much better. Does Amtrak run through anywhere close?" He hadn't answered my questions about Chay, but at this point, I didn't care. I wanted away as fast as possible.

"Sunny, I know this is difficult to believe for a human." There, he'd said it again. He'd said "human" as if he wasn't.

He'd picked up a stick, absently drawing symbols in the dirt beside me. "Judah wants and needs your help. Otherwise, he wouldn't have attached himself to you. And the fact that you can see him should be proof of that. Besides, I think he may hold the key to finding out what happened to Chavvah." He averted his gaze and bit his lower lip. "You haven't seen a coyote with gray-blue eyes, have you?"

"No, just the one with the white ear. But in my defense, I'd never seen a coyote in my life until I came here."

Billy Bob let out the breath he'd been holding. "Fair 'nuff." He nodded. "Let's focus on Judah. He has come to you for a reason. You have to figure out why."

I couldn't argue with the fact I could see this thing —I refused to call him Judah—but I still wasn't sure if it was a hallucination. And who was the coyote with gray-blue eyes? Chav had gray eyes. Did Billy Bob believe she was the same therianthrope, animal shifting thing that Judah was?

I leaned toward Billy Bob and touched his hand. Immediately, I was somewhere else.

Out in the deep woods, the smell of earth and spring grass scented the air. A middle-aged man with short gray hair sat with a young boy, also gray-haired, on a log near a trickling creek.

The boy looked up at the older man. "Grandfather, why are

all the wolves leaving." Grandfather? The man didn't look much past forty while the boy was at least twelve.

The older man stared off into the trees. "It's no longer safe for them. Nor us. Men have come to hunt them. It means they hunt us as well."

"I don't want to leave our home." The boy's mood soured with every word.

"Home is where you make it, Billy Bob. Nothing more. Nothing less."

The wild scents left, the breeze went away, the serene creek, all of it, gone. I found myself staring into the intense face of the shaman.

He held my hand carefully, like handling a snake. Very un-Shaman-like he said,

"That was freaky."

"What?" I was still adjusting to being back in the sweat lodge.

"Do you have some kind of seizure disorder?" Apparently the shaman was gone, and the doctor was in.

I knew from other people that when I went into a vision, sometimes my body shook, my eyes would roll back, and it could look pretty bad, but not always.

"No. I..." Oh, hell, why was I trying to explain myself to him? He was a few brain cells short anyhow, believing in were-creatures and all. Actually, though, it dawned on me, his belief in the paranormal might work in my favor. "You said that Chavvah told you about my abilities, right?"

"Yes, sort of. Go on." He nodded and waited for me to continue.

"Well, sometimes when I have a vision, my whole body gets involved. It's as if the vision triggers a grand mal seizure, but it's not really a seizure." I wasn't too concerned about him not believing me. I got the feeling the shaman believed in a whole lot of shit without much convincing.

I waited for Billy Bob to go off on some mystical explanation, but he just raised an eyebrow and stared at me curiously. "Interesting."

"That's it. *Interesting*?"

"And you had a psychic episode just now?"

"Yes."

Now, I wanted to tell him everything. Billy Bob made me feel relaxed and safe. I didn't feel as if he was judging me. Granted, it could've just been the pain medication still in my system, but I wanted to trust him.

"I saw you."

His eyes widened appreciably.

Throwing caution to the wind, I told him everything I'd seen.

"I see," Billy Bob finally said after a few moments of awkward silence. "This changes things even more, Sunny. When Chavvah had talked about bringing you to Peculiar, I was reluctant to support her wishes, but she felt so strongly, I agreed. But now that I see your ability is real and special, I think you were brought to Peculiar for a reason."

"I wasn't *brought* to Peculiar. No one or nothing brought me here. I drove to town all on my own volition." I didn't want to believe what Billy Bob was saying. Not about Peculiar, not about me, and not about Chav having a larger reason than friendship for wanting me to come here. But I had felt drawn to the place, hadn't I? Even before I drove into town.

Suddenly, I felt alone. More than ever I wished Chavvah was here. She grounded me. Kept me centered. The only other person…A twinge of tightness in my chest made it hard to breathe. Where was Babel? Why wasn't he next to me right now? He'd said that he was drawn to me, ached for me like no one else, but I'd been in this damn sweat tent for three days, and he was nowhere to be seen.

Fucking men!

"This is serious business, Sunny."

Damn right it was. "Yeah, seriously fucked-up." Had I said that aloud? I must have if the disapproval showing in Shaman Billy Bob's eyes was any indication.

"Judah's disappearance has been a mystery. I think if he's dead, he wants to be found so he can be put to rest. And I also think he can help us find Chavvah."

"Dead," I said dully, feeling a little shocky. Oh God. Could it be true? My hands, trembling, went to my mouth. How would I tell my friend when I found her…and Babel?

"You can see things that are beyond our abilities as shifters. I think Chavvah was right. I believe you were meant for this town."

How could he so readily accept my psychic prowess? It had taken me the better part of my pubescent years to come to terms with it. And just because he believed me, didn't mean I would automatically believe *him*. I mean, yeah, weird stuff had happened since I'd been in Peculiar, being attacked by a wild animal was just the topper. But ghosts? Were-people? People who could take animal forms?

As if he could read my thoughts, Billy Bob said, "If I prove to you that therianthropes and lycanthropes exist, will you at least try to believe everything else I've told you?"

"That seems reasonable." What was I saying? Reasonable-shmeasonable. What possible proof could he offer?

Shaman Billy Bob stood up and started to disrobe.

Oh, man! He was going to get naked. He was probably all old and wrinkly under the makeup and clothes. I didn't want to see a wrinkly old guy's body. "What are you doing?"

"I don't want to get tangled when I shift." The fur he wore around his shoulders hit the ground.

He was decidedly *not* old and *not* wrinkly in the chest. On the contrary, his muscles were smooth and wiry. Lithe even. He turned his back to me, then off went the leather trousers. His ass was shapely, firm and raised. You could bounce quarters off those buttocks. His body was that of a runner or swimmer. Taller than Babel and quite a bit leaner.

He glanced over his shoulder at me. "You ready."

"Uh, sure." I mostly expected nothing to happen, but he was easy on the eyes, which made it no problem to keep watching.

The air shimmered around him. I'd say it was a trick

of the light casting off from the fire, but it was solely concentrated on him.

A thick push of air breathed over my body as his skin danced, dark gray and white fur sprouting like tumbling skinny dominoes covering his entire body. In half fascination, half shock, I stared as he turned and his nose elongated slightly, but not completely wolfish.

Gray eyes stared back at me, so human. In the next second, he dropped to all fours, his body shimmering into a full-on gray wolf. I gasped. "Holy sweet mother."

The wolf sniffed around me. Absently, I reached for its thick fur. I needed to feel it, to know I wasn't crazy. It was remarkably soft and dry to touch, much like the coyote had been in my dream. And warm.

The fur disappeared out of my hand, and kneeling before me, Billy Bob once again looked human. His gray dreads dragged the dirt floor as he tilted his face upward to me and, even more shocking, the face paint was gone, and he wasn't the old man I'd imagined. The unlined skin on his chiseled face nearly took my breath away.

He was beautiful, manly beautiful, but beautiful all the same. Babel was ruggedly handsome while Billy Bob's face could have easily graced a Calvin Klein ad. He was the Jason Momoa of the Midwest. Wowza.

"Is that enough proof?" he finally asked.

Judah whined. I'd nearly forgotten the ghost coyote. I looked over at him, and he yelped a bark. Tingles shot through my fingertips, lips, and tongue. I felt light-headed. "Sunny?"

I turned back to Billy Bob.

"Can you believe now?" He'd already put his pants back on.

"I believe." I believed in werewolves. I'd seen one with my own two eyes. As to the part about me being there to help them solve some deep backwoods mystery? Well, that remained to be seen.

Chavvah Trimmel was my best friend. She had been my best friend for a lot of years. She knew everything there was to know about me, including the fact that I had a psychic gift. However, it was looking more and more likely that she had kept a secret from me. A really, really huge one. I wasn't sure how I felt about her deceit. It didn't change the fact that I wanted to find her, and I wanted her to be safe, but I wasn't certain what the future would hold for us beyond that. How could she keep this from me? I trusted her, but apparently, in our friendship, trust was a one-way street.

Billy Bob cleared his throat. "It's kind of cool if you think about it."

"*Cool* is finding a permanent cure for cancer. *Cool* is dating a millionaire. *Cool* is having perky tits when you're sixty-five. This—" I pointed at him. "—is so not cool." Okay, it was a little cool, but frankly, it also scared the crap out of me. I didn't want to be this person. The bigot. The one who couldn't get beyond someone's idiosyncrasy, but shoot, this was BIG. I'd have to digest.

Billy Bob kept me in the tent one more night before giving me the A-OK to go back to my apartment. He'd explained more than once how were-animals existed, and even though I accepted paranormal creatures walked the earth and kept whole towns for themselves, it was still difficult to fathom.

Apparently, they could shift at will. It was part of their nature, but once a month, on the full moon, they were forced to shift into complete animal form without choice. Unfortunately, the full moon had happened my second night in town. The puzzle pieces were falling into place. They'd wanted me to leave for two reasons: my own safety and to prevent the exposure of who and what they were.

I couldn't blame them. On either count. Damn Chavvah for not telling me.

Babel picked me up from Billy Bob's and drove toward town. I had trouble looking at him. I felt humiliated and embarrassed. I'd slept with a man who wasn't a man who could turn into what? I hadn't even asked him. Though...I glanced over. His blue, blue eyes stared out at the road.

"You're coyote?" Of course that made sense. Judah was a coyote. So, duh, why wouldn't his brother be the same? For that matter, Chavvah too. "You saved me."

He grunted uncomfortably. "Did I?"

"You don't remember? You pulled the other coyote off me the night I was attacked.

Unless there are more animals running around with your exact eye color."

"I don't remember."

"How can you not remember? Shaman Billy Bob said you guys could think like humans when you were in animal form." Was I really saying this out loud?

"What *Doctor Smith* didn't tell you is that on the full moon, we become more animal than human."

The way he'd said "Doctor Smith" gave me the impression I'd hit a sore spot. What didn't Babel like about Billy Bob?

I thought the shaman was a little weird, but totally cool. I let Babel continue without asking what his beef was with the lycan. It could wait. Besides, after not seeing him for three days, I was trying hard to work on being angry with him, but failing miserably. He was just so delicious to look at.

I sighed softly as I took in his broad shoulders. He was wearing a dark-gold sleeveless tee shirt and a tight pair of jeans. His look was finished off with a baseball cap and a pair of cowboy boots.

God! My mind was drifting to farmhand fantasies.

The young stud out bucking hay. The farmer's wife watches from the porch, waiting with an enticing pitcher of lemonade that will be the catalyst for her seduction. Sweat drips from his forehead as he stops work to stare across the yard at her. He lifts his shirts, exposing his tightly carved abs, as he wipes the sweat from his brow.

"Sunny," Babel said, piercing my fantasy. "Where'd you go? Did you have another vision?"

Yes. "No." I wished. I could stand to have that one come true. "I just got lost for a moment." *In your beautiful eyes and wonderful body.* "Tell me again."

"During the full moon, our minds," he tapped his head, "go to a place of pure instinct. Although bits and pieces of the night do show up as broken memories, it's more like pieces of a dream." He popped the clutch on his old truck and shifted down a gear. "It's why I think you shouldn't be here, Sunny. We're too dangerous for humans to be around full-time."

Jeezus. I knew his secret. He knew mine. But he was still trying to get rid of me. "Fine. Take me to the nearest bus station." I didn't mean it. There was no way in the world these jerks were going to get me to leave before I found my friend, but I was mad enough to make an empty gesture.

He adjusted the speed again, making the pickup lurch forward. I braced myself against the dash.

"I'm afraid it's too late for that," he said reluctantly.

"What? Too late for what?" The way he said it made me nervous. What did these creatures have planned for me? Then something else that I should have considered popped into my head. "I was bitten."

"Yeah." He rubbed my back as I dropped down and put my head between my knees.

"Will I..."

"Be turned into one of us?" he finished for me.

"Oh, it's too awful to think about." I clutched my head, willing all the bad stuff to go away. Oh, no. I couldn't be a werewolf or coyote or whatever. I could just imagine the amount of razors I would have to invest in. I hated to shave as it was, but if I was an animal, I'd probably get all hairy, and it was bad enough that I'd started to get chin hairs since I'd passed thirty-three—Holy crap, what if I started growing a full beard? I didn't want to get furry on the full moon.

I heard Babel's soft chuckle.

"It's not funny." I hiccupped.

"No worries, Sunny darlin'. We aren't made. Only born. The bite of a therianthrope won't turn you."

As the fear ebbed, again, anger was there to replace it. Asshole. "What are you guys planning on doing to me?"

"Doing to you?" He rubbed his palm against his jeans. "Absolutely nothing."

CHAPTER EIGHT

*V*ISIONS OF COYOTES, bears, and rabid beavers tearing my body to shreds danced in my head. No, not a real vision. Just my own worries wreaking havoc on my emotions. With the town just up ahead, I rabbit-punched Babel in the kidney.

In a normal dude, he'd have doubled over breathless, I'm sure. Apparently, wereguys weren't normal. He looked at me, annoyance plain on his face. "What'd you do that for?"

"Pull over." I wanted out of this truck and out of it this instant. I had stumbled onto a long-held secret, and while the wacky shaman might think it was fate, I had a feeling the rest of the town would view me as a threat.

"Sunny, we're almost in town."

"Pull over!" I shouted. Grabbing the door handle, I tried to push the door open.

Damn rusty piece of crap didn't budge.

"What are you doing?"

I rolled down the window. "I'm getting out." Unbuckling the seat belt, I climbed up into the open window. "You can pull over and let me out. Or I can jump."

Who was I kidding? We were only going about twenty-five miles per hour, but even at that speed, the fall would probably kill me. If I managed to not get myself run over in the process.

Babel grabbed me by the shirt and yanked me back down into the seat. "Don't be stupid."

Stupid? He had *not* just called me stupid! "I feel sick. Babel, pull this truck over, or I'm going to ralph all over you."

The truck slammed to a stop, and I flew forward. Babel's arm was the only thing that kept me from banging my head into the windshield.

"You all right?" I heard Babel ask.

"All right? All right? Am I all right?"

"That's what I asked."

"No, I am not all right! Are you an idiot?" My chest started to hurt, and I began to hyperventilate again. "I. Am. Freaking. Out." I tried to get my breathing under control.

Now was so not the time to have a panic attack. "I need air."

"Maybe I should take you back to the doc?"

"No!" I didn't want to go back to Billy Bob's. Even with Chavvah still missing, I had the sudden urge to escape. I wanted to go home. And not Peculiar—San Diego home.

"Just let me out. Let me out. Let me out."

"Okay, okay." I heard the panic rising in his voice. He reached over and pushed the door open on the passenger side.

I fell out onto the asphalt road and scrambled to my feet. I was never so glad to be wearing my tennis shoes. It was going to be a long walk.

Babel was out and on the other side next to me before I could get my bearings.

"The nearest town is thirty or so miles that way?" I pointed west.

"You'll never make it."

"What? You going to hunt me down like a dog?"

His chin jerked back as if I'd hit him. "I just meant, it's a long, hard walk from here."

"I'm sorry." My chest still hurt, but my breathing eased. "I made a mistake. I shouldn't have come here." There was definitely a sorry-for-myself, verging-on-whiney factor going on.

"Sunny." Babel's voice was kind and gentle. It made me even more nervous because it reminded me of how people talk when someone has just died. "You don't know how much I hate that you're in this position. Chavvie had no right to bring you into this world."

A sharp bark drew my gaze. I sighed. "Not now, Judah. Go away."

"What?" Babel asked wearily, then his voice became strained. "Judah?"

"Yeah." Then. "Oh." I realized Babel didn't know his brother was among the deceased. The wind kicked dust up just as I inhaled. I coughed, covering my face with the collar of my T-shirt.

"Is it like one of your…episodes?"

"Uhmm, well, not really, but sort of."

"Just now, though." He pulled me up, my face mere inches from his chest. "Did you have one now? About Judah? Do you know where he is?"

"No, no. Nothing like that," I tried to explain, but how did I tell him that his brother's ghost was stalking me in coyote form?

"You're keeping something from me, Sunny."

No shit. "I…" I didn't feel right not telling Babel what I knew, even if it hurt him.

"The coyote I've been seeing…"

"Yes." His bright blue eyes lanced my heart with their intensity.

I stroked his cheek then took his hand. His fingers felt so warm against mine. I hadn't noticed before how much heat his skin gave off. I guess I'd just attributed the temperature to the fact that everything in Missouri was damned hot at the moment. I bit my lower lip and steeled my courage. "It's Judah's ghost. I'm sorry, Babel. I really am."

He shook his head, his face grim. "Do you know what happened to him? Has he said anything?"

Sighing, I put my arms around him and rubbed my face against his chest. I fit perfectly against his body as if he'd been made for me. "I'm sorry. He's in coyote form, and while he barks and whines, I've got no idea what he wants from me."

His thick fingers laced my hair at the nape. Tilting

my head back, he closed his lips on mine. Heat moved thick like a living, breathing entity between us. There was no werecreatures, no ghost, and no Peculiar. Just Babel and I locked into a moment of desire. I wanted to lick him from head to toe right there on the dusty road. Caution and common sense be damned.

A daunting howl sounded from behind me, snapping me back to reality.

Babel had been a one-off. Not lifetime-commitment material. If I allowed myself to fall, I knew I'd fall hard (and probably crack my head and break a few bones in the process). Besides, he wasn't even human. On top of that, he could be the end of my friendship with Chav. She would not want me banging her brother. It went back to that girl code. Regardless of the physical chemistry between us, these issues seemed an insurmountable problem to overcome.

Reluctantly, I broke the kiss. "We can't."

"We already did." Grief glittered in his eyes, but he forced a thin smile. Wow, he was trying to lighten the mood. Either that or lust was clouding his judgment.

Smacking Babel's chest, I stepped away from him. I glanced at Judah's ghost. "We have eyes on us right now, and I'm not into exhibitionism."

"You really can see him?"

"Yeah. You don't seem surprised that he's, you know…"

He finger-combed his mussed mane of hair. "I've known for a while my brother was gone. Not just missing. He might not have wanted to live in the human world, but he always kept in contact with our folks and me. Judah wouldn't have just run off."

"I get that. But you believe me? I'm not used to that. Most people think I'm a crackpot."

He lowered his eyes. "If your abilities are real, then there is a real chance we can find Chavvie. I couldn't help Judah, but I don't want to let my sister down."

I didn't want to let anyone down, but I'd lived with this wretched psychic curse for most my life, and it was nothing if not unreliable. I worried that I would fail Chavvah, especially now that I knew Judah was dead.

"I'm starving. Feed me and then we'll see if I can justify some of this hope you have where I'm concerned."

Chavvah's cabin, where Babel was staying, surprised me. It was tidy and neat.

"Make yourself at home." His voice was distant as he rummaged the cabinets of his kitchen.

I watched him put fettuccini noodles on the counter. He opened the freezer and pulled out a bundle wrapped in white butcher's paper. "That's not meat, is it?"

He held up the parcel. "Only the best. Prime Grade-A beef from the cattle ranch up the road." Tossing the meat in his hand, he smiled. "Hope you're real hungry."

I shuddered. "I'm a vegetarian. So no beef for me." Then another thought hit me. There were werecoyotes, wereopossums, wererraccoons, deer, squirrels, bears. Oh, holy hell! "Are there werecows?"

Babel's eyes went wide, his jaw clenched for a moment. Then the corners of his eyes crinkled, and he began laughing, and not just a chuckle. This laugh bordered on a guffaw with several snorts added in for good measure. "There're no such things as werecows, Sunny," he finally managed when he could once again breathe.

"Well, how in the hell am I supposed to know? Up until recently I would have said there's no such creature as a were-anything." I threw my hands up. "You people need to come up with a damn manual or at least a *Werebeasts For Dummies* book."

"We're not beasts."

"Aw, I'm sorry. Did I hurt your hairy little feelings?" Big, dumb stupid-head. Teach him to laugh at me. Ha ha!

He growled, proving my beast point. "So, no beef?"

"Pretty much." I grinned. I couldn't help myself.

Babel, as it turned out, was a whiz in the kitchen. He made up a feast of pasta and veggies rivaling any of the meals I'd had at those fancy-schmancy vegan restaurants in California. Plus, all his kitchen wizardry had the added advantage of allowing me a private showing of his perfect ass. I was getting hungry, but not for food. Yum. When he was finished, and I'd managed to pick my tongue off the floor and put my eyeballs back in my head, he offered me a cold bottle of beer.

"Do you want a glass?" he asked as we walked out to the front porch to eat and take in the beautiful evening.

I sat on the swing, a two-seater, and marveled at the clear sky. I didn't think I'd ever seen stars look so close and bright before. "Bottle's fine."

"My kind of gal." He took up residence on the other side of the porch swing.

I'd been thinking about Billy Bob's transformation from human to half-beast to wolf. I wondered if they all could change so quickly and efficiently. He seemed like such a nice man. Why didn't Babel like him? I didn't know a delicate way to bring it up, so I asked point-blank. "What's your problem with Billy Bob?"

"Other than his name?" Babel snorted. "Aw, Doc Smith is all right. He's competent at what he does. It's the whole Shaman-priest thing that bothers me."

"Really? Why?"

He shrugged and took a swig from his beer. "I'm a Christian."

Not what I was expecting. I was raised a neo-pagan, but spiritually I was bereft.

"And Billy Bob?"

"He perpetuates the old religious customs that keep shapeshifters and others like us, you know, different from humans, in the dark ages."

Others like us. What others? And did I really want to know? I shook my head. "What kinds of customs?"

"Worship of animal ancestry. Spirit walks. That sort of thing."

"Oh." Well, with everything I'd seen and been through, who was I to question Babel or Billy Bob's faiths? To each their own and all.

"So, Judah's ghost has just been hanging around? No rhyme or reason?" Babel changed the topic so abruptly, it startled me. He really didn't want to talk about the shaman.

"Not that I can tell." I felt weird talking about his dead brother. Especially, since Judah hadn't left my side since he'd shown up on the road. It dawned on me though, the one place he'd led me had been to Sheila Murphy. "Do you think Sheila might've had something to do with your brother's disappearance?"

He paused a moment, as if to think about the question carefully. Finally, he shook his head. "Sheila's a lot of things. Spoiled, wild, a free-spirit, and often a bitch. But she's no killer."

A stab of jealousy went through me. He sounded as though he admired her. And, damn, I was a fool. He'd had sex with her two days before he'd had sex with me. Did Sheila think her and Babel had a relationship? I pushed the awful question away, and concentrated on more productive thoughts. Babel had said Sheila was no killer, but I had wounds on my shoulder that begged to differ. Or at least I was pretty certain it had been Sheila. Those eyes were too much like hers. She would have killed me and had me for dinner the night of the full moon if Babel hadn't pulled her off.

But he seemed so adamant about her character that I didn't think I could get him to agree. Instead, I changed the subject. "Why do you want to leave Peculiar?"

Babel shrugged before standing up. He paced back and forth, his gaze never wavering from me as he moved. When he finally stopped, he shook his head with a denial that seemed to filter all the way through him. "This isn't my world."

I snorted beer through my nose. Not attractive. "Sorry."

"S'okay." He took the bottom of his T-shirt and wiped the beer from my face. I leaned forward into his touch so that his palm brushed my skin. The natural heat from his hand spread through me from nose to toes. I'd read books before where the heroine's "loins were aching." I always thought the description was a total corn-fest. Not anymore. My loins ached. Oh, jeezus, they totally ached.

If Babel noticed, he didn't react. He wiped his hands on his jeans and said, "I can see how you'd think it was strange. I grew up with humans. I like humans. Hell, some of the people I care about most in the world are human." He rested his warm palm on my cheek.

I leaned forward to fully meet his caress.

"That's not to say that I don't like therians," he added. "That would just be too self-loathing. But, I guess, I just don't want to hide myself from the world."

The last bit hit a little close to home. Chavvah had known how unhappy I was in California. I'd wanted to escape, just another way to hide, from the world I'd come from, so when she'd proposed the restaurant in Small Town, Midwest, I'd jumped at the chance. And look how that turned out. Here I was, the only human in a town full of shapeshifters. I really couldn't fathom what Chav had been thinking.

Chav.

Guilt throbbed in my gut. I should be out there looking for her every minute of every day until I found her. I had been more than useless since my arrival in town. The only things I'd managed to do were have sex with her brother and nearly get myself killed. But what could I do?

I really wasn't Nancy Drew. I didn't know how to investigate the ingredients on a box of honey buns. How in the hell was I going to find a missing person? Why hadn't Chav just sent a longer text? Something with a big, fat, get-a-clue moment?

Instead of, "Sunny, I need u," would it have killed her to add a few more letters, such as, "Sunny, I need u. I'm being kidnapped or followed by John Doe." Had she been kidnapped? Or was she choosing to stay hidden?

My gut knotted with anxiety, but my head told me that the Chavvah I knew, the one who'd become my best friend, was too smart to get herself trapped.

I didn't understand how she could love a place so much, or how Judah could have loved the same place, and yet, something so sinister lurked beneath the surface. Heck, the place did have a way about it. Even I'd been drawn to the town immediately. Why was Babel so reluctant to embrace its charm?

"You don't have to stay here, ya know." I shrugged. "Hide, I mean. It's not like anyone in the outside world can know what you really are."

"And what do you think I am, Sunny?" Babel rolled his neck, cracking bones in the process. "I'm a man first. And while I have to hide the animal side of myself, out there I can follow my dreams in a way that I can't here. I have ambitions that move beyond this kind of place. I mean, I went to college, got a degree. I couldn't ever use it here. There's not a lot of call for a public relations analyst in this type of community. Do you get that?"

Public relations analyst? What the heck? Maybe there was more to Babel Trimmel than I'd first thought. I did understand, though. He liked being among the free and the brave, having the ability to pursue his life, liberty, and happiness. Being in Peculiar was like being in another country. It had its own citizens, politics, and rules.

I risked another sip of beer, letting the cool amber liquid trickle into my mouth. "I get it. I just look out at this peaceful front yard with all its trees and no neighbors, and wonder how anyone could want to live anywhere but here."

I'd also seen the backyard view from the window in the kitchen, nothing but a sparse lot of trees and a gorgeous lake. I could totally live here, and when I found Chavvah, we'd...My gut ached for my friend. I'd been less than useless since I'd arrived in Peculiar. Finding out no one was human had been a big pill to swallow, but at least it gave me more information to investigate when I got back into town.

Oh. Town. It dawned on me that I had no idea what the good denizens of Peculiar planned on doing with me. They wouldn't want to take a chance on their second nature getting out. And no matter what a boon Billy Bob thought I was, I figured most of the town wouldn't be feeling quite as warmly toward me. "What do you people plan to do with me, by the way?"

"Do with you?" His eyes softened around the edges and warm heat from his gaze melted me to my toes.

"Well, I don't know about *you people,* but there are several things I'd like to do with you."

His voice had dropped two octaves, the way it did when he was lusty and sexy, and it fondled my horny button like no man's voice ever had. It made me want to be fondled in so many, many wicked and naughty ways, but truthfully, I wanted to know. I had dawned on me more than once that I knew a major secret, and it was a secret people might be willing to kill for.

"Stop that." Although his teasing actually made me feel better, I didn't think Babel was the kind of guy who would try to sleep with a woman who was about to be dead meat. Then again, I would have never thought Babel was the kind of guy to sprout a tail either.

He sat down next me and traced the skin of my arm to the bend of my elbow with his fingertips. Goosebumps raised on my forearm. "Well, it's not like we haven't been...intimate."

He said "intimate" as if it was some magic word. I closed my eyes, enjoying the feeling of home I got when Babel touched me. In a way, it was just like with Chav, not the sexual attraction part, but the part that drew me to him like a kitten to a box. Why did he make me feel safe? If I knew nothing else, I knew the feeling was probably a result of an adrenaline rush. I barely knew Babel's mind or the way he thought or felt about anything real. I knew he had a gorgeous body and that he knew how to use the damn thing, but beyond that, our relationship was more about our connection to his sister than about anything between us. I opened my eyes and moved his hand away then walked to the edge of the porch.

He came up behind me, his arms wrapping around me and folding me into him. Leaning my head against his shoulder, I gave into the press of his chest against my back as his thickly muscled arms wrapped me in a cocoon that was a mixture of safety and lust. The avocado in his California roll. Oh, how I wanted to completely give myself to Babel. Especially when the sculpted muscles of his thighs grazed my ass. The pool of moisture between my legs indicated the flesh was definitely willing, even if the spirit wavered.

As he rubbed himself against me, the rigid planes of his hips and groin pressing into me added to my growing need to boink him immediately. I turned in his arms. I would let him take me, possess me. I was weak against his seduction.

The phone rang in the house, trilling loudly, and breaking Babel's spell on me. I groaned and nestled my face against his chest. "You better answer that. It could be important."

He nibbled my jawline and kissed me. His mouth was wet and delicious with cold beer. "The answering machine can get it," he said.

Oh, God, I wanted to run my fingers all over his body and dig the tips into his firm flesh. To have him fill me again, to ride me until I vanished into a delicious orgasm that would make all the bad stuff fade, was beyond tempting.

The answering machine picked up, and while I couldn't make out the actual, "leave your name and number part," my skin burned when I recognized the person leaving the message.

"Babe, call me, sweetheart. I am aching for you."

Hearing Sheila stopped my breath and my heart. I stepped away from Babel and out of his grasp.

"Fuck," he whispered. "Sunny, it's not what you think."

"You have no idea what I'm thinking," I said, my voice cold even to my own ears. My shoulder ached and I rubbed it. I wanted a hot shower. More to put distance and a door between us than for any other reason. Total bastard! "I want to go back to the apartment."

Babel came up behind me. "You can stay here tonight." There wasn't the same lasciviousness in his voice as before. It was an offer now, nothing more.

"I want to be alone." Really, I didn't want to be alone. Not after the attack.

"Sunny." Babel's voice was soft and low, gentling. "You should stay, at least until tomorrow." He touched my hair. "I'll sleep on the couch."

The offer was tempting, not because I wanted him, but because I really was scared. A lot of stuff had gone down over the past several days, and while I liked to think I was bad-ass, it just wasn't true. I hated myself for feeling like a damsel in distress. I wanted to say screw it, and make him take me home. I wished hard for my vehicle. If it hadn't been busted up so badly from the wreck, I'd drive to the nearest roadside park, lock the doors, and sleep away my worries.

Regrettably, I had no such options. So, for safety

reasons only, I decided to stay. It had nothing to do with his bulging muscles, tight ass, or endearing dimples. I was a fool for having gotten myself involved with him in the first place—best friend's brother and way younger than me—I reminded myself.

But the thoughts didn't stop me from needing to be with someone tonight, as in proximity, not sex. "Okay then."

CHAPTER NINE

I ***WALKED INTO*** *the kitchen with the worst tunnel vision of my life. Not even six Black Martinis at The Bitter End had produced such a fuzzy peripheral. I noticed immediately the kitchen wasn't Babel's kitchen or my own.*

Where the hell am I?

I opened my mouth to ask, but instead the words "Where do you keep your spatulas?" came out and they were said with a distinctly male voice.

Huh? I looked down at my large hands and hairy knuckles.

This can't be good.

There wasn't a response to the question, so I began rummaging through the kitchen drawers. Really weird, since all I wanted to do was get the heck out of whomever's body I was in. In one of the drawers, under a pile of cooking utensils, I saw a red ledger. I could feel the quiet curiosity of my host's mind.

Flipping open the book, I saw dates, initials, and monetary *sums. Big, really big sums. 07/15 JT $15,000, 07/25 RC $17,500, 07/19 GH $20,000, and so on, the numbers and letters continued. Whatever the money was for, the price kept going up.*

"Hey, sugar," my host said. "What's this book about?"

I was glad he asked. I was curious myself. I put the ledger back in the drawer where I found it and pulled a spatula from the next drawer I looked in. "I hope you like your eggs over easy."

Before I could turn around to see who "sugar" was, I woke up with a foggy brain.

I was on Babel's couch, my head pounding still from the dream. At least I was pretty sure it was a dream. I remembered the word "sugar" but the rest had already started to fade.

The couch had been fairly comfortable, so I wasn't completely pissed at myself for convincing Babel to sleep in his own bed. Not that there weren't several times during the night where I'd woken up and thought seriously about making the journey to the bedroom, but good sense kept me in place. And other than a minor crick in the neck and some quiet regret, I'd survived the night on *Temptation Island*.

I can't say I was completely delighted at Babel's self-restraint. Not that I wanted to have sex with a player. I'd promised myself after the last guy that I wouldn't fall for the same bullshit again. So why did I want to give up my scruples for Babel? It couldn't just be about his looks. I've never been that shallow about guys. I'd almost allowed myself, during dinner the night before, to imagine a relationship with him. I could be so dumb sometimes.

Since my clothing options were limited, Babel loaned me a black T-shirt and a pair of basketball shorts that were ridiculously big on me, but at least had a drawstring. The shirt smelled wonderfully of candied orange peels. I'd never smelled a fabric softener or detergent quite like it. Bunching the shirt in my fists, I took another whiff. Babel was full of pleasant surprises. *No,* I admonished myself. *I will not think fondly of him. I will not think of him at all.*

Getting up at six in the morning was not one of those pleasant surprises. An ungodly hour and Babel was already in the kitchen rustling around when I wandered in. *Holy hard body, Batman!* He only had on boxer briefs, and wow, in the light of day, and for the third time, I had to marvel at all the dips, and curves, and cuts of his muscles. Even with his hairy chest, every part of him was the very definition of *definition*. "Don't you have clothes?"

"My place," he grumbled.

"Chavvah's place," I countered.

"My sister," he said.

"My..." I had nothing. He'd been staying here before I arrived, and until we found Chav, he had more of a claim than I did. "Thanks for putting me up last night."

"I asked you."

"Yeah, I know. But still."

"You look great." His eyes drew to slits in that dreamy yummy way.

"I like your fabric softener." Lame. Super lame.

"Yeah, it's good." He chuckled and shook his head.

Great, well, we agreed on laundry products. A match

made in heaven. Aside from the whole "he's leaving to go back to his real life, Chavvah would hurt me, and the whole other woman" thing. Oh, and the fact that he was a lot younger than me. By a lot, I meant…"How old are you again?"

He faltered for a moment at the unexpected question. "Old enough."

I nearly choked on the sip of coffee I'd just taken. "Huh." I tried to sound nonchalant.

"How old are you?"

Didn't he know it was rude to ask a woman her age? Next, he'd want to know how much I weighed. "Old enough." Thank heavens I'd resisted saying, "Too old."

He raised a questioning brow, and I wanted to punch him in the face. Needless to say, he was smart enough not to give voice to his doubts.

"Want some grits?"

I scrunched my nose. I'd heard of grits, but I'd never actually had them. "I don't know."

"You either want them, or you don't." He pulled a pan from the oven and a cylindrical container from the cupboard.

"What do they taste like?"

"I can't believe you've never had grits. You're in for a treat. They're warm and soft and buttery."

The way he described them, they sounded like a much-needed hug.

"And." He smiled, dipping his head toward me. "No animals will be harmed during the process."

I nudged him. "Yeah, yeah. Whatever."

He poured white granules into the pan and added

water, turning on his gas stove. "You a total vegan, or can I add cream? It's the secret ingredient."

"Not so much a secret now that you've told me. And, no. I'm not a total vegan. I can do byproducts, just not meat." I didn't go on to explain about the crazy bloody butcher visions that turned me off meat in the first place.

"Got it. No meat."

The thumb handles just below his hip bones were deeply carved grooves leading to much more exotic and southerly locations. They were calling my attention. I licked my lips, contemplating what it would be like to lick the crevice down to his man-bits.

"Speaking of meat."

His grin went crooked. "Oh yeah?"

"You're a horn-dog." Who really needed to put some damn clothes on.

"You're half right."

"The dog part."

"Nope." Babel moved in fast, catching me completely off guard. I froze as he kissed me hard. He turned the heat off on the stove and turned it up in the kitchen. I'm not sure when it happened in all the groping and clinging, but it wasn't long before my T-shirt was on the floor and the basketball shorts were down around my ankles.

Going to his knees, Babel kissed my breasts, my stomach, my...I didn't want him to stop. "Stop," I whispered, my fingers enmeshed in his thick hair.

He peered up at me—desire, passion, and a dark

carnality filled his eyes. His voice thick, with a slight growl, he said, "I want you so bad, Sunny."

Oh, man, I wanted him as much as he wanted me, if not more. "I can't."

He sighed heavily, wearily. His fingers squeezed my hips before he stood up and turned back to the stove. He certainly knew how to take "no" for an answer, much to my chagrin. I watched, stunned at my own stupidity, as the small flame under the pot flickered back to life.

More regret. I put the T-shirt back on, but stepped out of the shorts hanging around my ankles and kicked them aside.

"So, you can change whenever you want?"

"Change?"

"You know." I wiggled my fingers. "It's not just on the full moon."

Shaman Billy Bob could change at will; he'd proven that to me. He'd also made the distinction between lycans and therians. I wanted to know if there were differences.

"I can *change*, as you say, when I want." He shuffled his feet uncomfortably. "I've never really talked about this part of my life with a human before. Hell, I don't even think I've talked about it with a therian."

"I don't want to pry." Yes, I did. I wanted to pry hard. I'd somehow gotten myself entangled in a world completely different from my own, and I wanted to know exactly what kind of people, er, animals, or beings I was dealing with.

"It's okay. Really. Just feels a little weird is all. We're

brought up with one restriction. Keep the secret. Above and beyond anything else."

"I wish Chav had told me." I felt my eyes welling. I missed her so damned bad it physically hurt. This was exactly the kind of time I needed her the most. I wanted to call her. Hear her voice. Have her tell me to I wasn't losing my mind. I also wanted to give her the bitching of a lifetime. BFFs did NOT keep these kinds of secrets from each other!

"She wanted to, Sunny. We talked about it, and I'd tried hard to convince her to cut ties with you."

His words hurt. "I can't believe you—"

He quickly added, "Before I knew you. Before I knew you had secrets of your own. Chavvie didn't want to keep this from you. But when you grow up like we do, it's not easy. And keeping our secrets is more than just about us. There are therian communities across America that would be affected if our existence got out."

I guess I could see his point. It actually made me feel better about Chav not telling me. It still hurt a little, but I understood now that it wasn't just *her* secret she'd have been revealing. Looking back on it, I remember several times where I knew she'd wanted to tell me something. Something important.

God, it had to be a monster of a burden to grow up with a covert life.

I knew from babysitting experience when I was younger that kids aren't the greatest secret keepers. How did the shifters manage to keep their young from spilling the beans? "You went to regular school? How did you never tell anyone? If I was a kid with that kind of ability, I'd want to tell everyone."

"I was home-schooled until I was a teenager." He shrugged his massive shoulders and stirred the grits. "When I was old enough to understand the differences between myself and the humans, my parents let me attend high school."

"I was home-schooled."

"Yeah?" He smiled for a second. Fleeting, but nice.

"My parents were New-Agers. They were all about the learning experience being a natural process, not some restricted, dictated indoctrination. Their words." Sometimes, I wondered how I would have fared among other teenagers. Would I have been popular or picked on? Babel didn't look like the kind of guy who is easily bullied. "I bet you had a wild time in high school." He definitely looked like a coach's wet dream. Probably all the girls had wanted him and all the boys had wanted to be him.

He scooped the grits into two bowls, added a dash more salt, a pat of butter, and finished with a generous amount of heavy whipping cream. "It was different."

"Different, huh?" Steam wafted from the bowl he handed me. "Mmm, smells good enough to eat." And after the first bite, I decided grits might replace donuts as my favorite fruit. Warm, buttery, creamy, and artery hardening. Everything I loved in a food.

"Yeah, I didn't really fit in. Sort of an awkward teen." He grinned, shoveling a spoonful of the grits into his mouth. "I didn't come into my own until college. Now that was a wild time."

And not all that long ago, I reminded myself. "What does it feel like?"

"Normal. For me anyhow. How do your visions feel to you?"

"I see your point." I wondered if he'd get weirded out if I asked him to shift for me?

Before I could figure out how to ask, Babel set his empty bowl in the sink. "I'm going to jump in the shower, then I'll take you back into town."

"Hoo-kay." Our eyes met as he turned to me, his face shining with humor as he rubbed a hand down his stomach. Visions of slippery suds sliding down his chiseled, muscular chest, lathering against the lovely soft hair covering his pecs and leading to a happy trail that made me very happy played in my mind. I didn't think I could resist joining him if I stayed in the house. "I'll get dressed and wait for you outside." He bristled, but didn't try to stop me.

The morning air was brisk and chilling against my skin. I'd put my jeans and shirt back on from the previous day. I hadn't been rolling around in the mud with them, so they weren't dirty, but I'd wished I had a fresh change. I leaned against the porch rail and closed my eyes. It was so peaceful. I couldn't understand how anyone would want to leave. There were so many reasons why hooking up with Babel was a bad idea, but in my heart, I knew his relationship with Sheila wasn't our only stumbling block. He wanted to leave. We'd find Chav. He'd go. I'd die a little. It would take more than pastries and ice cream to recover from losing him. It was easier not to have him in the first place.

Doomed from the start—it was the tag line for any relationship that might happen between us. We were just too...Wrong.

The woods were set off just a little way from the house, and a patch of wildflowers caught my eye. Judah appeared next to the plant, as if he'd been sitting there the entire time. He dug at the ground around it, making me curious. I wandered over to get a closer look, the dew from the grass wetting my shoes. The leaves were the color of cabbage with purplish tints, longs stems, and the flower came to a point at the top with what looked like an unopened blue and muted red bud.

I touched it.

It was dark. The moon was high, and even through the thick shrub of treetops, I could tell it was full.

Howling in the distance and men shouting. I jumped behind a nearby tree. I knew I was in a vision, but it didn't stop my heart from trying to beat out of my chest.

Four men with rifles and gear traipsed lightly over the crisp brush near me. It was too dark under the trees to see their faces.

"We've got a live one, boys," I heard one of the men say.

"Finally one of these things is giving us a run for our money. Clever bugger," another added.

"Where do you get these creatures, John?"

"Trade secret." I could hear the smile in his voice.

"Hush now, boys," the man in front said. "We've got more tracking to do." Who were they hunting?

I knew they couldn't see me, but I crouched down behind the tree as they passed by. Everything felt so real and surreal all at the same time. My hand tangled in a plant. I looked down—the same kind of wildflower.

In the next instant, I was in a different place in the woods. An animal jumped over a nearby log and cocked its ear. It was a coyote, and I recognized his red fur and sharp eyes. "Judah?"

He pawed at the earth with sharp toenails. He didn't look over. He didn't hear me.

A gunshot echoed through the woods. I heard them laughing. They were closing in, whoever they *were. Judah's head cocked sideways, and he sniffed the air.*

"Hey, boy," I heard a man's voice sing out. Come out, come out, wherever you are."

"Run," I told him. "Run."

Another blast resounded. Judah's body dropped to the ground next to me, the side of his head bloody from the clean kill shot.

"Judah!" I screamed, choking on a sob as the bile rose in the back of my throat.

I heard my name repeatedly. I glanced toward the voice. It was Babel. He leaned over me, shaking my shoulders. The sun was out. It was daytime again. It was the present again.

I threw up.

"Babel." I could feel the wet tears streaming my cheeks as he held me.

"I heard you shout Jude's name. What did you see, Sunny?"

"They killed him," I said, the sob catching in my throat making my words harsh and raw. "Oh, God, they killed him."

It had been a full moon the night Judah died. He'd

been trapped in animal form, with animal thoughts and instincts. The killers had been human. They had to be, otherwise, they'd have been in were-form as well, and I didn't know many four-legged creatures who could accurately shoot a rifle.

I couldn't get Judah's lifeless body out of my head. I was so angry over what had happened, and for the first time in my life I wanted to physically hurt someone, to render them limb by limb. Those hunters hadn't been trailing Judah on accident. Judah had been murdered, and from the way they talked, he hadn't been the first.

CHAPTER TEN

"**WHY DO I** have to talk to Sheriff Taylor? He doesn't even like me," I whined. I felt like a kid being sent to the principal's office.

Babel shook his head, driving straight to the municipal building. "You have to tell him what you know."

"Can I at least go home and change clothes first?" It wasn't really about the clothes. I knew this. I was angry and grieving, and my useless vision had shown me just enough to be horrifying, but not enough to be helpful.

"No."

I rounded on Babel. "First, I resent the fact that you think I don't have any say-so in this. Second, I'm not saying a fucking word to anyone until I have my own clothes on and no longer look like a rapper-wannabe." I'd puked down my jeans and shirt, so I was back in Babel's oversized clothes. A large t-shirt and a pair of sweatpants that kept falling down my ass.

"Tough." He'd been a man on a mission since I'd

revealed the vision of Judah's death. I didn't blame him. As angry as I was, he had to be in a rage. I was such a shit right now, but I didn't know how to cope with my gift or what it had revealed.

I wanted to take the bastards down as much as Babel. But in talking to the police, I'd have to tell them *how* I knew what I knew. They wouldn't believe me. Hell, Babel didn't believe me when I first told him. It took some convincing, even when it was obvious he *wanted* to believe. They might be supernaturals, but it was like asking them to believe in aliens. It would be a big-ass waste of time. "But, I don't want to talk to the sheriff," I repeated for the umpteenth time. For the life of me, I couldn't understand what he didn't understand about that. "He's going to think I'm making shit up."

"We'll make him believe."

Great, we were a "we" now—a real, live Fred and Ginger, Bonny and Clyde, the Captain and Tennille. "Lovely." I sighed.

We—now he had me thinking "we" also—slid to a parallel halt in front of the sheriff's office. I stayed in the truck, hoping that in Babel's concentrated efforts for justice, he'd forget about me.

No such luck. He pulled the passenger door open and practically yanked me out of the vehicle. "Let's go," he said.

As if I had a choice. If he or anyone laughed at the way I was dressed, the fur would fly. Pun intended.

"Nice to see you again, Ms. Haddock," Sheriff Taylor said amiably, as we walked into the station. "Glad to see you looking well."

"Is that a dig?"

"Not at all." His eyes, dark, nearly black, held concern even as his mouth quirked in a friendly smile. I noticed once again the darker circles under his eyes.

"What animal are you?" I blurted without thinking.

The office went dead silent, the sheriff, the three deputies, and Babel all staring at me as if I was an alien. It wasn't like I'd asked them to take me to their leader. Maybe it was insulting to ask or something. "I'm not trying to be impolite. I'm just curious."

I heard one of the deputies mumble the cliché, "Curiosity killed the cat." I glanced at him and saw the open hostility animating his face. His badge showed the name Thompson. Ruth's last name was Thompson, and...wait...could this be one of her two oldest boys? Either Tyler or Taylor.

Whichever he was, the pictures I'd seen of Tyler's wedding didn't seem to fit the Deputy Thompson in the room. He was a big guy, tall, soft-looking but not fat, short blond hair and brown eyes. He scowled his contempt. Thompson reminded me of Enos from *Dukes of Hazzard,* minus the jovial personality.

Great. I had a fan.

"You're a cat?" I asked the sheriff, trying to lighten the mood.

"Uh, no," the sheriff said with more indignation than I thought necessary. "And I'm not an animal."

Mood lightening was a bust. "Oh, for shit sake. You guys are really sensitive. What kind of therianthrope are you?" They all kept ogling me like I'd just asked them to strip to their undies. "What?"

"Sunny," Babel said. His voice held a warning note.

The sheriff held up his hand. "Raccoon."

It was a good thing I hadn't taken a drink of anything at that moment because this was a total spew moment. As it were, I managed to stop at a snort.

Sheriff Taylor narrowed his eyes. I'd heard raccoons were vicious—better watch my step. "Sorry." I couldn't hide my smile, but then I remembered why I was there in the first place, and my smile faded.

"Sid," Babel interjected and redirected, "Sunny has information about Judah's disappearance. It might lead us to Chavvie." More call for gaping stares.

The sheriff, whose first name was Sid, cleared his throat. "Both of you. My office."

He didn't wait for us to respond as he turned on his shiny black heel and headed to a small room at the back of the station.

After a few minutes of explanation about me being psychic, seeing Judah's ghost, and the revealing vision, Sheriff Taylor raised his brow. "You know how crazy this sounds?"

I slapped my palms flat on my thighs, which made my shoulder throb. "About as crazy as a town full of people who can shapeshift into animals, I'd suspect."

"Sunny," Babel warned again.

"No." Damn it, I was tired and getting fed up with the whole business. "I told you he wouldn't believe me. I could have been back at my apartment, soaking in the tub right now."

"Now, girl," the sheriff said. "I'm not saying I don't

believe you, but the whole thing just seems a little farfetched."

"You're absolutely right. I'm not psychic, I'm not seeing Judah's ghost, and I didn't get a vision depicting the most vicious crime I've ever heard of or seen." I stood up. "I'm just another weirdo whack job in a town full of weird whack jobs. If you'll excuse me." Babel stood up.

"No," I said again. "You stay. Have coffee with *Sid*. I'll walk home from here. I think I can find the way." Before I stepped out the door to the office, I turned back for one last comment. "Believe me or don't believe me, Sheriff, but be warned, these men know what you all are, and they still killed Judah like he wasn't anything but big game to be slaughtered. I got the distinct feeling it wasn't the first time they've done it, and it won't be their last. You guys have been all nervous about a human living in your town, exposing your secrets? Well, you've got much bigger problems than little ol' me."

I felt vindicated but no less easy as I walked out of the police station. Deputy

Thompson stepped out behind me and grabbed my upper arm. "Let sleeping dogs lie, Ms. Haddock. No one ever benefited from having their pasts dug up."

I flashed on an image of him punching Judah square in the nose. "Tyler or Taylor?" I asked.

His eyes narrowed. "Tyler," he said hesitantly.

"Well, Tyler. I really like your mom. Because of that, I'm not going to mention to her or anyone else how positively discourteously you're treating me. Now let go of my arm. I'd like to leave now."

He released me and went back inside. I really did want to go back to the apartment, lock all the doors, and curl into the fetal position until my world went back to normal.

I'd never return to that kind of normal.

It was like when a close friend or family member dies, and your idea of normal has to change. I didn't know if mine could ever change enough to be comfortable with knowing what I knew now.

"Sunny!" I looked at the beckoning call. Ruth was sitting on a bench across the street, waving her petite hand at me.

"Hi," I hollered back genially, then turned to walk up the street. I liked Ruth. A lot. Probably more than anyone else I'd met in town, and because of that, I felt kind of betrayed. I know why she didn't tell me about what she was. I knew it was the same reason Chav hadn't told me. Also, she'd tried to warn me several times, but still... "Sunny!" I heard her shout again. When she caught up to me, I stopped.

"Hey, Ruth. Did you need something? I was just going home to clean up and take a nap. It's been a rough several days."

I remembered the kiss between her and Judah. I winced. Ruth had been close to him. I didn't know how to tell her he was dead.

It wasn't my problem. No one had hired me to be the town crier. Of course, Judah picked that moment to return. I walked toward the door and nearly tripped as he popped up in front of me.

"Shit," I mumbled.

"You say something, Sunny?" Ruth asked, gnawing her lower lip. Her tawny brown hair was pulled back into a neat ponytail and showcased her beautiful, delicate bone structure. I was still in awe that her figure was supermodel-hot even after nine kids, but the fact that she wasn't human probably made all the difference. At least, I hoped so. No one should be that flawless *and* human.

"No, just wishing whatever acid trip I'm on would wear off already." She smiled, and it lit her deep brown eyes. I couldn't smile back.

Her smile faded a little. "I just want to apologize for everything. I couldn't tell you, darlin', but I really wanted to. I really want to be friends, Sunny. But I understand if you don't."

My heart defrosted. I felt the gush coming on. As if someone opened the floodgates to let out the overflow, I started crying. The act of which surprised Ruth *and* me. Her lithe arms wrapped around my shoulders.

"It's okay, honey. Just let it out." She patted my back in a motherly way, making it even harder to put the brakes on my tears.

"I want to go home," I finally managed to say.

I meant the apartment this time, not California. The Golden State would have to wait on Sunny Haddock. Looking at Judah, who'd distanced himself a little when my hysteria started, I knew I couldn't leave until I found Chavvah and his murder was solved.

"Come over later for tea or something," I told her. She agreed to meet with me, and I was glad. I wanted more information on Judah, as I was certain his death was the reason behind Chav's disappearance, and Ruth might be able to give me some insight.

Even though the tub was small, the bath had been deliciously fine. Water warm enough to redden my skin, and I'd added a touch of lavender for the mother of all headaches forming behind my left eye. I'd resisted the urge to put on my most comfortable pajamas since Ruth was coming over and instead settled for a pair of tan low-rise knit trousers, an emerald-green tank top, and a pair of strappy sandals the same color as the shirt.

The bell rang at the door downstairs. "I'll be right down," I called to Ruth. I checked my hair in a small mirror I'd mounted next to the door (I liked to give myself one last glance over before leaving anywhere). I noticed it was a little frizzy in the Missouri humidity and the color was a bit duller than I like, but it still looked nicely coiffed.

I skipped down the steps to the restaurant area. I nearly missed the last one when I saw who was waiting for me. It wasn't Ruth.

Babel stood in the center of the room looked haggard and worse for wear. There was bruising around his left eye, and his lower lip was split and swollen.

Queasiness fell over me, but my panic overrode my usual squeamish nature. Like the head cheerleader fretting over the quarterback, I ran to him. "Are you all right? What happened?"

"I'm fine." He turned his head when I tried to touch his cheek. "Just a misunderstanding."

"Looks more like gang warfare." I dropped my hand. I couldn't blame him for pulling away. My heart was at war with my head. I didn't want to be with a player, someone who could jump from one woman's bed to the next, but I wanted Babel. I settled on a truce for the moment. "Are you part of the Sharks or the Jets?"

Babel crooked a smile. I melted a little. And yay, he wasn't too young for the reference. "Which do you belong to?"

"The Jets, definitely."

His eyes lowered onto me in a penetrating gaze. "Then me too."

He was adorable, and hot, and sweet, and funny, and I didn't want to like him so much. Every time I was around him, I became the magnet to his steel. *I will not flirt with him.* "You say the nicest things." *Ack! I flirted.*

Without warning to him or myself, I let adrenaline and raw need launch me into his arms. Our mouths met with crushing sweetness. I felt the heat from his bruised lips. I knew it was wrong, even as slid my tongue along his front teeth and he opened his mouth for me. His hands kneaded my back, up and down from my shoulders to the base of my spine. Whenever a guilty reminder that he was with Sheila, or at least she thought so, tried to make its way to the surface, I beat that sucker down with a mallet.

His fingers laced into my hair. He pulled my head back a little and gazed down at me.

"You make me want so much, Sunny," Babel murmured.

I knew the feeling all too well. Drawing my palm over his bruises, I sighed. Sheila was a lunatic and a bitch, but if I allowed myself to act without thought to who it might hurt, was I any better than her?

He nodded toward the apartment and wiggled his eyebrows. "So, upstairs."

"Babel..." My words were cut off by the tinkling of the doorbell. Shit, I'd forgotten about Ruth.

Again, it wasn't Ruth.

CHAPTER ELEVEN

THE MAN STANDING in my restaurant looked wild and savage if you didn't count the civilized blue jeans and gray one-pocket T-shirt. It was obvious someone else besides him did his laundry. His hair was long, black, and unkempt.

He had a scraggly beard with too many days' growth that crept up the sides of his cheeks, and his amber pupils were just a tad more yellow than his corneas. Even from across the room, I could smell whiskey oozing from his pores. His lips pulled back in an ugly snarl.

This was it. This was the hour of my demise. Death had come for a visit, and it seemed he was really pissed. At me. Ack.

"Not open yet," I said in a pleasant voice, trying to hide the strain in my vocal cords. Babel moved in front of me. The pose he took reminded me of Wolverine getting ready for battle.

"Stay out of this, Trimmel." The man's voice was gruff from too many cigarettes or drinks, I wasn't sure which, but it had the effect of making me quiver to the bone.

"Go home, Brady."

Brady? Why did the name sound familiar?

The man stalked farther into the restaurant. He pointed a shaky finger at me. "I want you to leave my boy alone."

Boy, boy? I checked my mental inventory, trying to figure out exactly what boy he could be talking about. The only person I'd spent any amount of time with had been Babel. Surely this wasn't his father. "I think you have the wrong girl."

He walked closer, making me take a step back. I tasted my heart in my mouth. Thank heaven's Babel was there. I'd have been freaking out big time if I'd been alone.

He pointed again. "If Jolon comes back around, you just send him on his way."

Babel spoke up again. "You don't mean what you're saying, Brady. Go home."

Jolon? Who the heck? Oh, Jo Jo. "I don't know what you think I…"

The wild man cut me off. "You don't pay a seventeen-year-old fifty dollars for unloading a few boxes, gal. So whatever you paid him for, it's not happening again. Are we clear?"

I don't know which offended me more, his insinuation that I'd paid his seventeen year-old son for sex, or the fact that he'd think I'd need to pay for sex.

I loved being angry. It drowned out the fear. "Now you just wait one minute!" I snapped, advancing on him. To my surprise, he backed away. "Maybe I overpaid for a little help, but I in no way defiled your child. I resent the implication, Mister...whatever the hell your name is!"

Stunned, he supplied the information. "Brady Corman."

"Mr. Corman. You have a lot of nerve coming into my establishment and accusing me of stuff." I poked Brady in the chest. His bloodshot eyes went wide. "And while the people around here haven't been super friendly, no one has been so rude!" I poked him again.

He raised his hands, open palm as if to surrender. "Calm down, missy."

"Don't you *missy* me." I wanted to slap him hard enough his mother would feel it in her womb. "You picked the wrong damn woman on the wrong damn day to mess with."

He stumbled back in retreat and tripped. I stared, stunned, at the collapsed man on the floor. Suddenly, he didn't look so dangerous. He looked...Broken. I took a deep breath and counted to three. I held my hand out to him, and he eyed me warily. Finally, he nodded and grasped my palm in his. The world went fuzzy. Again.

"Rose Ann," the well-dressed man in a blue suit said. His ebony-black hair was shortly cropped, his face clean shaven, but the golden eyes were unmistakable. I was seeing a past Brady Corman.

A perky blonde in a simple but beautiful blue sundress came bounding out of the back room. "Oh, you look so handsome." She beamed at him.

"I'm nervous as hell," he replied.

She whacked him on the ass, and he feigned surprise.

"They are going to love you," she said fiercely. "Just like I do."

Brady nearly pulled me over getting off the floor. The vision had ended, and once again I had no idea what it meant. I couldn't get over the contrast. How had that clean-cut man in my vision turned into the recluse before me?

"Rose Ann," I whispered.

Brady Corman's eyes grew haunted, his mouth grim. He released my hand then headed toward the door. He turned back before leaving. "What do you know of *my wife?*"

"She loved you," I said, perplexed. My response seemed to stun him for a moment. He opened his mouth a little as if to say something more, but closed it just as quickly and fled the shop.

"Wait!" Babel called to Brady. He gave me a look that sent my adrenaline-filled body into a twitter. "I have to go after him. At least to warn Jo Jo of his state."

"Go." I didn't know what Babel thought Brady would do, but I didn't want to be the cause of suffering for the kid.

Ruth scooted through the door right after, a look of sheer astonishment on her face. "Was that Brady I seen light out of here?" She shook her head. "I haven't seen that man in town in a coon's age."

"You know him?"

"Well, of course, hon. Anyone who's lived in Peculiar for any amount of time would. He used to be the mayor."

Now it was my turn to be astonished. "That man used to be mayor?"

"Oh, yes." Her face lit up at the prospect of being able to confide in me. "It's sad, really. His story that is. I feel even worse for Jo Jo. The boy hasn't had an easy time of it, let me tell you."

"Really." I had a feeling she was going to tell me whether I wanted to hear it or not. Luckily, I wanted to hear all about it.

"It's a doozy of a tale. Brady Corman seemed to have it all. Good looks, good marriage, or so we all thought. He was well-respected in town. He's my age, you know. My husband and he used to run around together when they were teenagers." Her voice grew quieter for a just-between-us-girls moment. "I had the biggest crush on him for the longest time when I was young."

I smiled at that. From the vision, seeing Brady in his prime, I could totally see Ruth finding him unabashedly handsome. "Never dated him?"

"Oh, no." She sounded scandalized, but she looked delighted. "He only had eyes for Rose, even then." She sobered. "Poor man."

"Do you know what happened?" Even though I'd heard she'd run off, I wanted to hear Ruth's version of Rose Ann's story.

"No one knows for sure, but the gossip is she ran off with a lover and never came back. Sometimes it's hard to know what to believe."

I could tell Ruth was a believer, but she didn't want to sound unfair. "Wow. That's a tough pill to swallow." And hard to imagine, from what I'd seen in the vision. She had definitely been a woman deeply in love with her man.

"You're telling me." Ruth pulled up a stool at the counter and sat down. "Brady just never recovered. I'm afraid to the point of neglect in every other part of his life. His work, his house, his son..." She tsked.

"I can't imagine," I said for lack of anything more appropriate.

"I felt so bad for Brady. Rose Ann just went off like she was going to work one day and never came back." Ruth pursed her lips. "She'd been working as Neville's legal assistant in Lake Ozarks for several years. If she was running around on Brady, that's where she would have met the guy."

"The mayor's a lawyer?" That explained a lot about his slick personality.

"Yes. He's a nice man, though."

"You don't think Rose Ann and him..." I let the question linger.

"No, no. Nothing like that. Rose Ann went off while Neville's wife was dying. I've never seen a man so devoted."

"Dying? Was she human?"

"Lands, no. Maggie was a coyote, like him, but she had a type of cancer some of our kind are prone to get."

For a second, I was stunned. I'd never even considered the idea the therianthropes or lycanthropes could get sick. I'd somehow built into my mind they were more like the supernatural creatures of the movies.

"I thought you guys were—" Immortal monsters? How could I phrase that in a way that wouldn't be offensive?

Ruth smiled wistfully as if she knew what was on my mind. "We aren't like regular folk, in that we live a little longer. But we don't live on forever, nothing much does. We can get sick and die just like everyone else."

"But you're stronger, faster, and can heal most things quicker, right?"

"Girl, you make us sound like comic book heroes." She laughed. "But you're mostly right."

"So, silver bullets? That's not true?"

Ruth rolled her eyes. "I'm sure it'd kill us just as dead as hot lead if it hit the right spot."

Another myth busted.

I brought the conversation back around to Rose Ann Corman. I can't explain why, but I knew she was somehow important. "So, not Neville then." Neville being a widower made me feel more kindly toward him, and it made me feel a little judgmental. I'd assumed he'd had it all, money, power, friends, and good looks.

"No, he wouldn't have." Her voice took on a note of conspiracy. "Not then, anyhow."

Whoa-ho. At least I hadn't been completely wrong about the mayor. He might not have been strutting his stuff back then, but he was a total playa now.

"Really?"

"Heck, yeah." She grinned. "I don't want to be uncharitable, but about a year after his wife died,

Neville started to really cat around, if you know what I mean. I don't think he'll ever settle down again."

"And Brady?"

"Ed tried to help him out, but Brady just withdrew into himself. If it weren't for Jo Jo, I don't think anyone around here would give him much thought anymore."

"Jeez, that's really sad." My heart ached for Jo Jo, and Brady and Neville to some degree. They'd all lost so much.

"Yes, it is. I thought him and Ed would always be friends," Ruth said, gazing directly into my eyes. "But, friendships are like a garden. If you don't work at cultivating them, and keeping the weeds down, they eventually die out."

I grinned. The analogy had been succinct, if a little cliché. "Then how about we get to planting our own little garden?" Placing my hand over hers, I added, "I'll get the tea on."

"Great idea," she said brightly. "So, tell me about yourself, Sunny. I only really know what Chavvie told me. I'm interested."

It was nice of Ruth to ask, whether she was genuinely interested or not. So, I told her all about growing up in a hippie commune, the lying, cheating ex-boyfriend, and how Chav had been there for me through the worst of it. Some of the stuff she'd told me made me a little more wary of the small-town culture. I was used to living in an anonymous world. I mean, sure, rumors could start in a small circle of friends in San Diego, but to have a whole town know your business fifteen minutes before you did was awesome and awful all at the same time. Ruth seemed to know just about everything about everyone. Although, it made me wonder, how come nobody seemed to have a clue about where Chavvah was?

Neville Lutjen had been mayor for eight years, since the year after Brady Corman had fallen apart. They were both coyotes, she revealed. She and Ed were deer, which nearly surprised me as much as Sheriff Taylor being a raccoon. Delbert and Elbert Johnson were opossums. Sheila Murphy was a coyote, which duh, I could have guessed. Becky from Beck-E's Bakery was the only bird in town, a red-tailed hawk.

If I had to be an animal, a hawk wasn't a bad way to go, though my feelings for Babel probably put me more in the cougar territory.

The very large and boisterous Blondina, owner of Blonde Bear Cafe, and her three boys and daughter were none other than black bears. I'd be checking her roots the next time I went in for salad.

We'd nearly talked about all the town people I'd met and a few I hadn't met.

"What about Billy Bob? He is a whole series of contradictions. How can a doctor with concrete knowledge of science be a spiritual leader as well?"

"Oh, Doctor Smith. He's something else, lion." She raised an eyebrow and grinned. "Mighty fine-looking man."

I had to agree. "There is no shortage of hotties in this place." I couldn't help but think of Babel. Tall, broad, and a sensuous mouth he certainly knew how to use. His wild, thick hair drove me crazy as well. My mouth watered as a mental image of him naked played in my mind. "My lord, you guys know how to grow them right."

Ruth laughed. "The doc is such a nice man."

"Oh, yes. The doctor." My train of thought had definitely jumped the track.

"Very solitary, mind you. But you know, he delivered all of my babies. He's got a great bedside manner." She sighed for effect. "Oh, if I were a single woman." Then she laughed again.

"Well, I *am* a single woman, but I plan to stay that way for a while. I'm not into the whole ex-man-to-the-next-man thing." Although it had been two years, and a new man would be less "rebound" and more "new game". Either way, I didn't want another relationship.

"What about Babe?"

I choked on a sip of tea and landed myself into a coughing fit. "What about him?"

"Well, I just thought you two…Maybe I got it wrong."

"You thought wrong." Not really. "There's nothing between us." Except for the mondo chemistry. I'd been around really good-looking men before but never had I felt so connected to any of them, so it wasn't just his great body or pretty blue eyes. It couldn't be. Possibly I was feeling transference. I was putting my affection for Chavvah on to Babel. Though, I'd never wanted to lick Chavvah from toe to top. Hmm.

My body craved Babel in a way that made me feel like a bulimic in a grocery store. Maybe I was having a mid-life crisis and just reacting to attention from a young man. I wouldn't be the first woman to have these desires. Hell, I probably wouldn't be the first woman in town to have these particular fantasies about Babel.

I refilled the kettle and put it back on the stove. "Why do you ask?"

"Honey," Ruth said. "Call it a gut feeling."

Jeezus, I thought I was psychic, but Ruth had intuition in spades over me. I shook my head. Babel was a passing fling, nothing more, and less and less fling-ish as time progressed.

"I'm not interested in him," I lied again. "Besides, he's planning on moving back to the city, and I think he was seeing someone already before I got here."

Ruth's mouth formed a perfect little "o." Her mouth turned down at the corners only slightly in disappointed. "A girlfriend?"

"No, not really. Oh hell, I don't know." I didn't want to get into it. Thinking about Babel with that really awful woman made my stomach churn. I clenched my fist as I thought about ripping her hair out at the roots. I didn't want to be the other woman, but it was hard to feel sorry for the cow. Or coyote. Whatever.

"I'm not trying to make you feel bad, Sunny. I'm sorry I asked."

"No, you're fine. I don't mind that you asked. More tea?" I offered.

"Better not. My bladder's near bursting." She gestured toward the small bathroom in the corner of the restaurant. "Mind?"

"No, of course not. Go ahead."

As I watched her trot over and close the door, I

hoped to hell there was toilet paper in there, because I hadn't checked. I supposed Ruth would let me know if she was without.

As if Ruth's exit was his cue, Judah came trotting out from behind the counter and whined, then walked back around. I followed him. His nose poked in and out of the baseboard of the display case. Frankly, it was disconcerting. We were having another

Lassie moment. Whatever was under that board, Judah was working hard to get at it. I prayed it wasn't a mouse. While I didn't believe in cruelty to animals, rodents made my teeth hurt.

He whined more, and I felt like a coward. Whatever lay under that board, he obviously thought it important. "Fine," I huffed.

I glanced over at the closed bathroom door and decided to act. I got down on all fours and pulled at the board. With very little prying, it came loose. The board was a little less dusty than its surrounding. I hadn't been the first person to find it. It was too dark to see inside the small space, but I steeled myself and stuck my arm in, patting around with my hand. Cold metal chilled my fingers. The object wasn't so big I couldn't maneuver it around, and after a few moments, I managed to pull it out. It was a box; more exact, a cash tin with a locked front.

Maybe Chavvah had put something in the box that would explain all the mysteries. I would find her, we'd catch who killed Judah, and Babel could leave. I felt sick to my stomach.

"What'cha got there?"

I startled at Ruth's question. I'd been distracted by morose thoughts and hadn't noticed her return. "Uhm, a box I found." Stating the obvious.

"Ooo," she cooed. "I wonder what's in it."

"I don't know. Maybe money or something." I didn't really think so, but since I hadn't told Ruth about Judah, I didn't want this to be the way she found out.

"Found money's always the best. That's why my husband and kids always make sure they check their pockets before giving me their laundry."

"There's a locked latch on it."

"No problem." She pulled a bobby pin from the back of her hair. A little strange considering she was wearing it down.

I raised my brow in question.

"This?" She sniffed, grinned, and held up the bobby pin. "You just never know when one of these buggers might come in handy."

"No friggin' doubt," I said, impressed when she had the lock popped in seconds. I made a mental note to add bobby pins to the other junk in my purse.

Ruth pushed the box toward me. "You found it. You get the honors."

I rubbed my hands together in anticipation, then carefully opened the box as if it was booby-trapped.

Inside lay a folded diner check, a wad of twenties, and a necklace with a gold heart charm. Okay, so there'd been money and jewelry, but I couldn't help but feel as though it was a little anticlimactic. I unfolded the diner check and let out the breath of was holding. There was a series of numbers and letters. They looked really familiar.

I cast a sideways glance at Ruth, who hadn't spoken since we'd exposed the contents. "Ruth?"

"Huh?" My voice snapped her out of it whatever la-la land she'd drifted off to. "Oh look, hon. There's money, and what's that you've got in your hand. Anything good?"

She hadn't mentioned the necklace, but I let it slide. "I'm not sure. It's one of those checks that you take orders on, but nothing on it looks like bacon and eggs." The sequences were a weird pattern of 150000715JT, 175000725RC, 200000719GH, then 250. It had been scribbled hurriedly, and I could barely make out the last zero.

"That's Judah's handwriting, I'm pretty sure." Ruth chewed on the inside of her cheek. "I wonder if it's bank numbers, or some covert offshore account, or passwords to something?"

"I think you've been watching too much television."

Ruth huffed. "Well, I'm just saying." She ran her delicate fingers through her soft brown hair.

I chuckled. "Okay, Robert Langdon. Sometimes numbers are just numbers, not the Da Vinci code."

"Ha! Don't think I don't know what you're talking about. I'm not saying it's anything sinister, just kind of neat. Nothing really happens in Peculiar." Forget drifting, Ruth permanently resided in la-la land.

CHAPTER TWELVE

I'D GONE ON a walk for some fresh air after Ruth left. Just up the street from Johnson's General Store, I saw Babel's tiny car—the one I'd seen him in the first day I arrived in Peculiar. He'd been driving a truck the last couple of days, so I wondered if the car and the truck were his, or if he'd borrowed one or the other from someone. Who would the car belong to? Sheila, maybe? It pissed me off, completely and unreasonably. I hated feeling so possessive over someone who wasn't mine, but I couldn't help it. I wanted to beat his ass for making me want him.

I looked around expectantly for Babel, then mentally kicked myself for being disappointed that his podunk ass wasn't anywhere to be seen. For no good reason, I crossed the road and started walking toward the car. Okay, there was a good reason or at least an okay reason. I wanted to see Babel. Hell, I needed to see him. He might not be mine, but I was beginning to think that I was his.

Delbert Johnson, or it might have been his twin Elbert, greeted me before I could get past their store.

"How do?" he asked, taking a long drag from a cigarette. His smile crinkled around his eyes, genuine and bright, and a little mischievous. It was contagious. This was a jolly man, and Peculiar could use a few more like him.

"I'm good. You?"

"Fine as frog's hair," he remarked, tossing his cigarette butt on the sidewalk and dashing it with the toe of his boot. He looked up the street toward Babel's car then back to me. "Enjoy your afternoon." With a wink, he dismissed me as he went back into the store.

The car was sitting in front of a craft store. As I got closer, I noticed someone occupying the driver side, sort of slumped down. Babel had been in a fight or something earlier—the split lip and bruises had been a flashing neon sign to that effect. What if he'd been hurt worse than he'd let on? He could be bleeding internally, dying alone in a ratty little beat-up car as his coffin. Why did Ruth have to tell me that therians could die just like anyone else?

As I ran the short twenty feet to the car, I made deals with any deity that would listen. If Babel lived, I would give him up completely. I wouldn't interfere with his relationships or try to stop him from leaving town when the time came. I wouldn't be selfish. I would...

The driver-side window was down, and Babel had his head resting against the steering wheel. I stared at his gorgeous, scruffy face, remembering how good those soft whiskers felt against my thighs. He looked so peaceful. I'd heard people get that way when they're going into shock.

I tapped his shoulder gently. "Babe?" I didn't know why I used his nickname.

Twisting his neck sideways, he peered up at me through a thatch of hair angled across his face, his intense blue eyes red and watery. "I don't know how to tell my parents."

Crap. I caressed his cheek, and he nuzzled his face against my palm like I was a touchstone. "I am the worst person in the world." He'd been so calm, focused, when I'd told him about my vision earlier, that I hadn't even considered what *knowing* Judah was dead would do to him.

"I'm so sorry." I opened the driver-side door and knelt down next to him. I wanted to wrap my arms around him and kiss the sadness away. Instead, I placed my hand on his leg. The heat radiating from his thigh through his thin, worn jeans made me shiver.

Babel put his palm over my hand. When I tried to pull away, he gripped me tightly. My fingers clenched involuntarily against the firm muscle beneath. The wild look in his gaze was predatory and violent.

"Babel." I forced myself to relax. I didn't try to move my hand again. "You okay?"

It sounded lame, even to my own ears, but frankly, he was scaring me. I didn't like the feeling. Babel still hadn't answered me, and I fought to keep my free hand from grabbing the handle.

Silently, he stared at me. I looked away when I could no longer meet his stare. His fingers changed, elongated over mine. His palms became thick and rough, scratching the skin on the back of my hand. My pulse raced, and my fear doubled.

"Stop," he growled, his voice taking on a distinctly inhuman quality.

"You stop," I quipped, trying to sound brave. "I'm not the one going all doggy bits."

"No, but you're making it hard."

I glanced at his hand, it had become unrecognizable. Like something out of the *Howling*. Beyond that, the bulge in his pants was pronounced. Apparently, I was making all sorts of things hard.

"I'd like to go now." *Said the fly to the spider.* "Uhm, if that's all right. You know, things to see, people to do…" Wrong cliché. Oy.

Once I'd watched this nature documentary on PBS, and the host, John Somethingoranother, had said that when faced by a wild animal you should hold perfectly still. Don't run. I think he'd been talking about a bear, so I wasn't sure if it would work with a man-beast situation. But I froze like an ice sculpture just in case. Even when his right hand whipped across his body with ungodly speed and fisted my hair, I kept my movement and noise to a flinch and a squeak.

Babel leaned in close, his nose pressing against my neck. He inhaled deeply. The exhalation came out as an agitated rumble. His tongue flicked my jaw.

I released a shaky breath as my lower parts clinched. "Babel. Please don't." It might have been more convincing if my fear hadn't been mixed with a tinge of excitement and a dose of lust.

He made a chuffing sound right before his hot mouth pressed against my lips. Sirens went off in my brain, but my body responded. Babel's tongue slid along the crack of my lips, forcing them apart. He tasted of maple syrup. Mmmm.

The heat from his skin warmed mine. A swooping sensation rolled in my stomach. Before I could stop myself, I grabbed a handful of his shirt, closed my eyes tightly, and leaned into his chest. I apologized to all the deities I'd made deals with for being a liar liar pants on fire, then met his kiss with a fevered rush. He let go of my hand clamped to his thigh and wrapped his arms around me.

My tongue brushed a sharp and elongated canine followed by a sharp sting and the salty taste of blood. A coil of nausea unwound its way to my throat as visions of Babel and Judah as children playing ball, sharing meals, and secrets. Babel looked up to Judah like most little brothers. The depth of his grief choked me, and at that moment, I knew I would do anything to take it from him.

So I swallowed it, every bit of his grief. I took it into my body, my mind. I don't know how, or even if it was real, but I could feel the tension leave his muscles. His hands slid up my ribs to my breasts. The coarse pads of his palms took my breath, but the thick, sharp fingernails popped the bubble of fantasy and reality sank in.

I was making out on Main Street in broad daylight with *Manimal*.

When the rock cracked against the windshield, I realized I wasn't the only one to notice.

I scrambled back from Babel with a yelp. Outside the car, Sheila Murphy already had her arm reared, ready to throw again.

"Oh, shit." I ducked as another rock whacked against the windshield. "You fucking bitch," she screamed. "I'm going to kill you!"

"She's goddamn crazy," Babel muttered.

"Ya think?" Holy crap. Crazy was stalking in my direction. I popped the lock down on the door. Sheila's lips contorted into a maniacal smile.

"Oh, shit," I repeated.

Tempered glass shattered in all around me in little chunks as Sheila put her fist through the window. I scrambled across Babel's lap to the passenger side. Babel jumped out, and in a single bound, he leaped over the car, landing directly behind the woman trying to tear my head off.

My heart went to my throat, thick and pounding, as she grabbed my ankle and yanked me half out of the car. I screamed, because, well, I was half out of my mind with terror, then kicked out with my free leg and got a lucky strike to her face.

She didn't let go. Frankly, I think it just pissed her off even more. Before she could wrench me completely out onto the sidewalk, Babel wrapped his forearm around her neck, and with his other hand, he snatched her loose from my ankle.

He tossed Sheila like pizza dough, and the woman went flying into the brick wall of the craft store. With another leap, Babel was crouched next to her. Instead of getting up and trying to kick the shit out him, Sheila surprised me. She started sobbing.

Babel took her in his arms, and let me just say, I felt like the world's biggest boob. The woman tried to kill me, for the second time, and Babel was comforting her. I hated him so much. *Hated* him! Maybe I didn't have the right to feel betrayed—we were not going steady, and she'd seen him first, obviously—but he'd really pissed me off.

"Now, now," I heard him say softly. "Why'd you have to go and wreck my car?"

Not, "why are you messing with Sunny?" Not, "leave Sunny alone!" Or something helpful like that. The bastard was only troubled about his beater.

Sheila cried harder, her mess of long brown hair falling haphazardly across her face.

She looked more beautiful, if possible. I hated her so much.

"I heard about Judah," Sheila said, her voice all choked and gravelly.

A tiny wince of guilt fluttered inside. Very tiny. I'd managed to get my legs to stop shaking long enough to stand up from the car. I used that momentum to walk across the street toward my shop.

"Sunny," Babel said loud enough to get my attention.

I didn't turn around. I didn't want to see him holding her. They were grieving. Fine. They had a shared emotional bond that didn't include me. Fine. But it didn't mean I had to stick around to watch. Assuming he was watching me go, I waved my hand to let him know I was all right but kept pace all the way to the door.

Inside the restaurant, I sat on the floor with my back to the wall. I worried for Babel. For a big strapping guy, he had a lot of emotions buried deep. I wasn't so sure I could help him, especially since he'd almost shifted on me. Maybe I was bad for him, and vice versa. Probably Sheila understood him in ways I never could. When I stopped feeling sorry for myself (well, not completely), I cracked the front door and took a peek.

Babel, Sheila, and the car were gone. Fantastic. I stepped out onto the sidewalk. Yep. Gone. Fuckers. I hated them both.

Turning back toward the restaurant, I saw Delbert and Elbert outside their store, chuckling and talking softly to each other. I wondered if it was some twin-speak thing going on.

"What are you guys up to?" Maybe they hadn't seen the Terminator reenactment.

"Just chewing the fat."

"Just shooting the shit," they said almost simultaneously. It was hard to tell where one began and the other ended.

"Hmmm."

I strolled across the street to them and looked each man over. I noticed one had a slightly thinner face, though it was hard to tell under the snow-white beard. The one with the heavier face had a tiny blond freckle next to the outer corner of his left eye.

I pointed to the freckle. "Which one are you?"

Talking with the Johnsons was calming for some odd reason. Besides, they were a much needed distraction.

The thinner-faced brother laughed. "You're the psychic. You tell us?"

"Ha. Ha. Very funny." So, my little problem had become town gossip. Two could play this game. "You two are hilarious for a couple of opossums." Put that in your pipe and smoke it, Johnson twins.

They didn't seem in the least offended. "Well now, you're a little spitfire for a looney."

I rolled my eyes. How much did they really know? How much did the whole town know? "What? Did you all have some sort of town-hall meeting about me?" Freckle snorted. "Sure." His brother nodded with a knowing grin.

I touched the thinner-faced Johnson on the arm and got a quick flash. I smiled back at him. "Delbert, Peggy's gonna be pissed if you go fishing and miss dinner one more time. She's a pretty delicate woman, but I have a feeling she could take you in a fair fight."

Delbert's smile faded, for two beats of a heart. Then he chuckled. "Wooo," he hooted. "Nice one."

Elbert shook his head. "I like you, Sunny. Watch yourself. Sheila is an unpredictable bitch, and Brady... Well, he's become a bit...unstable over the years." He patted my arm warmly.

Awww, I made some more friends. I guess they had seen the fight along with Brady Corman's little tirade. Nosey neighbors.

"Thanks." I frowned. "Did you know Judah well?"

"Well enough, I suppose." Elbert again.

"Did you see or remember anything weird around the time he disappeared?" The sheriff and Babel had probably asked this question already, but it couldn't hurt to ask again.

"Nothing I can think of."

"Me either." A little twitch over Delbert's eyebrow made me reach out and touch his hand, and I got a flash of Judah under the awning with the twins, all of them laughing, then nothing more. The visions were coming much more frequently and less hard-hitting, but still pretty much useless

"What about Chavvah? Did she seem okay when you saw her last? Did she say anything? Was there anyone hanging around more than normal?"

"Whoa, missy. Slow it down," Delbert said.

Elbert sucked his teeth. "I can't really recall seeing Chavvie too concerned, though she was upset that one time..."

"Yeah, I remember," Delbert added. "Doc Smith had just been with her, along with Neville and the sheriff. Not sure what went on there. You'll have to ask them. That was probably the last time I saw her."

"I saw her a couple of days after, going out of town in her little yellow Bug."

I'd forgotten Chavvah had a Volkswagen. I hadn't even wondered where it had gone. Some detective I was turning out to be, and jeezus, why hadn't I talked to the Johnson twins sooner? I hugged Delbert, then after, I gave Elbert the same. I'd never seen men turn so red. Even their ears were the color of beets. I smiled.

When I put my hand on Delbert to apologize, I had another flash of vision. *Judah coming out of the restaurant at night. He looked angry, his fists clenching and unclenching, the sound of jangling keys clinking with each tight movement. Sheila Murphy came out next; she was tucking her shirt in. Eww. She tried to kiss Judah and he pushed her back. He jumped in his truck and took off, leaving her out in front of the store.*

The vision stopped there.

I gazed up at Delbert. "Did you see a fight between Sheila and Judah?"

His brows raised then he shook his head. "More times than I can count. Nothing new there."

I didn't doubt fighting had been a regular thing for anyone and Sheila. She was a whole bag of nuts and then some. But did I really believe she could be responsible for Judah's death? Maybe? She definitely had the temper and temperament for it, but the grief I'd seen earlier had been real, not manufactured. Besides, she might stab him with a butcher knife, maybe, but the whole hunting thing was calculated.

"Yeah, I guess so," I finally said. I was really grossed out by the fact that she'd had a relationship with Judah. She'd been sleeping with him, I could tell that much from the vision. And now she was sleeping with his little brother. Yuck and yuck. "She really is a crazy bitch."

Elbert laughed. Delbert smiled, but it was tight, fake.

"Oh, nearly forgot." He went inside his store and came back out seconds later with a manila envelope.

"Neville Lutjen stopped at your shop earlier when you weren't there.

He had these." He handed me the envelope. "I told him I'd give it to you."

"Thanks," I said. Maybe it was the licensing paperwork. I really hadn't given much thought to the restaurant. If I couldn't find Chav, it wouldn't matter anyhow. "See you guys around."

Back in the apartment, I set the envelope on the small kitchen table. Soon, I grew bored, bored, bored. Chavvah hadn't had cable installed in the building. I would have killed for my *Supernatural* DVDs, but I was too lazy to find the box they were in. (Watching Jensen Ackles was my comfort food.) So, I retrieved the diner check with the secret codes and tried to decipher it, still not completely convinced I'd be able to make heads or tails of the clue. If nothing else, it was a great way to keep from thinking about Babel and how exactly he and Sheila might be comforting each other.

Some of the numbers seemed familiar, but I couldn't figure out from where. I tried treating the numbers and letters like an anagram, but there were too many zeros for a word puzzle to work. It couldn't be a binary code, too many other numbers besides zero and one. Maybe the letters were the key: JT, RC, GH. JoT, ReC, Go Home? Nah. In desperation, I tried holding on to the slip of paper, hoping for some kind of revealing vision—after all, I'd been getting them regularly since I hit town.

Nothing.

I sighed.

Hell, Judah could have been playing a mad game of Sudoku for all I knew, and the scribbles of letters and numbers could mean absolutely nothing. It was seven in the evening when I finally gave up. I tucked the diner check into my pocket and decided to go back downstairs to get the metal box. Maybe I'd missed something in it earlier.

I didn't think I would, but I missed California. Here it was, a Friday night, and I had no real friends to call, no date to speak of, and I'd never felt so intensely alone. I heard a bark at the bottom of the stairs. Okay, so, intensely alone except for one ghost coyote.

I stepped out onto the hardwood floors. "Hey, Judah. Got something new for me?"

A shadow of movement to the right caught my eye. I barely had enough time to look over when a large, dark figure slammed me against the wall. I didn't see that coming. Silly, silly, me.

The *thing* towered over me, his body a warm press of fur hard against me. Its hot breath blew against my face. My knees began to shake uncontrollably even as I willed them to stop.

Sharp fingernails dug into my arms and shoulders. I couldn't tell what he looked like, or even if it was a he. I'd been assuming, but it was too dark. It pressed its malformed mouth to my hair and spoke. "You need a lesson in minding your own business."

Horror, sheer and discernable, ripped through me. I had a major visceral reaction to the guttural voice. Pure fear. I tried to yank away from the shifter, but it was too strong. The lesson came as a swift backhanded slap across my face. My jaw snapped as I crumpled to the floor. I heard the snick-snack of fingernails clicking while the hairy beast seemed to ponder what to do with me next.

Unable to speak, to ask why or even plead for my life, I pulled a Rover as I went limp and played dead. A thunderous kick landed on my ribs. The air whooshed from my lungs as pain burst in all directions, making me think death might be a better option. He didn't touch me again. Kicking me had been his parting soliloquy.

I lay still for a good half hour, the numbness had soon worn off and the pain in my face was nearly debilitating. Somehow, I managed to drag myself up on an elbow then finally I was sitting up against the wall. I tried to speak, to call for help, but my lower jaw refused to work and my tongue was swelling inside my mouth.

As it were, I had a couple of choices: lie here until someone found me, drag myself upstairs and use my cell phone to call for help, or try to get to the police station three blocks up the road. Lying there and waiting was my favorite option, because the other two involved painful movements.

Where was Babel? It was unreasonable to expect him to ride in wearing a white hat and rescue me, but if I ever needed the rescue, now was the time. Babel would take charge. He'd know what to do. I'd never been needy, but as the pain worsened in my face and ribs, I knew I needed help. I *wanted* the help to come from Babel, but at this point any ol' hero would do.

I considered going upstairs for the phone, but I couldn't form words, and the blood in my mouth meant

I'd probably bit through my tongue (the swelling didn't help either). So, I had to drag myself out onto the dimly lit street and travel the short distance to the police station.

I shuddered at the prospect.

Thrice now, I'd been attacked. Once by a shifter in full animal form, then Babel's psychotic girlfriend (who was probably my first attacker as well), and now by a shifter in its half-n-half state of transformation. What if it waited outside for me?

I had no idea whether it had been a male or female. Could it have been Sheila? Maybe it had been Tyler Thompson. He'd been downright hostile. Or Brady Corman? Or someone I hadn't even figured into the equation.

I recalled Delbert and Elbert. The town had had a meeting. They knew I was a psychic, and while I was certain there would be a bunch of people who wouldn't believe, I was beginning to think there might be a few who wouldn't want to take a chance on me discovering something they wanted to keep hidden.

Through the pain, anger rose to the surface.

The front doorbell jangled. I froze. *Oh, God. He's come back.*

CHAPTER THIRTEEN

I **STILLED MY** heavy breathing, but it was hard to be quiet with a clogged nose and a swollen tongue. For the umpteenth time, I felt certain I was going to die. Feeling around the floor, I couldn't find anything to use as a weapon. If I was going to get mauled again, I wanted to do some damage as well.

"Sunny?" I heard a young man's voice. Familiar. Jo Jo.

I whimpered my relief. I tried to say his name, but it came out as a muffled mess.

"Son of a...Sunny. Just hold still." Jo Jo kneeled next to me.

I winced when he touched my face. He tried to keep the horror out of his voice, but couldn't keep it off his face. I hurt too bad to care.

"I'm going to get the sheriff," he said with sudden determination. "Try not to move."

Grateful, I nodded. The pain made me sorry for the gesture. I don't know if I'd passed out, but it seemed like a very short time had passed between Jo Jo finding me and the sheriff and his men coming in. Someone had turned on the lights.

Sheriff Taylor cradled me in his arms and carried me upstairs to my bed after a few photos were taken of me and the scene. The sheriff placed me gently on the comforter. His wife, Jean, brought in an ice pack. When had Jean gotten there? Misery played across both their faces, and I wondered how bad I really looked?

Jean smoothed my hair as she held the cool bundle to my cheek. Sheriff Taylor wore jeans and a casual shirt. It was the first time I'd seen him out of uniform. He'd been off duty.

"We're gonna get who did this, Sunny. Don't you worry," he said softly.

Jean tried to smile, but it came off as a grimace. "Doc Smith is on his way. He'll be here soon. You just hang in there."

I hoped soon meant immediately. I could use some of Billy Bob's good drugs. Even with the blood, my mouth felt parched. I took hold of the ice bag and pointed to the cubes. Jean, with expediency, produced a small chip. I slid it past my lips, unable to get my jaw open more than a crack.

Goddamn, it hurt!

Where the hell was Billy Bob? Didn't he have super powers or something too? I mean, hell, a lycanthrope should be able to run here in a couple of minutes.

One of the men in the living room shouted, "Doc's here."

It was about friggin' time. Now that the shock had worn off, my whole face throbbed.

Jean patted my arm. "It's going to be all right, dear. It's over now."

Jean Taylor thought it was over? I'd been threatened and attacked. By who and why? Until those questions were answered, it felt far from over in my mind.

Sheriff Taylor stayed until Billy Bob arrived to care for me. He told me he'd post a man downstairs for my protection. While I hadn't seen Tyler Thompson, I hoped to hell he wouldn't be the guy the sheriff chose. Especially since, if I had a suspect list, he'd top it.

Billy Bob walked into the room with a flourish normally reserved for the regal. My eyes widened as he plopped an old fashioned black doctor's bag on the bed near my calves. "I'm going to look you over, okay?"

I managed to grunt an affirmative. He started at my scalp—no lacerations, he confirmed—then my jaw. He made a humming noise as he pulled a syringe from his bag, along with a bottle of clear liquid. He drew the plunger back until the syringe was full.

"This is some Lidocaine. It's going to pinch a little, but it'll make you feel better."

His hands warm and dry, he gently pushed the area in front of my left ear and injected me with the burning liquid. I squeezed my eyes tightly to keep from squirming or trying to clench my teeth. He repeated the procedure on the right side.

The pain abated. I let out a grateful sigh that stopped when Billy Bob pressed his thumbs along both those spaces and exerted pressure. Inside, I screamed as I felt my jaw snap back into place.

"Awww," I managed past my thick tongue. My jaw still hurt like a bitch, but at least I could move it again.

"Don't open your mouth wide for a couple of days, and make sure you put a hand under your chin if you yawn or laugh. Your mandible was dislocated, and you'll have some swelling from possible muscle and tendon tearing that will need to heal."

Man, this guy was in full-on doctor mode. It was really hard to think of him as the same painted man who'd kept me in a sweat tent for a couple of days. He put on gloves and pulled out a tongue depressor from his kit.

"I'm going to look in your mouth now. It's not going to be comfortable, but the Lidocaine set at your mandibular joints should help some."

With one hand he held a small light, the other the depressor, which he used to move my tongue around. "You're a lucky woman."

So lucky. I wanted to smack him. Lucky would have required me to *not* get the crap beat out of me for the second time in a span of a week.

"Only a lateral tear on the left side of your tongue from where you bit it. And the tongue is one of the quickest healing appendages on the body." I wanted to tear his appendage and see how lucky he felt.

He moved closer to my face, and I thought he was going to numb up my tongue like he had my jaw, but instead, he kissed me.

Holy crap! His tongue swirled around mine. In my

shock and awe, I nearly failed to notice that my mouth was feeling better and better with each swipe. When he finally quit laying the lip-lock on me, my toes were curled, and my tongue felt less swollen and painful.

"Why did you do that?" My surprise must have amused him because he grinned.

Now that the pain was better, I noticed him. Really noticed him. He looked positively amazing. He wore tight black jeans and a button-down navy-blue shirt that set off his incredible gray eyes. He had his dreadlocks pulled back off his face, and the sight of him nearly took my breath away. I bet he wouldn't be as much of a challenge as Babel. Billy Bob was actually a grown-up. Although, just thinking about Babel made my heart sink. I wasn't ready to move on to someone else. Not yet.

"Lycanthrope saliva has healing properties," he replied, buckling his black bag.

"Uh-huh." I was still confused. But I definitely understood what Ruth meant about a "great bedside manner." Woo-wee.

He shrugged. "It was a hell of a lot more fun than spitting in your mouth."

"Ewww." And I completely agreed. Then another thought occurred, my shoulder had healed up pretty damn quick as well. "That poultice you made for my shoulder..."

"Yep," he confirmed.

Great, who needed a medical license when you could salivate super-healing ju-ju? I wanted to be repulsed, but I settled for appreciative. "Thank you. Again."

"My pleasure." He brushed my hair back with a finger then traced down the side of my face and neck. His gaze softened. To me, he felt safe, not like Babel.

Babel.

The thought of Babel made me shrug off Billy Bob's touch. My head said Billy Bob was definitely the better choice as far as guys went, but my heart was all in on Babel, even if I couldn't have him.

Shaking his head, Billy Bob picked up the ice pack off the nightstand and put it back on my face. "Ice, rest, and ibuprofen. And try to keep your mouth closed. I'll be back in the morning to check on you."

"Thanks again, Doc." I pursed my lips with consternation as he left my bedroom and apartment.

I am such an idiot. Billy Bob was good looking, didn't seem to have a lot of baggage, and he was an actual grown-up without a psychotic girlfriend. And while he hadn't asked me out or come on strong, I'd seen the look. The one a guy gives when he's interested. Billy Bob was definitely interested.

I rationalized my reluctance as part of my "no men" mantra, but my heart knew better. I ached for Babel, and damn it, I wanted it to stop. Conflicted, yet resolute, I took one of the pain pills Billy Bob had left on the nightstand with a glass of water and closed my eyes to the day.

When I woke up, a large, warm body pressed against my back. A hairy arm crossed my chest while soft snoring played in my ear. Hazy still, I couldn't figure out where I was or whose arms I was in. I turned my aching face to my bedmate and saw my *happy place*. "Babel?"

His eyelids opened on his handsome face. "Hey there," he said softly. "I came last night but I didn't want to wake you. You all right?"

I nodded, fighting back the tears that wouldn't come the night before. He wrapped his arms around me, and I let him hold me tight. For a brief moment, I let him be a man to my woman and took his comfort for all it was worth.

That is until I heard a throat clear. I looked up.

Babel went rigid, and his voice was hard. "Hi, Doc."

"How are you feeling this morning, Sunny?" Billy Bob sat on the edge of my bed, the Babel-free edge—his full concentration on me.

"I'm still pretty sore," I said with a tight mouth.

Billy Bob leaned in close to examine my face and Babel's arms tightened around me. While there were worse situations than being sandwiched between two gorgeous men, I had a feeling they would kill each other before they threw any action my way.

As Billy Bob touched my cheek, checking for swelling I guessed, a low rumble emanated from Babel. Billy Bob snarled back.

Come on! What the hell?

"Oh, for daisy's sake, Babel," I said through gritted teeth, admonishing Billy Bob with a narrow-eyed stare. "Go wait out in the living room until the *doctor* is finished checking me over."

Was I the only one in the room who remembered that I'd gotten knocked silly the night before? These guys were awfully territorial considering neither had any real claim to me. Sheesh!

Babel skirted off the bed, grabbing his shirt from the nightstand as he left the room without even a glance back.

Billy Bob leaned forward for a closer look at my jaw, close enough to touch, but not touching. Good man. "So, do you want another kiss?" he asked with a grin.

Maybe not so good. But there was a part of me that twitterpated. "No." Up close, I noticed some fine lines at the edge of his eyes.

The first time I'd met the Shaman-doc, I'd thought he was old because of the hair, then young because of the *GQ* body and pretty-boy good looks. But now, now I wasn't sure at all how old he was. Hadn't Ruth said he'd delivered all her children? How in the world was that possible?

"What are you thinking about?" He placed his finger between my eyebrows. "You're going to get hard lines if you keep up that kind of concentration."

"How old are you?"

"How old are *you*?" he countered.

"I asked first." I smiled and wished I hadn't. Too much pressure on the jaw.

"I'm forty-seven."

"Damn, men have all the good aging genes." Hell, yeah, I was jealous. I was over a decade younger than Billy Bob and I certainly had a bit more age to my appearance. Of course, he looked like he was still in his twenties.

"Your turn."

"Uh-uh, no way." The corners of my lips tugged upward in a small smile.

"Come on." He winked. "Doctor-patient confidentiality and all."

"You think you're slick enough to get it out of me, huh?"

He skimmed my cheek with his thumb. "And then some."

My breath caught as he moved his lips toward mine. He was fun and easy, without attachments. In other words, he was not Babel Trimmel. And while he was hotter than August on the sun, again, he wasn't Babel. My body ached only for one man.

Jo Jo walked in and the doc went full stop. "Sunny." Jo Jo hesitated. "Is this a bad time? Babel said I could come in."

Of course he had. Admittedly, I was put off, but Jo Jo's timing had probably saved me a lot of embarrassment down the road. "Nope. Not a bad time." I held out my hand to the teenager.

He smiled and took it. "I'm so glad you're all right. The sheriff made me go home last night or I would have stayed. I'm sorry you got hurt. So sorry."

Guilt was written all over Jo Jo's pensive face. Even with all the tattoos, piercing, funky dye-job and the sleeveless black T-shirt, he looked like a scared kid.

I knew in that moment—Jo Jo thought his dad attacked me.

I wanted to do something to ease his mind. Even if his dad had been the culprit, it wasn't Jo Jo's fault, and he shouldn't have to carry the burden. "I didn't get a chance to thank you. You're my hero."

"You're welcome. I'm just sorry I didn't show up sooner. I'd have kicked some major ass."

Billy Bob stood up and took a step back. "I'll let you visit for a few minutes, then Jo Jo, Sunny's going to need to rest." He stepped out of room.

"Oh, Jo Jo," I said softly as the boy sat next to me on the bed. He bowed his head, avoiding eye contact.

"I'd come by last night to tell you how bad I felt about my dad talking to you like he did. He didn't mean nothin', Sunny. I swear it." He was so sad. A sad young man. Why hadn't I seen it before?

Squeezing his hand tighter, I could feel my eyelids fluttering in spasms and *I was running.*

A blonde woman, Jo Jo's mother, ran past me at a faster pace than I could manage, but I tried to keep up. The fear in her brought about a surge in my adrenaline. She jumped over logs and bushes like a gazelle, but it was a clump of grass that tripped her up. She fell, sprawling face-first onto the damp ground.

"*Get up, Rose Ann," I said. Why wasn't she fighting them? Couldn't she turn into a big were-creature and whip the shit out of them? "Fight! Don't give up."*

Two men grabbed her arms and dragged her backward, laughing to themselves at some clever personal joke. Why couldn't I see their faces! *I felt nauseous. Her pink suit dress was torn and filthy, her beautiful blonde hair dirty with nature, and her shoeless feet were cracked and bleeding.*

I saw all of her, but none of them. I wanted to scream with frustration. Then I heard one of them say, "Maybe we pumped her too full of tranquilizer for the change?"

And the other said, "Yeah, if he was even telling the truth about her. Just because he *can, don't mean shit."*

"Well, if she don't, we'll just have to hunt his ass down."

"Please," Rose Ann whispered. "Don't. I have a family..." One of the men smacked her head with the butt of his rifle.

"Rose Ann!" I roared.

Much to Jo Jo, Billy Bob, and Babel's surprise. Apparently, I was back in the real world, and I'd brought the tail end of the vision with me.

"Oww," I said. The shout had hurt.

Jo Jo leaned off the bed and threw up. Rose Ann had been hunted like Judah, only now I knew one of her own people had sold her out. A man. Had Chavvah found out who? Is that why she disappeared? Had she been taken as well?

Oh, no! The full moon had happened a week ago. Was she dead already? Was I too late for my friend?

I would find the bastard who'd sold out his own kind for sport, so help me, and I would make him pay.

CHAPTER FOURTEEN

BABEL HELPED JO JO to the bathroom to clean up. The guilt over his father possibly hurting me, and the shock of hearing me scream his mother's name had been too much for the boy. I didn't blame him for throwing up—I didn't know what was keeping me from doing the same.

I tried to put the pieces together, everything I'd seen and heard since I'd gotten to Peculiar. None of it made any sense. It was as though I'd been given a jigsaw puzzle that had most of its pieces missing and even worse, extra pieces from other puzzles. Nothing fit.

The key had to be in the recent attack. Most towns, especially small ones, had their share of problems to hide, but this secret had someone bothered enough to assault me. Obviously, whoever it was didn't want me dead, because if that had been the case, I'd be a corpse. This had been a warning to scare me and it worked. I was scared.

I now suspected everyone and anyone in town, except Babel. After all, he'd only arrived after his brother's disappearance. And while my choice in men had never been top-notch, I couldn't believe Babel could do anything so dastardly.

Billy Bob didn't make my list of suspects either. It's not that he didn't have opportunity; he'd been around the town a very long time. But I couldn't fathom any motive. Besides, he's the one who encouraged me to help Judah make his peace. Jo Jo wasn't on my list either. Too young, too vulnerable, and he loved his mother too much.

Everyone else was fair game, though. I didn't know these people from Shinola. Not only were they strangers, but they were also a whole 'nother species. Two people in this town had been hunted for sport, possibly more—my stomach lurched at the thought of Chav being hunted—and for certain one of them was dead.

Sheriff Taylor arrived with Tyler Thompson in tow. Seeing the deputy sent flutters of fear through me. He was high on my "who would want to hit me" list.

I avoided looking directly at Tyler. Jo Jo's silent pleading kept me from implicating his father. I would let the teenager have his say after the police left. It wasn't as if I felt I owed him, but a small part of me felt a kinship to the disenfranchised Jo Jo.

I was still in my jeans and light green tank top from the night before. There were brown spots of blood from my mouth spattered across the ribbed cotton fabric. For the first time, I didn't feel faint at the sight. Maybe it was true, the whole saying, what didn't kill you made you stronger. I just wasn't sure how tough I wanted to be.

Neville Lutjen showed up next. It was turning into a real party. He wore a tan suit with a light-blue shirt and a chocolate tie. "How are you doing this morning, Ms. Haddock?"

Oh, so formal. He was in civil servant mode. "Fantastic, Mayor. Don't I look fantastic?"

He cleared his throat nervously. "Well, I, well," he stammered. "I just wanted to check in. I'm sorry about what's transpired here in our quiet little town. I assure you stuff like this doesn't happen here."

I begged to differ. I was living proof stuff just like this happened in Peculiar. "I'm not holding you or the town responsible, Mayor. The only person who can be held accountable is the person who attacked me."

Neville shuffled his toe against the floor, shifting uncomfortably. "Even so."

He put his palms together and tapped his fingertips. He looked like he'd rather be anywhere but here. I remembered what Ruth said about Neville's wife, her long-term illness, and death. In my state, I must've reminded him of her.

"Thank you for coming by, Neville." I forced my mouth into a tight smile. "I appreciate your concern."

He dropped his hands to his side and grinned. "You're mighty welcome, Sunny. The Red Hat ladies sent over several covered dishes. They're in your refrigerator. Just holler if there's anything I can do for you." He winked.

I'm dead serious here. If I hadn't been so flabbergasted, I'd have laughed. Billy Bob clapped his hands together once. "Everybody out. Sunny needs to rest."

Finally, a boon for my sanity.

"I'll post a man outside the apartment," Sheriff Taylor said.

"Not Deputy Thompson." All eyes turned to me. Including the deputy.

"Is there something you want to tell me, Sunny?"

"He doesn't like me very much, and I'd prefer my protection to, at the very least, be cordial with me." There, I'd said it. I put the elephant in the room, and they could all like it or lump it.

The sheriff glanced at Tyler Thompson, who had the good sense to look mildly ashamed. Then the sheriff nodded. "Okay. Not Thompson. Anything else you can remember?"

I pretended for a moment to think about it, but the truth was I couldn't tell him anything concrete. Nothing I could prove. The stuff about Rose Ann, I wasn't ready to say out loud.

The police vacated my apartment slower than I'd have liked, but eventually it was just me, Billy Bob, Babel, and Judah, who was watching me from the bedroom doorway. I huffed at the ghost. It seemed there was no getting rid of him. I desperately wanted to shower the filth from the night before. "You guys can go. I'll be all right." I wanted Babel to stay, but I wasn't going to ask. He'd been cold and distant since Billy Bob had arrived, and I'd barely seen him throughout the morning. I didn't have a right to feel so put off, but I did anyway.

Billy Bob grabbed his bag and nodded to me. "Take the pain pills if you need them.

Try not to overtax yourself."

After he'd left, it was down to the two brothers. Babel picked chipped white paint off the door molding. "I'd like to stay."

My heart fluttered. If I didn't watch myself, batting eyelashes would soon follow. "I'm really tired, Babel." *Please stay.* "I'd just like to take a hot shower and sleep." *Please stay.*

He walked toward me, his usual swarthy swagger gone. Insecurity looked sweet on him. I wanted him to stay so badly it made my mouth dry. Everything about Babel made me want to hold him, have him hold me, and never let go. But there was Sheila. They shared a past I could never compete with, and I didn't think it was right to try. She'd be a better match for him. They were both therianthropes, and I was just a human.

Everything that I'd gone through since coming to town, the trauma and danger, couldn't dampen down the emotions I felt for Babel. That was perhaps the most dangerous bit of all. I was falling for him. Hard. To the point of distraction. To the point that everything else be damned. I avoided eye contact. I knew if I looked into those blue, blue eyes, I might not be able to say what I had to say.

"Babel, I'd like you to go now."

"But Sunny..." I heard the hurt and misery in his voice.

"No." I held up a hand. "Just go." I closed my eyes and waited until the door to the apartment closed before opening them again and sighing. Wrong man, wrong place, wrong time. The story of my life.

Judah curled up in the corner of the bathroom near the small vanity as I went inside.

"Get out."

He whimpered and rested his chin on the linoleum floor.

I shook my head. "Fine. Then hide your eyes."

Like a good spirit, he obeyed. I dropped my clothes to the floor and stepped into the shower and let the warm stream wash away my cares. It worked. For a whole second.

Judah started whining. I turned off the shower, anxious he might be warning me. Had someone come back? Armed with a scrub brush in hand (it was either that or the small bottle of shampoo, and the scrub brush was heavier), I peeked around the shower curtain.

No one stood waiting on the other side. I gave Judah a cross look, but he ignored me, pawing at the floor through my jeans. "What now?" I asked, my exasperation growing.

Grabbing the towel from the hook, I wrapped it around my chest and stepped onto the cold floor. I leaned down trying to figure out what about my pants the stupid ghost found so damned interesting.

The folded corner of the diner check jutted from the edge of my jeans pocket. I pulled it out and showed it to him. "This? This is what you wanted me to find?" He barked.

Great, now if I could only learn to speak fluent coyote, we'd have this whole mystery wrapped up in no time.

For the second time, he'd brought me to this clue. The numbers and letters made absolutely no sense to me. I suppose it was too much to ask that he'd left a letter along the lines of "I, Judah Trimmel, due to some sinister plot by insert guilty party's name here have been murdered in the most heinous of ways. Please bring my killer(s) to justice." Now that would have been helpful.

I could take the scribbles down to the police station. Put it in the capable hands of the sheriff and put my sleuthing cap in the closet. Seriously, other than the visions, it wasn't as if I'd been very good at the whole detective business. Hell, I wasn't even very good at the whole psychic thing.

Looking at the numbers again, I got a niggling feeling, like I should know what they mean. "Screw it," I decided in a breath. I'd take the damn thing down to the sheriff, and he could look into it or burn it, either way, I just wanted the mystery in someone else's hands.

After a disproportionate amount of time, I'd managed to put on enough makeup to cover most of the bruising growing on the sides of my face. Unfortunately, no amount of cream foundation could keep the swelling in my cheeks from making me look like a reject from *The Planet of the Apes*.

The black and white car outside my building was a little flashy. Pretty weird needing police protection in such a tiny town. I nodded to the deputy behind the wheel (Not Tyler Thompson, thank goodness!) as he started the engine to follow me, and I made my way down the street with few stares. Most of the people I ran into those few short blocks made a point of looking down at the ground or off to the side of me when they greeted, and passed with genial remarks like "nice day" or a simple nod hello.

If I could have jogged without jarring my head around, I would have. Anything to get away from the collective discomfort my presence aroused. When I reached the police station steps, I could almost hear an audible sigh from town.

The first deputy I came across was not Tyler Thompson. I was thankful for that small favor. His name was Eldin Farraday. He was youngish, thin and tall, and his kind smile made me feel better. He had me take a seat in the chair by his desk and went to the back to let Sheriff Taylor know I'd arrived.

A blackboard screwed into the sidewall of the station caught my eye. I hadn't noticed it the first time I'd been there. At the top, scrawled in chalk, were the underlined headers: Date, Incident, Resolution, Officer on Call. The following row had the date 04/23, Vandalism-Window Broke at Courthouse, open investigation, and the initials EF. Which I took to mean Eldin Farraday. There were six incidents total, with my assault being the last, and ST—Sid Taylor—as the officer on duty. I'd been reduced to just another "open investigation."

Dates, incidents, initials.

I stood up and walked to the board, smearing the

sheriff's initials with my thumb as the numbness of realization swept over me.

Dates, incidents, initials.

The dream.

I pulled the diner check out of my pocket and grabbed a pen off the nearest desk and translated the sequence of numbers and letters. 150000715JT, became 07/15 JT $15,000, then 175000725RC became 07/25 RC $17,500, and finally 200000719GH became 07/19 GH $20,000. The dream at Babel's had been a vision, not a dream, and the curious ledger had been real.

My throat felt tight as if I'd swallowed a marble. I rubbed the paper between my palms, hoping for a psychic episode that would clear it all up for me. But I knew better than anyone, my gift didn't work that way.

I heard the sheriff's deep voice. "Sunny? Did you remember something else from last night?"

Turning to Sid Taylor, I stared dumbly at him and held out my hand. A breeze from an oscillating fan in the corner of the room blew the diner check from my fingers and onto the floor.

Whether from psychic mojo, or just intuition, I knew what had been in the ledger— what Judah must have figured out. The letters represented people, the dates were when they were taken, and the monetary amount had been the prices for their lives.

CHAPTER FIFTEEN

"**SUNNY, I DON'T** know what you want me to do here." Sheriff Taylor ran his thick fingers through his salt-and-pepper hair.

"I want you to do your job." My rebuke ruffled him, but I'd been sitting in his office for two hours while he sifted through mounds of folders for the last five years.

Sheriff Taylor twisted in his seat. "Young lady. I've done what you suggested, and other than Judah, there haven't been any missing people in town that fit those initials or otherwise. You don't think I want to find out what happened to Judah? He was a friend of mine. I can't tell you how many sleepless nights I worked to find out what happened to him."

He leaned back with a heaving sigh. "Sometimes, the hardest part about this job is knowing that some cases will never be solved. I'm afraid whether Judah took off on his own, or something bad happened to him, we might never know."

"He's dead," I said as bluntly as I could, all my anger directed at the sheriff. "And that list has something to do with the reason why. You're the police. Get to policing."

It hadn't been fair to take my frustration out on Sid Taylor, but it seemed like every new development led to more questions instead of answers, and I was getting sick and tired of feeling sick and tired.

"Sunny," Sid said as I stood to leave. "Don't forget your scrap of paper."

I shook my head in dismay. "Keep it."

Tyler Thompson was waiting outside on the steps when I exited the building. Bile rose in the back of my mouth as I braced myself for another confrontation.

"Ms. Haddock."

"I don't know if I can take any more today, Deputy Thompson. So let's make it brief." I tried to keep the animosity out of my tone.

"I just wanted to apologize, ma'am. For my behavior yesterday. It was rude and unwarranted." He sounded sincere.

Huh. "Okay. I accept your apology, Deputy."

"And," he said, chewing the inside of his cheek. "Thanks for not telling my mom about it."

Before I could respond, he headed back into the station. Inside I laughed, because a real chuckle would have hurt, and I was already sorry for all the talking I'd been doing. It was hard to stay mad at a guy who had a healthy fear of his mother. Although, his apology in no way crossed him off my list. Maybe he was apologizing for more than just being impolite.

Cars and trucks drove past me in the easy, slow way they do in small towns. I saw a man standing outside my restaurant door, he turned and smiled charmingly. Neville Lutjen could be disarming most of the time. He had the type of personality and bravado to ingratiate himself with people. Real likable.

I didn't trust him as far as I could throw him.

It had less to do with the man before me and more to do with the fact that he reminded me of my father. One of those guys who always knew the right thing to say and do. He could diffuse a bad situation, even one he caused, with a wink and a smile. People, especially men, with that ability were inauthentic.

"Hello, Mayor Lutjen," I greeted as I neared the front door.

"Call me Neville. Please." His voice held its normal warm quality, but I noticed he'd kept his hands to his side. It was the first time he hadn't offered me a handshake or tried to touch me in some manner. I'd seen this reaction before in people who found out about my ability. It made them wary of making skin-to-skin contact with me.

I took my keys from my purse to unlock the front door, glanced at the police car, and waved to the officer on duty as he watched me.

"Can I help you with something?" I asked Neville.

"Uh, well, I just wanted to check on you. Make sure you were okay."

"About as well as I was when you popped in earlier."

I opened the door and discovered I'd forgotten to turn on the restaurant lights before I'd left. Or had I forgotten? Was someone or something lurking in the darkness waiting for me?

"Well, if I can help in any way."

"Thanks, Neville. I'm feeling better now. Still a little afraid." Peering inside, I thought of a way to make the mayor feel useful. "Could you have a look around inside before I go in? Maybe turn the lights on? I'm just a little nervous."

Men loved it when you appealed to their protective he-man nature, and Neville was no exception. He beamed a large, bright white smile in my direction. "Why, of course. I'm happy to be of service, m'dear."

Flipping on the lights, he made a big to-do about checking every nook and cranny, even the back door. Which I'd found had a terrible lock on it and no deadbolt. I'd stick a chair under the handle tonight, and buy new locks for it tomorrow, I decided.

Neville finished checking the apartment, and gave me the "all clear."

Instead of breaking into my best faux southern drawl and telling him how "I've always relied on the kindness of strangers," I simply said, "Thanks."

I really needed to get the cable hooked up if nothing else than to get out of my head a little. Then another thought, did they have cable in Peculiar?

I looked around the desolate restaurant, my dreams of veggie-deli-dom with my bestie drifting away from my grasp. Where was Chavvah? I knew if she could have called or texted she would've. I was scared that I'd lost my best friend. I was scared that I'd have to tell Babel that he'd lost his only remaining sibling. I was scared none of us would recover from the hidden truths in Peculiar.

Tucking my tail (no pun intended) between my legs and running seemed to be my modus operandi. I'd ran away from the community I grew up in because it hadn't given me the freedom I so desired. When Chavvah had suggested Peculiar, I'd jumped on the idea so I could run away from a painful relationship. And now I wanted to leave Peculiar because...

Well, for once, I had great reasons for wanting to skedaddle from a place. Everyone but me was a were-animal, something super-sinister way above my pay grade was happening, and on top of those reasons, I'd been attacked twice. But still, did I want my whole life to be a series of getting while the getting was good?

Of all the places to make my stand, I was choosing Peculiar. *Idiot*.

It was noonish, and the rest of the day seemed a wash. What to do with myself for the remainder of time became the issue. So, I was determined to get rid of Neville and start really cleaning the restaurant area. Maybe I'd find another clue while I was at it.

Either that or nap. A nap sounded good.

"Well, little lady, I'm off." Neville, chipper and nearly giddy, moved toward the door.

"Thanks for your help."

"Always a pleasure to help a neighbor." He gave me a gallant nod and a wink.

Oy, another wink. Inwardly, I groaned. I was ready for Neville to take his shiny happy ass out. The lanky boy in the doorway kept him from going.

"Great timing, Jo Jo," I mumbled.

Neville hung near the front as Jo Jo shuffled nervously toward me, completely ignoring the mayor. "Sunny, I need your help." His eyes were red as if he'd been crying.

"What's happened? Are you all right?"

"Fine. I'm okay." He wiped his nose with the back of his hand. "I got into a fight with my dad."

"Over me?"

"Kind of." He leaned in closer, suddenly aware we weren't alone. "He didn't do it. I know what you think. But I'm sure he didn't."

I patted his shoulder. "Don't worry about me," I reassured him, even though I didn't feel so reassured myself.

"You mentioned my mom. You had a vision?"

Reaching for Jo Jo's hand, the one he didn't wipe the snot from his nose with, I gave his fingers a squeeze. I didn't want to tell him what I'd seen. No kid should have to know his mom had such a horrible end. "What kind of help do you need?"

"I want you to come out to our property."

The alarm must have been plain on my face, because he added, "My dad's not home. Probably won't be all night. It would only take a little while."

"What do you think I can do at your house, Jo Jo?" I tried to keep my question even and calm.

"I want you to do your magicky mumbo-jumbo and see if you can give my dad...some peace." He looked down at his toes, fully expecting a rejection.

I didn't know if I would *see* anything to illuminate

his mother's disappearance. But I didn't have the heart not to try. "Okay."

That garnered me a small smile. I wanted to ruffle his short leopard-spotted hair.

Nah, too condescending.

"No promises," I warned him.

"None." He shook my hand. "Agreed."

Neville cleared his throat. "I've got a meeting, but I'd be happy to take you out to the Corman place, Sunny. Since you don't have a vehicle."

I winced at the reminder. "Uh, well..." Did I really want to spend a trip confined in a vehicle with Neville? Not really. I looked to Jo Jo for help.

"I've got my truck out front. I can drive."

"Excellent." Though, I wasn't sure if having a seventeen-year-old chauffeur was any better. "You go on to your meeting, Neville. I appreciate the help!" I tried for perky, and his rewarding smile said I'd managed.

"All right then. See you later." He waved and tilted his head to Jo Jo.

"Bye," Jo Jo said.

As I got into Jo Jo's truck (after telling the officer on duty where I'd be and fending off his protest), the teenager started his engine.

"You should put on your seat belt," I told him while buckling my own.

"The pickup was old and used when I bought it. Seat belt doesn't work, never has."

"Huh. You might want to think about getting that fixed."

He grinned and put the truck in gear. The tires

squealed as he peeled out. Oh, boy. Seemed like I'd arranged for afternoon entertainment after all.

I don't know what I'd expected, a shack or a stick house at the very least. I was more than a little surprised when Jo Jo drove the long mile down his driveway, which opened up to a large unkempt field and a gorgeous, sage-green two-story Cape Cod style house with a three-car garage.

As we pulled up and parked, I noticed the paint peeling a little, and one of the gutters around the side was down. In my heart, I knew at one time this place had been immaculate.

"You sure your dad isn't home?" I unbuckled the safety belt I'd been white-knuckled since we'd left town. I wished I had called Babel to let him know what I was doing and where I was going. It would've made me feel safer having him know. Well, if Jo Jo and I disappeared, at least the mayor would be able to give the police a jumping-off point. What I really wished was that I hadn't sent Babel away in the first place. Why did I have to be so stubborn at the worst possible times?

"Yeah," Jo Jo answered. "He always takes off after a big fight. Sometimes he doesn't come back for days."

"I'm sorry, Jo Jo." My parents never yelled at me or hit me, so it was hard for me to understand what he was going through.

"Why? You didn't make him act like he does."

I found it hard to reconcile the Brady Corman of my vision with the one who'd presented himself at my shop the day before. He hadn't always been a drunk. Jo Jo had at one time had a mother *and* a father. I promised myself to keep that in mind while trying to stumble into a "helpful" vision.

Inside the house, the decor had seen better days. There were coffee stains, or at least I hoped they were coffee stains, on the light-blue chenille cushions of the Old Country style sofa. All the furniture matched. Before Rose Ann had been taken from them, she'd kept a beautiful home.

I didn't have to a have a psychic event to know how much love she'd put into her house.

As I walked around, I'd get a flash here and there. Rose Ann cooking, brief intimacies between her and Brady, how proud she was when they'd brought Jo Jo into the world. All her happiest moments, but nothing sinister lurking at the edges.

I just didn't get it.

"Anything?" Jo Jo asked hopefully.

"Sorry. Nothing yet."

The living room and the kitchen didn't get me anywhere. I doubted the bedroom would be better. When I got inside, I saw a flash of Jo Jo helping his father from the floor to the bed, pulling the peach ruffled bedspread up to the drunk's chin. I closed my eyes as though that could keep the bad stuff away.

It didn't.

Judah's ghost prowled around the floor, sniffing in all the corners. I'd wondered if the coyote would show up or not. He drew my attention to the side of the oak dresser and my chest tightened.

What terrible thing would I find?

My heart beat heavy, hard enough to feel the surge

of each pump in my ears as I crept toward Judah. He didn't move from the spot, so I had to reach through him. The space where his body was felt slightly cooler than the rest of the room. A shiver ran from the nape of my neck down my spine. Like backing up into a spider web.

Way high on my creep-o-meter.

The edge of a wooden frame peeked out from behind the dresser. I pulled on it and broken glass fell out and punctured the palm of my hand.

"Son of a bitch," I swore as the blood welled to a ball. Where was lycan spit when you needed it?

I heard Jo Jo's quickening footfalls. "Sunny?"

"I'm okay," I told him, holding out my hand. "Got a bandage?"

"Sure." He disappeared out in the hallway and I pulled the picture frame completely out.

It was a young Brady and Rose Ann in traditional bridal attire—he in a tux, her in a gown. For furred-folks, this town seemed pretty normal. Hell, more normal than the way I grew up.

The coyote seemed intent on the wedding photo. "Come on," I said to Judah. "Can you be a little more helpful? For shit's sake." He whined and sniffed the photo.

Great, dead and sentimental. I shook my head, but examined the picture once more. Maybe there was something written on the back. Nope. The back just had the photography studio mark on it. I flipped it back over. They really had made a beautiful couple.

And that's when I saw it. The necklace.

I couldn't be one-hundred percent certain it was the same as the one in the metal box, but if it wasn't it was a very close twin—gold chain with a small heart.

I folded the picture up, put it in my purse, and sent quiet apologies to Rose Ann Corman wherever she was.

"Anything?" Jo Jo asked again as he brought me a first-aid kit.

"Sorry, no." I didn't want to tell him about the necklace and get his hopes up. It was just one more piece to the whole wacky puzzle, and for all I knew, meant nothing at all.

"It's time to get back to town, I think."

Poor kid. I wished I had the answers to give him.

Back on the road, I prayed we'd get to town in one piece. I'm not saying Jo Jo was a bad driver, just a little erratic. We had a few "Hail Mary" moments, making me think I'd have to get a stronger dye to cover the gray hairs he was giving me.

"Slow down, Jo Jo. It's not a race."

He didn't respond with words, but his foot let off the gas a bit. A dark SUV, midnight blue or black, I couldn't tell, was heading up the road toward us in the opposite direction. I hadn't seen it before, but no surprise there. "Neighbors?" I asked.

"No," Jo Jo said. "At least, not unless the Berringtons got a new Suburban. Man, those are total swag."

I was trying to decide if swag was good or bad when I noticed the Suburban had picked up speed and was moving to the center of the road.

"Where did you get your license?" Jo Jo yelled. "K-mart?"

"Are they going to get over?" The large SUV kept getting closer and closer, kicking up dust from the gravel road like a professional fog machine.

"They'll get over," Jo Jo assured me.

I didn't feel assured.

"Watch out!" I screamed as the truck seemed intent on a head-on collision.

"Oh, shit!" Jo Jo yelled and cranked the steering wheel to the left, just missing the dark machine of death. We landed nose down in a three-foot embankment on the side of the road.

The crash sent me forward, but the seat belt kept me from doing more than hitting my forehead on the dashboard. Jo Jo hadn't been so lucky. There were no airbags in the truck, and the teenager hadn't been wearing his seat belt. His head was cut to shit from where it had hit the windshield, tiny shards of glass speckling his face as blood gushed from a large cut on his forehead. He was unconscious, and as tough as I was getting, I felt that lightheaded feeling coming on.

The SUV sped off down the road, not even stopping to see if we needed help. Bastard. I don't know how the driver hadn't seen us.

How in the hell had I managed two freakin' attacks and two motor vehicle accidents all in the same week? *Fuckity-fuck-fuck-fuck!*

"No," I chastised myself out loud. This boy had spent his life with one disappointment after another. I would not be just one more adult who failed him. I hadn't brought a jacket, and modesty seemed like the least of my problem, so I took my blouse off, cream-colored and one of my favorites, and pressed it to his forehead.

Shaking his shoulder gently with my free hand, I tried to rouse the wounded teenager. "Jo Jo, wake up." I tried again, and then again. Maybe he'd done damage to his brain. What did I know? The extent of my medical training included a crash course in the Heimlich maneuver when a restaurant customer had started choking. I needed a doctor.

Since the doc wasn't here, I took steps to help Jo Jo as best I could. I kept pressure on his gash with my right hand—because in the movies, that was the first thing they always did—while I reached into my purse with the left and dug out my cell phone.

Flipping it open, I refrained from voicing the stream of expletives running rampant in my head. (Besides, it would be pretty hard to compete with the quadruple f-bomb, so why try?) No bars! What the hell was wrong with Peculiar? Hadn't they ever heard of cell towers? Maybe they had a shifter-to-shifter phone service I wasn't aware of. If I started howling, would anyone come running?

After a minute, the panic waned a little. My cell phone worked in town. We must've just been in a dead spot.

I rolled my shirt and put it around Jo Jo's head like a bandana and tied the back. I took my hands away to examine the makeshift bandage. It seemed to be holding, but it was hard to tell with all the other smaller cuts if the bleeding was stopping or not.

It would have to do. Jo Jo needed help. Real medical help, and I wasn't qualified.

"Hang in there, Jo Jo." I stroked his hair, comforting, like I'd seen his mother do when he was a baby. "I'll be back. I promise."

My arm and jaw were killing me by the time I'd finally managed to hold a signal. (You try walking nearly a mile holding a cell phone up in the air.) I couldn't even switch sides because my other shoulder was weaker from where I'd been attacked. My face, of course, still hurt from the night before, and the desperation of my circumstances seemed to compound the ache. I'd probably only been walking twenty minutes, but it'd felt like two hours in the hot June sun.

I brought the phone down to make the call, and the friggin' bars disappeared. Shi-it!

I thrust it back up, and the signal came back. Why couldn't this be easy? Why couldn't anything in my life be easy?

Because it wasn't. I'd deal with it.

Dialing Babel's number wasn't an accident. Billy Bob and Babel were next to each other in my address book. I didn't hang up when his phone started ringing. If he answered, at least he could get help. Even if he were angry about me sending him away, he wouldn't turn his back on Jo Jo. "Please answer," I begged softly.

I heard a faint "hello." Shoot, I needed to put him on speaker.

"Hold on!" I hollered. "Don't hang up!"

"Sunny?" I heard him say clearer as the speaker engaged. "Why do you sound funny?"

"'Cause I'm in the middle of freaking nowhere! Jo Jo's hurt really bad. He's knocked out and bleeding a lot." Panic mounted inside me, and I forced it down. "Help me."

"Where are you?" He sounded as anxious as I was feeling.

"I don't know. I swear all these country roads look alike. Why can't you all use freakin' signs like normal people?"

"It's all right. Tell me where you were going?" He didn't even yell at me over the "normal people" comment. I was glad one of us was calm.

"I...We were going back to town. Coming back from Jo Jo's house."

"Okay. I know what road you're on. I'll find you. I'll be there soon. Just hang on."

He hung up, and my arm went limp at my side. The cell phone slipped out of my hand, and the screen cracked and went black when it hit the rocky ground.

"Nooo," I shouted to the tree frogs and crickets. *Breathe, Sunny, Breathe.* I picked the broken phone up and put it in my pocket. Babel was coming. He'd save Jo Jo. I ran back to the truck. I had to get back to the boy. I had to make sure he still needed saving.

I hauled ass as fast as my legs would work. My bra was soaked with sweat by the time I made it back to the wreckage. *Don't be dead. Don't be dead*, I pleaded silently to animal ancestors, God, and all the earth deities I'd grown up with in my parents' community. I hoped if any of them existed, at least one would hear me. Of course, they might be pissed about me not completely holding to my earlier bargain.

Jo Jo looked so pale and listless when I reached him. My hand shook as I touched his neck, trying to find a pulse. He still had one.

"Thank you," I mouthed to whoever had been listening. I heard the roar of a car coming down the road in the distance.

"Help is on the way," I told Jo Jo. "Stay with me, buddy." At least I hoped it was help and not the SUV back for another swipe at us. The more I thought about it, the more I thought it had run us off the road on purpose. Relief washed over me when I saw it was Babel's car, broken windshield and all. I got out of the cab of Jo Jo's pickup to meet him.

Ho-boy, he looked pissed as he stalked toward me. My hero.

"Why didn't you call me to go with you to the Cormans?" he began his rant. "I live a damn mile from here." His nostrils flared. Why did he have to be even sexier when he was angry? Gah!

When I came back to my senses, Babel was still ranting. "After the way Brady came after you yesterday, are you out of your mind going out there alone?" He stopped for a moment, sniffed the air, then made a sharp chuffing noise. "And where's your shirt?"

Great. He caught my horny hormones on the wind. "How am I supposed to know that you live a mile from here, huh? I'm in the middle of the boonies with an injured teenager, and you're pissed because I didn't call you to babysit us?" I glared at him. "As to my shirt, do you think I was making out with a seventeen-year-old? Seriously?" First Brady, now Babel. What the hell did that say about popular opinion?

Babel raised an eyebrow. In response, I picked up a walnut-sized rock and chucked it at him.

He rubbed his chest where the projectile hit. "Ow."

"My shirt's keeping Jo Jo from bleeding all over the damned place, you idiot." Why had I called Babel? I could have called Billy Bob instead, and hell, it probably would have been the best thing for Jo Jo, but instead, I'd wasted my phone call on one moody coyote intent on punishing me with word, if not deed.

He went around the driver's side of the truck and checked on Jo Jo. "He's still breathing, and his pulse is strong."

"Thank you, Doctor Trimmel," I grumbled, though I really was glad Babel had checked on Jo Jo. It made me feel like he wasn't a complete shit-head.

"I can't believe you didn't call me."

I snorted. This conversation was disintegrating into absurdity. "This is so much bullshit."

"What did you say?"

"I said bullshit."

He growled at me.

I dug my broken phone out of my pocket and threw it at him. "Don't you growl at me! You might have a bigger bark, but I have a bigger bite." Not really, but I was really pissed at him for acting like he owned me.

He'd dodged the crippled device easily, strode forward, and closed the gap between us faster than I could react. His arms swept around me. He crushed me to his chest.

"Goddamn," he murmured. "Damn."

"Babel." I craned my neck, no small pain there, to look up at him. His eyes were wild, but not animal-wild like before. He looked so handsome, in a tortured, *One-Flew-Over-the-Cuckoo's-Nest* way. In a moment of weakness, I allowed myself to sink into him, taking all the reassurance he gave. His chest felt warm against my cheek, and I could hear his heart thudding beneath my ear.

He stroked my hair. "You shouldn't be alone."

"I'm not alone. You're here."

"Not what I'm talking about. I'm worried. You shouldn't be living alone. You need someone around. Someone who can take care of you."

Oh, no, he didn't. Moment of comfort over. It didn't matter to me that he might be right..."I'm a big girl, Babel. In case you hadn't noticed."

"Sunny, don't be like that. I only meant—"

"I know exactly what you meant. I'm not the helpless heroine in some bad B movie who needs to be rescued every five minutes." Okay, my track record hadn't been great this past week, but usually, I'm very capable.

"It's not that you're a woman, Sunny." His arms dropped to his side. "You're human."

The way he said it was like a punch in the gut. He'd said it like me being "human" was insurmountable. I was fragile cargo. Easily damaged. "You're just figuring that out, Einstein?" I snapped. I couldn't believe what I was hearing. Lucky for Babel, the doc pulled up before I really went off on his stupid, albeit sexy ass.

Billy Bob examined Jo Jo, then looked at my bloody, bandaged hand. "Did you hurt yourself?"

I shook my head. "Most of the blood is from Jo Jo. Is he going to be okay?"

Babel tried to put his arms around me, and I moved away from him. I didn't need or want his macho support. Not now. Billy Bob got a little white thingy from his bag and snapped it in front of Jo Jo's face. The young man jerked awake. "Whoa, now," Billy Bob said. "Just some ammonia to wake you up."

"That stinks really bad," Jo Jo murmured.

"That's the whole point." Billy Bob smiled.

I was just happy the boy was awake. "A good sign, right?"

"Sunny..." Jo Jo said.

"I'm here. I'm fine."

"Stupid, goddamn truck."

Well, at least his memory was good. "Yeah."

"What truck?" Babel asked.

"The one that decided playing chicken on a June afternoon would be an ideal form of entertainment." I'd show them a whole new form of entertainment to rival the Spanish Inquisition if I ever saw them again. Vise grip to the balls sounded like an appropriate punishment. Actually, I might have to get more creative, squeezing their nuts until they cried "mommy" just wasn't satisfying enough.

Billy Bob put a neck brace on Jo Jo and gestured to

Babel. "Help me get him to my car. I need to get him back to the house to stitch his head."

They positioned the passenger seat down to fully recline and carried Jo Jo over, gently placing him inside. I went to the other door to get in the backseat. "I'll take you home, Sunny," Babel said.

"No, I don't want to leave Jo Jo alone."

The anger rolling off Babel was palpable, but now that the cavalry had arrived, I felt the full weight of the situation bearing down on me. Where was the Xanax when you needed it? Back at the doc's place, if I had to guess.

Billy Bob spoke up before Babel could protest. "You go with Babe. You can come check on Jo Jo later. But don't forget to head to the station and fill out a police report so they can try and find the person who did this to you both."

Sooo reasonable. Yeah. "Fine. Okay." I guess it was back to the police station for me. The place was starting to feel like hell sweet hell.

CHAPTER SIXTEEN

I **FELT A** little guilty about the deputy who was supposed to watch me. Sheriff Taylor reamed him up one side and down the other with threats like, "The next time I give you a job to do, and you don't, my foot's going to be so far up your ass you'll be spitting shoe polish for a month."

The man was a true poet.

I'd tried to speak up on the deputy's behalf a couple of times, but Babel would give me the look. You know, the one that says, "unless you want your ass in a sling as well, you'll keep out of it." The tirade lasted a little over half past uncomfortable and bordered on mortifying.

"Sheriff, am I a prisoner?"

He stopped berating the deputy and ogled me. "No, ma'am."

"Am I a hostage?"

"No."

"Then why don't you give the nice deputy a break? I

told him where I'd be, and while he insisted I should stay in town, as a free woman, I made my own choice."

The sheriff gave me a hard look. "Deputy Connelly, we'll talk more about this later."

Tyler Thompson walked over with a sheet of paper in hand. "No one in the town with a Suburban, dark or otherwise, Sheriff."

"Damn it." He shook his head and rubbed the dark circles under his eyes. "County?"

"There are nine registered in the county, but none that we can pinpoint as being the vehicle in question."

Sheriff Taylor's eyes narrowed in suspicion. "Anyone else know you all were going out to the Corman place?"

"Other than the deputy? No. Yes, Neville Lutjen was there when Jo Jo asked me to go. But –"

The sheriff picked up the phone from a nearby desk and punched in some numbers. "Yeah, Fran. Is Neville available? No. He's been in a meeting all afternoon? You sure he didn't go out for anything during? Okay. No, it's nothing. He doesn't need to call me back."

"You don't really think the mayor tried to run us off the road, do you?"

"Nope, not really. Just better to rule out who we can." Snapping his fingers, the sheriff got Deputy Connelly's attention. "Did you tell anyone where Ms. Haddock was going?"

"Uh, I called into the station about it, but that's it. Honest, boss."

If Connelly had called in, did that mean Tyler Thompson had known I'd be out there? Would he have really come after me like that and risk injuring or potentially killing Jo Jo in the process of trying to take me out? I watched the deputy carefully, trying to gauge his reaction. Nothing. I could read nothing on him. Except that he still didn't like me for whatever reason.

The sheriff fidgeted a pencil between his fingers. "It would have been nice if you'd gotten the license plate number."

"Well, between all the crapping myself, the ducking and the screaming..." I didn't want to be at the police station anymore.

"I think Sunny's had enough for the day, Sid," Babel said, echoing my thoughts.

Personally, I'd had enough to last me the whole year. Hell, my whole life.

The sheriff nodded, suddenly looking more tired than I'd seen him. "All right. I just have a few forms for you to sign, and you all can go."

I became aware of Babel staring at me as I dotted my I's and crossed my T's. The heat he poured into his gaze made me squirm.

I knew I looked a mess between my baboon-like cheeks, the oversized dirty T-shirt Babel had had balled up in the floorboard of his truck (better than showing up in my bra, and bonus, it smelled like Babel), and my matted hair from sweat and dirt road.

He didn't care.

The expression on his face was that of a man on fire. He'd gobble me up like homemade pumpkin pie, even as beat up and broke down as I appeared. My earlier anger at him vanished.

I handed the sheriff back his pen and looked sideways at Babel. "I'm ready." But for what, I wasn't sure. The tension in the car was thick and pressing. I could feel the weight of lust between us without even touching him. When we pulled up in front of the restaurant, Babel and I were fairly running for the door. He took the keys from my shaking hands and got us inside faster than I could have.

The next thing I knew, I was up against the wall, the heat of his body pressing against mine. His kiss was urgent, which I normally would have totally dug, but my jaw.

"Aww," I said. "Pain, pain."

"Sorry," he grinned. "Goddamn, but I want you, woman."

His caveman attitude, which would have ticked me off earlier, fueled my desire.

I jumped around his waist, and he pushed me against the wall again, knocking my shoulder. I groaned again. "Oh, seat belt bruise, damn it."

Gently, he carried me across the room and set my ass on the diner counter. I threw my other arm back and got another aching jolt for my trouble. "Son of a bitch."

Babel narrowed his eyes. "More pain?"

"Sorry," I said in a small voice, fighting the grimace. "Coyote attack." He stepped back and my heart dropped. Was he giving up? Was he right to? Babel leaned forward and kissed my neck. "Does it hurt here?"

"No," I said, feeling giddier than I was comfortable with.

He kissed my ear. "How about here?"

"Nope." Oh, man, we were having a total *Raiders-of-the-Lost-Ark* moment, and I was Indiana Jones! I squeezed his thighs between mine when his hand slid down between my legs. "How about here?"

Ho-boy. "No, doesn't hurt one bit."

He scooped me off the counter and carried me like a bride over the threshold.

"Where we going?" I asked, kissing the crease between his neck and earlobe. Oh, man, he smelled good enough to eat.

Babel made a rumbling noise that sent twitters down my stomach. "I'm going to take you upstairs and make love to all your parts that don't hurt, Sunshine Haddock. Is that good by you?"

Instead of saying "yes!" I asked the question, the one that would take us out of the moment. But I had to know. "What are we doing here?"

"I don't know about you, but I'm trying to get into your pants."

Okay, so he went for literal. Not what I was asking. I put my hand on his shoulder. I had to know that this was real because I didn't think I could do the "bang and bye" with Babel. Not now. If we did this, if we made love, my heart would be lost to him forever. There would be no turning back. At least not for me. And, Lord, I didn't even want to think about how I would explain it to Chav when we found her. A pang tweaked my gut.

Chav, where are you?

His fingers danced along my ribs. "Earth to Sunny."

I couldn't be with him if it didn't mean more than

just a fun way to kill time. "Is that it? Just in my pants and out of here?"

He grinned. "Well, there's several other things I'd like to do before the 'out of here' part." He brushed his hair back. The smile fading. "What answer are you looking for?"

What a romantic. "I don't know. I just..." What answer did I want? Did I want an undying declaration of devotion and love? Bad Sunny, I thought, reminding myself that Peculiar was only a temporary stop for Babel Trimmel on the road to bigger and better things. I couldn't let myself get sucked back into a relationship doomed to failure. Allowing myself to really care about Babel was a sucker's bet. The girl in me wanted to let it ride while the woman in me knew better.

I sighed.

Babel's smoky-blue gaze, along with his smile, nearly broke my will. He dipped his chin and kissed my cheek. "What?"

Ugh. I'd heard that tone before. It said, what are you going to *say* or *do* now to ruin this beautiful, happy moment?

Immediately, I was annoyed. "Nothing."

I'd played this game too often. I tell the guy what's wrong, and he uses it as an excuse to pummel me verbally and make me feel like the bad guy. I wasn't biting.

He stroked my leg. "Come on, something's wrong. Tell me."

Ah, lulling tactics. Where the male of the species

lures the female into his trap by baiting her with soothing and innocuous words of rationality.

Uh-uh. "Really. It's nothing."

"I can tell something's wrong." The temperature of the conversation dropped ten degrees. Here was the "if you don't want to have a confrontation, I'll just force it out of you" bit.

"Babel, it's all good," I fairly cooed, giving him the warmest smile I could manage. I curved my index fingers into two of his belt loops and tugged. "Come here."

He smiled then, the situation diffused. Whoever said the best offense was a good defense lied. The best offense was a good deflection. "Hey, I want to go out to Billy Bob's in the morning. Can you drive me?" I asked, stroking his soft hair.

Babel stiffened.

Situation back on.

"Why?"

"To check on Jo Jo, of course."

"I don't like the way Doc Smith looks at you."

Ohh-kay. The territorial thing again. Did he really believe I wanted to go out there just to ogle the fantastically beautiful Shaman-doc? Crazy, right? "I can't help how he or anyone looks at me."

He narrowed his eyes. "I don't like the way you look at him."

Remember how I said the day had started out so well? "Oh, give me a break." Apparently, my mountain man had a fragile ego.

"Don't deny it."

"Have I denied anything, yet?" For shit's sake, I'd fallen into his man-trap. I'd have tried for deflection again, but there was nowhere to go that wouldn't sound disingenuous.

"What do you want from me, Babel?"

"I want you to tell me you don't want him."

"Fine. I don't want him." I threw my hands up in frustration. "Anything else?"

Babel started pacing. For a coyote, his movements were nearly catlike and graceful. I found myself staring at the way he controlled every part of his body with purpose. He was hotter than a blowtorch in a room full of firecrackers. And just as explosive. I licked my lips then bit my tongue to keep from screaming, "Take me now!"

The next words out of his mouth were better than any cold shower. "I don't believe you."

Oh, no, he didn't. "You have a lot of nerve, buddy. You're going around with Sheila, then me, then back to Sheila, then back to me. I don't think I'm the dishonest one here.

So. Screw. You."

"You already have."

"Get out," I said, clenching my teeth tight.

"There's nothing between—"

"Get out!"

His expression changed from angry to stupefied and back to angry. He knew he'd taken it too far, but his man-genes kept him from apologizing. With a "whatever" flick of his hand, he left. Judah popped his head around the corner. How long had he been there?

He cocked his head at me as if saying, "bitches be crazy."

I grabbed a washcloth and threw it at him. He just kept staring at me with those sparkling green eyes as the damp rag soared right through his head and body.

"Just shut up," I told him.

Truth was, I felt like a crazy bitch.

CHAPTER SEVENTEEN

I HID UNDER the covers most of the night. Who's a fraidy cat? I am, that's who. Sick of myself, I threw the blankets off my head. Judah was still staring at me. "Fine. I'm getting out of bed." I was naked, so I added, "Go somewhere else so I can shower and dress. I don't need an audience."

The shower would have been much better with Babel in it, and my body ached a little more today. Post-crash stiffness and bruising along with a side of mauling. It dawned on me I was beginning to get used to bad shit happening to me. I didn't like it, at all, but it was becoming par for the course. I wondered what Peculiar would throw at me next. Thinking about the possibilities made my head feel like it would explode. Bereft of cell phone and vehicle, my avenues of communication were limited. I wanted to get in touch with Billy Bob and find out about Jo Jo.

Unfortunately, I wasn't ready to leave the Bat Cave, yet.

The pants I'd worn the previous day were crumpled in the corner. I took the wedding picture of Brady and Rose Ann out and unfolded it. There were some scratches from the frame's broken glass and a little blood from the cut I'd gotten on my palm.

I dusted it with my fingers and sighed. Rose Ann didn't leave her family of her own free accord. If the necklace were the same in the picture as it was in Judah's lockbox, it would at least be evidence. Another piece to prove that Judah had been on to something that could have put him in danger. I retrieved the box from behind the display counter and pulled out the necklace with the heart charm and compared it to the photo. They looked identical.

My peripheral vision narrowed, and darkness engulfed me.

Straw, dirt scented with urine and other foul body wastes inundated my senses. I reached out to the metal bars caging me. I heard a whimpering. The noise made me turn.

In the corner of the cage, a woman lay curled up. Her arms wrapped her body. The dress was tattered and dirty, but I recognized it and her. Rose Ann.

A clanging sound, like the metal cups in those prison movies, redirected my attention. A man with short blond hair, neatly trimmed, ran a rod over the bars. "It's almost time. The moon will be up soon, and the hunt will be on." Rose Ann rolled up on her knees and bared her teeth with a vicious growl.

Amazing. She still had fight left in her.

The man laughed, then two more men arrived. They were all wearing full hunting gear, including orange vests.

"She turning, yet?" one of the newcomers, a short, dowdy man with a bald patch and round glasses, asked.

He looked like an accountant, not a murderer for heaven's sake.

It dawned on me, all three looked like clean-cut businessmen, not the hillbillies of Deliverance *I'd imagined.*

Rose Ann growled again, and I stared as her body shifted from woman to mountain lion in a matter of seconds. She hissed at them.

I hadn't realized Rose Ann was a mountain lion. For some reason, I thought she'd be a coyote like her husband.

"Oh, shit," the balding accountant muttered.

"Carl," said the blond. "Let her out. We'll give her a head start for a challenge."

The third guy, banker type, dark hair, tall, soft around the middle, looked like a giddy teenager as he rubbed his hands together in anticipation before he climbed up on top.

The other two guys stepped far back against the wall. Guns ready if the mountain lion chose to turn on them here.

"Oh, Rose," I said, hating myself for being a human. I wanted the vision to end. I didn't want to see anymore.

Please end.

They opened the cage.

End.

She ran out the double bay doors.

End.

They waited approximately five seconds to chase after her. Ten seconds later, I heard three shots.

Oh God.

A minute later they dragged her carcass back into the building. They hadn't even given her a chance.

"Goddamn it, John," Carl laughed.

"That was fast. Not hardly worth the sport," the blond guy, apparently John, replied.

Carl lifted her lifeless head. "When can we get another? We'll take our time with the next one."

"You think she'll look good mounted?" the nameless balding guy asked.

End!

I was back in the restaurant, slumped with my back against the counter. Dropping the picture and the necklace to the floor, I wept for the loss of Rose Ann. Judah rubbed his ghostly body around my legs and whimpered.

I couldn't breathe. I had to get outside and into the light. I ran for the front door and threw it open, stumbling onto the sidewalk.

One thought pulsed in my brain—monsters are real. And not just of the supernatural variety.

Deputy Connelly, a very lanky, skinny man, stopped me as I came out of the restaurant.

"Where you off to, Ms. Haddock?"

Damn, I'd forgotten about my protection detail. "Just going to go visit Ruth

Thompson. I'll be back in a little bit."

"No offense, ma'am, but no way in hell I'm letting you out of my sight."

"Deputy. Truly, I admire your dedication. But I think I can safely make the five blocks to Doe Run Automotive safe and sound."

"Uh-uh," he said, rubbing his throat. "I can still taste the shoe leather from yesterday's ass chewing from the sheriff. So, wherever you go, I go. Okay?"

Like I had a choice in the matter. "I suppose." I shook my head, taking in the determined lawman. He reminded me of a cartoon I'd seen a couple of times. "Fine.

Come along, Deputy Dawg."

"Squirrel, ma'am."

"Huh?"

"Not a dog."

"Oh." Deputy Connelly was a weresquirrel. I'd have never guessed. "Got it."

"I'll give you a lift."

"No thanks." The breeze was perfect outside, and it wasn't too hot. "I'd rather walk if it's just the same to you."

"Suit yourself." Connelly tipped his hat to me and went to his car and started the engine. He waited for me to head up the sidewalk then drove slowly down the road, keeping about two car lengths behind me.

"Sunny!" I heard someone call.

It was Sheila. Fan-friggin-tastic. I did not need a dose of bitch today.

I kept walking. She caught up to me. Wonderful. "What?" I didn't even try for polite. She pulled her chin back, hackles rising. "I just wanted to tell you I was sorry—"

"For hurting me," I finished for her. "Fine. It wasn't your fault. Yada, yada. I get it.

Are we done?"

Sheila's eyes widened, and her lower lip quivered slightly. "You mean, you know?"

Weirdly enough, she seemed almost frightened. "It's the brown eyes. You have a very distinctive color to them. It wasn't hard to figure out." I was letting her off for the full-moon attack, so I wished she'd just go away.

"I didn't—"

Neville came out of Blonde Bear Cafe at that moment and smiled at both of us.

"Sunny," he said. "So glad to see you're all right. The sheriff told me what happened. I've heard from Doctor Smith that the boy is going to be just fine."

A sense of relief washed over me. In that second, I could have kissed the mayor. "Really? Oh, good. I'm so glad."

Sheila fidgeted with her belt buckle. "Well, I guess I'll let you go." She swiveled her eyes towards Neville.

The corner of his mouth tugged up into a half-smile. Oh, man! She was sleeping with him, too.

"Did you get those papers filed, Ms. Murphy?" Neville asked. "The ones for the

Community Preservation Project?"

"Not yet, Mayor. I'll have it done this afternoon," she answered.

Ms. Murphy and Mayor. *As if.* Who did they think they were fooling?

"See you around, Sunny," Sheila said as parting words.

Not if I see you first. "Bye."

"Well, back to the old grind." Neville smiled, his eyes sad. "Take care of yourself,

Sunny."

I watched him stroll down the sidewalk, nodding and smiling at people as he went along. I wondered how many people knew he was doing the bump and grind with his secretary. In this small town, probably everyone.

Ick. I didn't even want to think about it.

When I got to Doe Run, Ruth came out of the garage in full coveralls, wiping grease from her hands. "Girl," she said, giving me a light hug. "I was going to stop and check on you today. You didn't have to come all the way down here."

"It's not like you live that far," I said. "Took me five minutes." Not including the awkward run-in with Sheila.

"Do you want to come in for some coffee?"

"Tempting offer but no." *Please say yes.* "I was hoping I could borrow your car to run out to Billy Bob's."

Her forehead wrinkled.

So I added, "I want to see how Jo Jo is doing."

"Let me get cleaned up," Ruth said. "I'll go with you." Now *my* forehead wrinkled.

So she added, "I want to pick up some marshmallow root for my youngest. He's starting to get a cough."

"Sounds like a plan." Was there even such a thing as marshmallow root? I shook my head. It was too strange not to be real.

I told Connelly where we were going, and he followed us out to the shaman's house. Billy Bob's place was a sprawling one-level ranch house. Huge, let me tell you. I wondered why a single guy would need a home so large until I got inside. The whole left side of the place was a clinic. He literally worked from home.

"Very cool," I said with a bit of awe as Billy Bob led us down the corridor to Jo Jo's room.

Brady Corman sat in the chair next to his sleeping son's bed. "What are you doing here? Haven't you caused enough trouble?"

Before I could say anything, Ruth stepped in front of me. "You just watch your mouth, Brady Tyler Corman." She snapped her fingers. "I won't put up with your sass. Especially not with all Sunny's been through lately. She gives a damn about your boy, which is more than I can say for you."

Jo Jo's father winced as if he'd been slapped across the face. Which, in a sense, he had. Ruth had made her words a fist and verbally punched him in the nose. He glared at Ruth, and she glared back. They had a good old fashioned stare-off that lasted several tense seconds. Brady looked away first.

Go, Ruth!

"Well, I don't want to wake Jo Jo," I said, ready to leave now that the situation had become even more strained. "I'm sure he needs his rest more than the company."

"I'm awake," Jo Jo said, his eyes still closed. He flickered them open and looked at his dad. "I'd like to talk to Sunny alone for a minute."

Brady rubbed his face but stood up. I smelled the alcohol when he passed by me, his shoulder brushing against mine. I wanted to tell him that Rose Ann hadn't been a cheater. She hadn't voluntarily left him and their son. But since I couldn't prove it, there wasn't any point. Not yet.

Billy Bob massaged my shoulders for a moment, and the tension eased a little. Finally, he gave me a gentle pat and said, "I'll leave you to it."

Ruth left with him, I assumed to get her marshmallow root, and I was left alone with Jo Jo. I let him take my hand. "Are you doing all right?"

"Yes, thanks to you. The shaman told me if you hadn't been thinking quick, it could have been a lot worse for me."

I'd noticed Jo Jo addressed him as shaman and not doctor. "He's giving me a lot of credit for nothing. I just made a phone call."

"You did more than that, but never mind. Just... thanks. Thank you. That's what I want to say."

I'd put Rose Ann's necklace in my purse, thinking to give it back to Jo Jo, but I didn't know how to explain where and how I found it. I thought, especially at a time like this, he could use something of his mother. Firming my resolve, I took it out.

"I think you should have this." I placed the gold chain with the small heart charm in his hand. "It was your mom's."

Wetness formed in the brim of his eyes. "You keep it."

"I don't know everything," I told him fiercely. "But I do know this. Your mom never wanted to leave you. Believe me when I say, she wouldn't have left you if it had been her choice."

He gripped my hand tightly, fighting back the tears. "What do you know, Sunny?

What did you see about my mom?"

"Nothing I can prove." I pressed the necklace into his palm. "Not yet, anyways."

His eyes searched my face for more answers, but I couldn't give him what he wanted. Jo Jo was still a teenager. Once he learned the truth, any idealism he had left would disappear in the horror.

Finally, he nodded. He held the necklace in a tight fist and brought it to his chest. "Okay, Sunny. But when the time comes, I want to know everything. You may think of me as a kid, but I've had to grow up fast. I can handle the truth."

Some truths were hard even for adults. I was one, and I was barely handling it. I wanted to hug the grown-up right out of him. At seventeen, the only problems Jo Jo should've had were what acne wash to use and what girls to date. "You should rest. I'll check on you again soon."

I passed Brady on the way out. He glowered at me and I wanted to shake him until his brain rattled. I resisted the urge. I'd learned a long time ago, you can't change someone who doesn't want to change.

Ruth and Billy Bob were out on the porch waiting for me. He was disproportionally tall compared to her; hell, even when standing next to me, and I'm tall for a woman. It would have looked strange on Babel, who was perfectly proportioned for his height, but lanky really worked for the doc.

Ruth had a brown bag in hand, which I assumed was the medicinal herb she wanted.

"You ready?"

"I'm ready if you are."

Billy Bob's eyes sparkled like crystals when he stepped out into the sunlight. His dreadlocks, loose around his face, swept past his shoulders. He walked us out to Ruth's car and kissed my cheek. "The swelling's down," he said.

"A little." I smiled, but the sadness in my heart made it feel insincere.

Suddenly, Ruth said, "Oh, and I almost forgot. I'm having a potluck tomorrow night to welcome Sunny to town. I fully expect you to bring your sweet potato casserole, Doctor Smith."

A potluck. This was news to me, but it did sound like a good opportunity to read a few people, possibly get more information on Chavvah.

"I wouldn't miss one of your shindigs." Billy Bob smiled. "I'll be there with bells on."

Ruth squealed with delight then ran back to the patrol car and invited Connelly to the "shindig." I knew if I was going, the deputy would have little choice but to attend.

On the way back to town, I asked Ruth, "How long have you been planning this dinner thingy?"

She grinned. "About ten minutes."

Wow. "I really like you, Ruth."

"I really like you, too, Sunny."

Back at Ruth's, she invited me in for a minute. I was tired and ready to go back to my place, but she insisted.

I quickly found out why when Ruth produced a handgun. "I want you to take this for protection."

I already had Deputy Squirrel; did I really need a gun? "I wouldn't even know how to use one of those things."

"It's easy, honey." She held up the weapon with an experienced touch. She popped a magazine with bullets out by pushing a button on the bottom of the grip. While explaining the fundamentals, Ruth went through the motions as well. "This here is a Ruger .22 pistol. It has a ten-round magazine. You just load your bullets here." She pointed to the butt. "Stick the mag back in. Pull the slide back to chamber a round. Flick the safety off. Aim. Breathe. Pull the trigger to shoot."

Okay, so she didn't pull the trigger, but everything else. She put the safety back on and thrust the gun into my hands. It felt heavy and good to touch. I hated it. "I don't know if this is a good idea."

"Go ahead. You try it."

I managed to get through all the steps, the second time without prompting. It was so much easier to be armed and dangerous than I'd ever expected. I felt like Dirty Harriet.

"Do you feel lucky, punk? Well, do ya?" I said in my best Clint Eastwood impersonation (which really wasn't good on a good day).

"By George, I think you've got it," she said, grinning. I guess if I could channel Clint, she could channel Henry Higgins.

"Loverly," I replied, hoping we'd both stop before we broke out into song.

Ruth laughed. "I think you're smarvelous."

"And you..." I'd never been a fan of guns, but I wasn't a fan of getting my ass kicked all the time either. I put the Ruger 22. pistol, with the safety on, in my purse.

"...are swonderfully nuts."

"You like the classic musicals?"

"Yes, very much."

"We'll have to have a marathon one night. I have all the old musicals on DVD." As an afterthought, she said, "Oh, and it's semi-automatic. So, if some bastard tries to attack you again, don't be afraid to shoot him with all ten rounds.

Impulsively, I hugged Ruth tight. She was quickly becoming a really good friend when I needed one.

I just hoped the bastard who I was hypothetically emptying the magazine into didn't turn out to be her oldest son.

CHAPTER EIGHTEEN

*E*XHAUSTED, I LET Connelly drive me the few blocks back home. His front seat was littered with peanut shells, which struck me as funny. Squirrels do eat nuts. Also, he had a mullet. Again funny. Sort of like a bushy tail.

I thanked him for the lift and headed inside. Ruth made me feel really good about being here, which meant my version of normal was definitely changing. I decided to look over the papers Neville had dropped off. The envelope was upstairs on my small kitchen counter where I'd left it. When I emptied it out on the table, the contents left me gawking.

The pages were blank. Like someone had just shoved a stack of typing paper in there.

Sheila. Of course, it had to be that bee-otch. She was Neville's assistant, after all. Well, no way in hell was I letting her get away with this. I stuffed the blank pages back into the envelope.

I'd march down to the courthouse and give her a piece of my mind. She didn't scare me. Much. My shadow, Connelly, followed me. He waited out in the patrol car when I went inside. Although, as I approached the mayor's office, apprehension plagued me, and I wished I'd brought the deputy inside.

Who was I kidding here with my bravado? Sheila could totally whoop me. I took a couple of deep breaths and steeled myself for the confrontation. Knocking on the door, I felt the twinge of panic rising again. I heard Neville say, "Come in."

I held my head up high, threw my shoulders back, faked a confidence I didn't feel and walked into the lion's den.

Huh. No Sheila but Neville sat behind a big maple desk. The smaller desk in the room was vacant.

"Sunny, hi." He did not sound happy to see me.

"Hi, Neville."

He looked up but didn't get up. "Can I help you with something?"

I sighed heavily. "Well, I'd actually come down to talk to Sheila." *The bane of my existence.* "Those papers you dropped over the other day were blank, and I think she messed with them to mess with *me*."

"I'm really sorry, Sunny." His wide smile was back, and he looked relieved for some reason. "That Sheila can be a pisser. But she's usually very good at her job."

"I'm sure," I said, not hiding the sour note in my tone. I was sure she was good at a lot of things, but I'm not sure the job was one of them. "When will she be back?"

"I'm not sure." He tapped one thumbnail against the other and chewed the inside of his lower lip. "She took the afternoon off for *personal* reasons if you catch my drift."

I not only caught his drift, I was skiing it like an Olympian. All that was missing from his innuendo had been the *nod, nod, hint, hint, wink, wink*. I wanted to stick a spike in my ear to un-hear the intimation. He was implying she was off playing hanky-panky hooky with someone, possibly Babel. *My* Babel. I wasn't usually inclined to hurt people, but I was glad I left Ruth's gun back at the apartment, or I might have been tempted to shoot someone.

"I guess I'll stop by tomorrow. Will she be in then?"

"She's off tomorrow, but I'll let her know you were looking for her."

I saw a picture on the wall behind his desk. A beautiful woman, pale-green eyes, and gorgeous auburn hair. The style of her hair dated the picture to the late eighties.

"Is that your wife?"

"Yes, she was."

The "was" reminding me that she'd died. "I'm sorry, Neville. I shouldn't have asked."

He raised a hand to stop me. "Think nothing of it, darlin'. Life and death. It touches us all in some way or another." The sadness in his voice caught me by surprise. Gone was the charming, slick man, and in his place was the grieving widower. I wondered if the real Neville Lutjen would ever stand up.

He put his politician face on again and tapped his

fingers in a staccato beat on his desk. "I'll see you tomorrow night at the potluck."

I brightened. The small town grapevine was apparently more efficient than AT&T. "You heard about that already, huh?"

"Ruth is our own little Martha Stewart. I also heard you had another run-in with Brady Corman today. Ruth was a little upset about the way he treated you. Don't fret too much. He's become a shell since his wife took off on him, but he's harmless enough."

Was Neville concerned about my feelings? "Rose Ann worked for you, didn't she?" Hah, he wasn't the only one getting news from the rumor mill.

"Yes." He shook his head and clucked his tongue. "She was a beautiful woman.

Good at her job. It's just too bad about her extracurriculars."

He was implying the same thing about Rose Ann that he had about Sheila, but with Sheila I totally bought it. Rose Ann, well, I just wasn't sure. "Do you really think she took off with a lover?"

The word "lover" struck a nerve with him, as if he wasn't used to hearing a woman say it so blatantly. "Yes, I do. You've seen Brady. While he hasn't always been such a mess, I suspected that their marriage wasn't as perfect as they made out. At least, that's the feeling I got from Rose Ann."

Holy smack-down, Neville was as big a gossip as Ruth, but not nearly so nice about it. Even if she had been running around on Brady, I knew from my visions she hadn't left him for another man. Suddenly, I felt very discomfited about the whole conversation. "The Johnsons told me that you saw Chavvah a few days before she disappeared. They said she looked really unhappy. What happened?"

The question seemed to catch Neville off-guard. Good. He placed his palms flat on his desk and leaned forward. "I can't remember. Something about the permits, I'm sure."

He was lying. I could tell it in his voice. Which meant it had to be a real doozy of a lie. After all, politicians lied for a living. I didn't press for the truth. He wouldn't tell me anyhow, and I didn't want to make an enemy of the town's mayor. At least the question had gotten me a little payback for suggesting Sheila and Babel were out doing the hot monkey. "Well, I'd better get going," I said. "Thanks for trying to help with the paperwork."

"You're welcome. Think nothing of it." He didn't offer to walk me out, but did say in parting, "I'll see you tomorrow night."

"Looking forward to it."

I left the courthouse with a healthy sense of doubt. Had I been so wrong about Rose Ann? Not about her demise, but about the kind of wife and mother she'd been?

It shouldn't matter, I told myself. There was nothing she could have done in a lifetime of lifetimes to warrant such a horrifying death. And I couldn't shake the feeling that I knew something more and just hadn't put my finger on it.

CHAPTER NINETEEN

I ROUSED FROM sleep in the middle of the night with a chilling shiver. A daunting awareness crept over me as a light brushing noise sounded across the room. I'd always been afraid of rats, but now I had bigger beasts to be concerned about.

Maybe it was Judah? Even though he was a ghost, I'd heard him bark, whimper, and whine.

Shwish shhhh.

I heard the sound again, and it wasn't no ghost! Too late, I realized I was not alone. But how did someone get in? I'd double checked that I'd locked the door. I'd even had Elbert Smith come over in the late afternoon and put a slide bolt on the back door.

Deputy Farraday had taken over for Connelly when it was time for the young man to go off shift, part of the sheriff's whole twenty-four-hour supervision plan. So, where were the freaking cops when I needed them? I resisted the urge to scream. Slowing my breathing to barely audible, I slid my hand beneath my pillow where I'd hidden the gun Ruth gave me. I felt the cold steel of the Ruger against my fingertips. Did I really want to shoot someone? I'd never believed violence was the answer, but after getting knocked around a few times, I was beginning to think I needed to fight brutality with brutality.

The grip of the gun weighed heavy in my palm. I slipped my finger onto the trigger. My attacker would be a therianthrope. He or she would be faster and stronger than me. I hoped I could pull the gun out and get a shot off before the creature could get to me.

A rattling noise convinced me I had to try. I pulled the weapon out in a not so smooth motion. It tangled on the pillow case, but I managed to toss the pillow to the floor and raise the gun. I squeezed the trigger.

Nothing happened.

I tried to squeeze again, but it was like the damn trigger was stuck. Shit! The large shadow of the intruder moved against the wall. I tried to shoot it again. But still, the trigger wouldn't move. Fear gripped at my throat, choking my breath while my heart pounded in my ears, my hands shaking so bad I could barely keep hold of the useless fucking weapon.

The light came on. I screamed and smacked the gun against my hand to unjam whatever was jammed. When that didn't work, I threw it toward my would-be attacker. He ducked as the gun bounced harmlessly off the wall.

"Sunny!"

I'd been afraid to really look until I'd heard my

name. "Babel?" Jeezus H. Christ and all twelve of his disciples. "I could have shot you!" I panted trying to control the anxiety attack moving into full-blown hyperventilation. "What the *hell* are you doing here? You scared the shit out me!" Which I was hoping wasn't true, but I would have to check myself later.

He'd already moved closer to me and the bed, his eyes on the gun. "Those things work better when the safety's off."

Well, duh. My cheeks were hot with embarrassment. So much for my first time at playing Rambo. "How did you get in?" He'd obviously forgotten the whole "screw you" and "get out" moment we'd had this morning.

"I have keys, remember? Besides, Eldin said it was okay."

"Oh. Well." I huffed. "If Eldin says it's okay, then it must be okay!" If Deputy Connelly thought Sheriff Taylor was scary, just wait until Farraday got a foot up his ass from me. I wore high heels, and I would make sure those bitches hurt. That man would be lucky if he'd be able to sit by the time I was finished. He'd have to stand just to take a crap after I was done.

I held out my hand. "Keys. Now."

Babel sighed. "I made a promise to watch over you, Sunny. That's all I'm trying to do. I didn't mean to scare you."

Yes, I'd been scared, but one thought prevailed in my head, what if I'd shot him? What if I'd been responsible for hurting or even killing Babel?

"Stupid, stupid man." I was shaking all over now. I think I'd had a big enough shot of adrenaline to burn all

255

the calories I'd eaten earlier. Fear was not a diet plan, I reminded myself.

"Can I stay?" he asked.

"You can't. We can't." It wasn't even the anger talking at this point. It was defeat. Sheila was a cow, but I wouldn't be in a tag-team relationship with her and Babel.

Babel's gaze snapped to mine. He looked stricken. "Why? I don't understand why you keep pushing me away?"

There were a couple of ways I could go with this question. He was too young. Too my-best-friend's-brother. Too man-beast. I decided to go with the most honest response. The real reason I couldn't give in to my attraction to him. "I can't be the other woman." Why, oh why did I want him to hold me? Because I felt vulnerable and scared and sad. This too would pass. We would both move on with our lives, but I didn't think time or distance would ever be able to heal my heart.

"You can't be the what?" His shoulders rounded as he leaned forward. "What in the world are you talking about?"

He was close enough to touch now. All I needed to do was reach out. I hated that my entire being wanted his entire being. I scooted up the bed to put more inches between us. "You know. I've been cheated on. I can't do that to someone else, even if that someone is the spawn of evil."

Babel looked even more confused, if possible. "Are you talking about Sheila?" Okay, so maybe he wasn't so confused. Just clueless.

"No. I'm talking about Demi Moore." Gah! I threw up my hands. "Yes, I'm talking about Sheila. You know, your girlfriend!"

"She is not my girlfriend." His denial was like a knife twisting in my gut.

"Your lover, then. Fuck!"

He sat down on the bed and shifted his position until he was right up next to me. "She is *not* my lover." He lowered his voice, making it soft and gentle. Sexy.

"I think you already know that my visions are real, asshole. I know what I saw, and I saw things that make my brain bleed every time I think about it."

"She's not my lover," he repeated. His blue eyes drank me in. I felt myself growing weak and powerless. I took a deep breath through my nose and my stomach jittered. He smelled so good, all earthy and musk.

I would be strong. "Don't lie to me. What about yesterday? You totally threw me over for her, even after she attacked me."

"Sunny, I took her away from you, so she wouldn't hurt you. Sheila is insane. And yes, regretfully, I did sleep with her, but only the one time, and I was pretty drunk. She was Judah's girlfriend. They'd been dating for a couple months before he disappeared. She's kind of fixated on me, but only because she was in love with him, or at least she thinks she was."

He only slept with her the one time? "So, when you were comforting her..."

"I felt bad. I was having a hard time as you well know." Oh, I remembered just how *hard* he'd been.

"When she showed up all bat-shit and stuff, I was afraid she'd really hurt you if I didn't get her away."

"Really?" I sniffed. "You were protecting me?"

"Jesus, woman. You're frustrating."

Tell me about it. He was grinning now and looking so damned sexy I wanted to pounce on him. But I'd been suffering for days, and it was all his fault. Okay, maybe a little bit my fault, but I decided to let myself off the hook and blame him for the most part.

"Damned sexy, huh?" He wiggled his eyebrows and smirked.

Crap. Had I said that out loud?

Babel drew his large hand across his tightly tee-shirted chest. The corner of his mouth crooked up on the right, and he said, "You move me, Sunshine Haddock. I'm sorry if I ever gave you the impression that I might feel any other way."

Okay, I'd seen this tactic before. I liked to call it the "man-pology." And when he leaned over and stroked my arm with his fingers whisper-soft against my skin, I considered complete forgiveness. I couldn't let him off that easy, though. "A body built for sin does not give you an all-access backstage pass to the Sunny Show. Sorry.

Ticketmaster is closed. And the main event is all sold out."

"Come on, darlin'," he said softly.

Damn it! He knew he had me.

"You don't want to stay mad at me, do you? That's not fun for either of us."

"You know what?" I patted his shoulder. "I do want to stay mad at you. I don't need fun right now. And I want to go back to bed and sleep. So, get." I shooed him.

"I'm staying."

My skin went all goose bumps and shivers. "You're going."

"You're not safe." His eyes were soft at the corners, and his mouth was begging to be kissed.

"Farraday is watching the place."

"Farraday couldn't rescue his ass from the toilet." I chuckled. "Could so." At least I hoped he could.

"Could not."

We were quickly disintegrating into schoolyard tactics, soon it would devolve to "did so, did not, did so, un-uh, uh-huh." He kissed me gently.

"Hey," I said against the press of his lips.

"Woman, you talk too much." He kissed me again, his tongue slipping across my lips as I opened for him. I didn't usually like to agree with a man when he was being insulting, but in this case, I thought Babel was definitely right. The passion of our kiss grew intense. I didn't even mind the ache in my jaw. It was secondary to his hands roaming over my body.

He pulled me closer until I was on his lap, my chest plastered against his. Our kiss was filled with passion. He moaned against my mouth, making everything south wet and hot and needful. I wanted this man and I loved everything about him, even beyond the sharp angles of his gorgeously rugged face, beautiful blue eyes, a body any MMA fighter would be proud to have, and an ass you could bounce quarters from. He was sweet and gifted—he moved down my neck with his kisses and nips and licks—sooo gifted.

"Wow," I said, my brain too electrified for anything more intelligent. His slipped his hand between my thighs and I moaned my pleasure.

"Damn, Sunny," he panted, lust shining hotly from his eyes. "You're so goddamned beautiful. So sexy. I want you. I want only you."

Hot damn! My body yearned for him, and I maneuvered to make it easy for him when he tugged my nightgown up over my head and took my naked breasts into his mouth, first one then the other. I squirmed under his talented ministrations.

He rolled me onto my back and got between my legs. With one hand, he stroked me through my panties and I arched to meet his fingers. He stopped for a moment and I glanced down my body at him. His face was slack with desire as he kicked out of his jeans then knelt between my legs, one hand reaching up to caress my breasts while the heat of his breath penetrated the cotton barrier between his mouth and my sex.

My nipples hardened to attention as he pinched and rolled them between his fingertips. I groaned even louder when his tongue swiped at the fabric of my panties. Gah! His teasing of my sex was agony—blissful, orgasmic agony.

I fisted my hand in his hair and yanked him harder to me between my legs. He bit down gently and growled. He worked his way up my body, his fingers replacing his mouth at my nether region, as he took my nipple between his lips and sucked.

"Oh, God," I said, my voice a hoarse whisper. His fingers touched my lips and I sucked the tips. He moaned this time and the vibration against my breast drove me wild. I raised my hips, rubbing my wetness against his stomach.

He made a rumbling noise as his tongue swirled my nipple. He dragged his hands down my sides, his fingers from his right hand finding purchase on my ass, while the fingers of his left hand slipped beneath the fabric of my underwear.

"Off, off," I said, breathless with anticipation.

He didn't bother pulling them down my legs. Instead, he tore the panties in half, leaving me exposed. I gasped, my breath catching in my throat. Our first time together had been fun, but I'd had fun before. This, however, was beyond anything I'd ever experienced. Babel was a man possessed and his craving for my body set me on fire. The feeling overwhelmed me. He kissed me all over, inch by joyful inch, his mouth playing me like an instrument. *His* instrument. And he was definitely hitting all the right notes. I was slick and throbbing. Our bodies slid together as he spread my legs even wider with his knees and kissed my neck and jaw.

He paused, his blue eyes drinking me in. "You mess me up, Sunny. You mess up my world."

"Is that bad?"

"Hell no." He growled a low, possessive rumble. "I want to be inside you, Sunny. I want to make love to you."

"Yes," I heard myself saying without any real thought. My brain was too numb with passion.

"You're mine, Sunshine Haddock," he said, his voice guttural and deep.

"Yes," I repeated.

"Say it," he demanded.

I'd been waiting for this, waiting for him, my entire life. I just hadn't known.

"Say it," he repeated more insistently, pressing a finger inside me as his thumb played over my swollen nub.

"I'm yours," I said, then again. "I'm completely yours."

The tip of his shaft entered me and we both moaned. His mouth captured mine in a tangle of lips and teeth and tongue. He tasted delicious. My body arched and rocked as he stroked his shaft just a few inches inside me and over the sweet spot. I groaned, trying to curve into him, to force him deeper, but he outplayed me and kept up the torturous pace, the ridge of his length tormenting me to the point of rapture.

"Babe," I pleaded. "Babe, please."

Without any more encouragement, he thrust inside me, deep and hard, filling me so utterly completely. "Ah!" I cried out. "Yes, yes."

His paced quickened, and I rocked my hips forward to meet each thrust. Heat pooled to my stomach, groin, and thighs, our sex making me lightheaded and tingly.

"God!" he roared.

"Yes!" I shouted as I exploded in the hardest orgasm of my life. I shuddered and shook and clung to Babel, my hands fisting at the nape of his neck. I wrapped my legs around him, holding him tight inside me until every ounce of the orgasm subsided.

"Oh, Babe," I whimpered, and that was the trigger he needed. His animalistic roar echoed off the walls of my bedroom as he thrust hard three times, his chest bowing forward as he loosed his climax.

"Shit," he said, when he'd rolled over onto his back.

"Yeah," I agreed. We both laughed.

"You called me Babe," he said. I could hear the smile in his voice.

I rolled onto my side and propped myself up on an elbow. "I did, didn't I?"

"Yes." He kissed my left eyelid, then my right. "You did. It sounded wonderful."

I fought to keep from grinning. "I don't know what possessed me."

He stared down the length of his body, then down mine. "Oh, I know exactly what possessed you."

I playfully smacked him, then kissed him as a reward. "We were pretty damned awesome."

His expression grew serious. "You can't be a fling for me, Sunny. I hope you know you mean more to me than that. I'm in love with you."

"I know." I caressed his face. My heart thrilled at his words, and I wanted to shout out my own declaration, but I knew he'd never be happy staying in Peculiar, so I didn't know how we'd make this work. We'd cross that bridge (the only one in and out of town) when we came to it. Instead, I wrapped my arms around him and snuggled in close.

When we woke up the next morning, Babel was curled up behind me. "Morning," he murmured, kissing my ear. I smiled. I really loved the warm emotions swarming in my chest.

We cuddled in silence for a few minutes more, then Babel tilted my chin with his fingertips. "Ruth told me you had a run-in with Brady Corman." When had he talked to Ruth?

Reading my mind (no, not psychically), he said, "I saw her yesterday evening at the cafe. It's why I couldn't stay away last night. It drives me nuts not being next to you, protecting you. I want to keep you safe, Sunny. Don't you understand? I can't lose you too." He let his grief for Judah and his fear for Chavvah fill his expression.

"I'm not going anywhere." I tried to be reassuring. "I don't think Brady wants to hurt me. Not really. He's just got a lot of demons on him." And after what I witnessed about Rose Ann, I could understand why.

"Real demons? Do they exist?"

"No." I snickered. Then stopped. Hell, up until last week, I didn't think ghosts and were-creatures existed. "Not that I've seen anyways. I just mean, the man has problems. I feel sorry for Jo Jo. And his wife…Babel, I have to tell you something."

And I confessed everything to him—Rose Ann, my visions of the hunters, the necklace, the diner check, the dream about the ledger—everything. After I finished, I felt unburdened.

However, Babel looked really angry. "I'll kill those bastards."

Oh man, the way they'd caged Rose Ann, I hadn't thought. They must have done the same to Judah. Kept him locked up like an animal until it was time to hunt.

"Oh, Babe." I stroked his cheek.

He turned to me, the hard lines around his eyes softening. "I like it when you call me

Babe."

"Why?" I liked that he liked it, but everyone called him Babe.

He blinked, measured, as if in slow motion. "Because when you say it, you mean it."

I was having one of those hands-clenched-to-chest moments. The emotion overwhelmed me. Avoider that I am, I changed the subject. "You going to Ruth's tonight?"

"Do you want me there?"

He was playing with me. "Silly man. Of course, I want you there. I need a date, after all."

"Cool." He rubbed his thumb over the curve of my thigh. "You think Judah figured out what happened to Corman's wife and that's why he was taken?"

"I'm not a hundred percent sure, but yes, that's what I think. And I think Chavvah figured out who is behind all this. Babe, I think she might've been taken."

"Damn it. You can't even know how frustrating this is for me."

"I know." I smoothed my hand through his hair. "Me too."

"No, you don't understand. I gave up. After one year, I just gave up on Judah. Ready to just throw away my brother because I was done." His eyes brimmed with unshed tears.

"And now Chavvah..."

I finally understood. Babel was ashamed and angry at himself. He felt like he'd failed Judah. "Don't say that. Don't be so hard on yourself."

"I went back to Kansas City and left Chavvie to deal with all this. I'm worse than a coward. I couldn't face the not knowing and I ran away." He sat up on the edge of the bed and put his head in his hands.

I understood the desire to run. I'd been doing it my whole life. "I'm not a big believer in fate, Babe. But I'm here for a reason. We'll find these bastards and we'll make them pay."

I got up walked around the bed to him and tilted his chin up. I looked him straight in his baby blues. "I promise you, I won't give up until I know exactly who is responsible for what happened to Judah and Chavvah is safely back home." I hoped I wasn't lying about Chav, but after looking at those numbers again, I was pretty sure the "07" had been July. It was possible they only hunted in July, and July was a few weeks away, and still, it would have to be a night of a full moon. If I was right, Chav was alive.

Babel's hands fisted my hair. "God, you're beautiful."

Judah picked that time to show up. I waved him away with my hand as I took Babe's mouth hostage with a kiss that quickly grew passionate. I'd never had a man want me so goddamn bad before, and the feeling was completely mutual.

CHAPTER TWENTY

AFTER THE FULL Babel treatment for most of the afternoon, hubba hubba, he went home to change for the potluck. Tonight, I planned on doing it up right—curl my mop of brown hair, put on some evening makeup, and wear a dress with heels. I'd show Babel how hot the Sunshine could get. Also, I wanted to look sparkling for the townies. The potluck was an honor. Peculiar, with all its flaws and secrets, would embrace me, even if I had to twist their arms behind their backs to get it done.

It had been really nice of Ruth to put this together on short notice. I liked her so much. I hated that I suspected Tyler, her son, of attacking me. I could still feel that monster's hot breath on my skin when I thought about it too much.

You need a lesson in minding your own business. That's what the attacker had said to me. It nearly paralleled Tyler's request that I "Let sleeping dogs lie."

But how could he have been involved with Rose Ann's disappearance? Tyler would have been eleven years old at the time. If my theory was right, the person responsible for Rose was responsible for Judah. What if there was more than one person involved?

Between the gossip and the random vision or two, maybe something more than good eating would come out of the event. I would do anything to find Chavvah. I couldn't let what happened to Judah and Rose Ann happen to her.

Babel arrived promptly at six in the evening to pick me up. He looked handsome in a black button-down shirt with silver corduroys and a black pair of boots. The boots gave an extra lift to his butt that made it even more delicious—a feast for the eyes. He'd combed his hair back out of his eyes, and he'd even shaved.

Wow, I wasn't the only one sparkling.

I smoothed my black silk dress, just shy of my knees and sleeveless, and it had a slightly daring plunge in the neckline. The black pantyhose I wore were the kind that looked great from the thigh down but had the total control panel around the hips and waist.

This kind of dress needed the extra control.

I wore my grandmother's diamond earrings and a plain gold choker. I had a giraffe neck, and the choker helped the illusion that it was a little shorter.

Babel took a step back and gave me the once over. "You look stunning," he finally said.

"Ditto." I smiled, really pleased.

"You always say the nicest things." He laughed then finally kissed me hello. Arms were moving, hands were groping, and when I pulled back from his embrace, his neatly combed hair was back to its normal loose mess.

Oh, boy. Much more of this and the potluck would be shit out of luck because I didn't think we'd make it out.

"I hope the night doesn't last too long," I told him, my voice full of dark promise.

"From your lips..."

I grabbed my shawl from the stair rail. Babel took it and put it on my shoulders. So gallant.

Outside, it was a beautiful night with a large quarter moon dipping out of the clouds.

"Wanna walk?"

I'd only worn a two-inch heel, which made walking totally feasible. "Sure."

Babel held my hand as we strolled down the sidewalk toward Ruth's. Every block he'd stop and draw me into a kiss before moving on to the next. I felt giddy like a teenager. He made me feel young, vibrant, and vital.

Nearly twenty minutes later we arrived at the party. My hair was a little mussed, and I'd had to adjust my dress several times, but I didn't care. Ruth's yard was decorated with dozens of Chinese lanterns in blue, gold, and red, hanging from string lights that draped from one end of the drive to the other. I was shocked by the turnout. I think nearly all 1,027 residents of Peculiar had shown up!

Okay, that was an exaggeration, but there had to be at least fifty or more people milling around white-cloth-covered buffet tables set on the lawn. There were patio chairs and picnic tables gathered on the right side of the yard. "Holy wow. This is for me?" Suddenly, I felt nervous. What if they didn't like me?

Babel smiled and shook his head. "Come on." He dragged me to the buffet line.

While we waited our turn, I saw Connelly and waved. Crazy squirrel.

Poor Farraday had followed us in—God knows he got an eyeful—and had to show up to the party in his uniform since he was on Sunny-watch again.

I saw Tyler Thompson talking to a man I didn't recognize while he held two identical twin girls on his hips. Ruth's grandchildren. They had on the cutest yellow dresses.

Please don't be the bad guy.

His wife—I recognized her from the wedding photos—went over to him and took one of the girls. They all chatted, perfectly normal. Like there wasn't a serial killer in the bunch.

Jean Taylor stood in line next to me. "Mmm, mmm. It all looks so good," she said.

"It really does." I was surprised to see the sheriff wasn't with her. Should I take his absence as a rejection? "Is your husband coming?"

Jean bit into a slice of cucumber. "Uh-hum. He had to finish up some work, he said. But he'll be here after a bit."

Ruth came out and went to stand between Tyler and his wife. She kissed both her grandbabies on the cheek and gave them a tickle. Turning toward her guests, Ruth saw me. She grinned and nearly bounced her way through the throng of people to get to Babel and me.

"I'm so glad you're here!" She looked around. "It's great isn't it?"

"Great doesn't even come close." I hugged her. "More like spectacular." My anxiousness had a side-effect. I had to pee. "Can I use your bathroom?"

"Honey, you don't ask that a party. You just go."

With a parting look at Babel, who just shook his head at me, I followed Ruth out of the food line and up the steps to the house. A tawny-colored fawn with white spots on his hindquarters ran past me out the door. I jumped out of the way.

"Linus!" Ruth yelled. "What did I tell you about changing in the house?" She patted my arm. "I've got to go take care of this, Sunny. Hope you don't mind. The boy will change back buck naked in front of everyone if I don't stop him. The bathroom's the third door on the right."

"By all means. I can find my way."

The house was full of people as well. Neville stopped me inside the hall. "Sunny, you look splendid this evening."

I curtsied. "Why, thank you, Mayor Lutjen."

"Have you tried any of the food?" He took a bite of a barbecued meatball on a toothpick. "It's really good stuff." The whole house was as packed as the yard, but running into the mayor on the way to the toilet was unexpected.

"Not yet. Had to take a nature break, if you catch

what I'm saying." Of course, the pee-pee dance I was doing should have illuminated for him.

"Oh, then, by no means let me hold you up, young lady." I grabbed the door handle to the bathroom. It was locked.

"Occupied," a voice said from inside.

Fantastic. I wondered how bad it would look if I had to hold myself.

I leaned against the wall, squeezing my thighs tightly together.

"I want to talk to you."

I looked at Tyler Thompson's furrowed brow and nearly peed myself right there.

"I don't know why you don't like me. But it's not my problem."

"I want you to stop filling everyone's heads with nonsense."

"What nonsense? People have died, and you're acting like it's a personal attack on you. I don't get it."

"Whatever happened to Judah, he probably deserved it."

The vision of Tyler punching Judah in the nose flashed in my head again. Along with the vision of the bullet smashing into Judah's skull. "Don't you say that. Don't you ever say that again. I don't know what happened between you and Judah, but no one deserves to be hunted and killed like an animal."

"What?" His surprise shocked me.

"You are a police officer, Tyler. I can't believe the sheriff hasn't shared that little revelation with you." Of course, if the sheriff didn't believe me, he might not have. "Judah was caged until the full moon then hunted like some exotic beast to be slaughtered. Is that what you think he deserved? What could he have done that could possibly make you think such terrible things?"

Tyler's cheeks reddened, his eyes wide in disbelief. "No. That didn't happen." He backed me against the wall. "Liar."

"Tyler Edward Thompson!" Ruth to the rescue. Where had she come from? And how long had she been listening? Ruth grabbed her son by the arm and yanked him away from me. She slapped him hard across the face. "You will not talk that way to a guest in my home. And you will not talk to Sunny like that *ever*. Do you get me, boy?"

He rubbed his face and kept his eyes averted to the floor. "Yes'm," he mumbled as he quickly left the house.

Cripes. I never wanted to be on the wrong side of Ruth's anger. I could see why Tyler hadn't wanted me to tell her about his behavior at the police station. Da-yum.

"I'm really sorry about all that, Sunny. The boy's got a mean temper on him sometimes, but he really wouldn't hurt no one. He's got more bark than bite."

I wasn't nearly as sure. "I don't understand why he dislikes me so much. Or why he hated Judah. I thought you told me they were friends?"

Ruth sighed. "They were. Until the evening Judah confessed he loved me. I tried to tell him I didn't feel the same way; after all, Ed may not be the prize pig at the fair, but he's a good husband. Judah caught me unaware and kissed me. Before I could stop him, Tyler had come in from the garage. He and Judah got into a terrible fight. Please don't think too badly of my son."

"Does Tyler think you were...more involved?" Because all this animosity over a kiss seemed really crazy.

"I told him there wasn't anything going on, but I don't think he believed me. When Judah disappeared two years ago, Tyler seemed to become less angry. At least with me. Until you got to town. I think your gift frightens him. He's afraid you're going to tell folks stuff he doesn't want known."

Tyler was being a mean son-of-a-bitch out of some misguided attempt to protect his mother's reputation. I didn't know if I bought it completely, but he was young, only twenty. Rationality and youth didn't always go hand in hand.

"I'm sorry, Ruth." Damn, there was a lot of apologizing going on. "You know I would never spread gossip about you."

"I believe you."

The bathroom door opened and Elbert Johnson (freckle near the eye) walked out.

"Whew," he said, waving his hand. "Might want to light a match when you go in there."

"Land sakes, El," Ruth chided. "That's what the spray is for."

"Oh, my damn, Elbert." I plugged my nose as the stench worked its way into the hall. "Are you sure you don't have a little skunk in you."

He just chortled as he walked away, fanning his hand behind him.

CHAPTER TWENTY-ONE

WHEN I GOT back outside to Babel, he was sitting at a picnic table with two plates. One all vegetarian. The homespun atmosphere nearly made me weep with joy. *Chavvah would love this so much.* I wished she were there to share the night with me and Babe.

"I made you a plate," he said. "What took so long?"

"You don't even want to know." I didn't know if Tyler was completely off my list of suspects. After all, he still could have been the one to attack me. But he seemed way too surprised about Judah to have known about the hunt. I looked around the colorfully lit yard at all the happy townsfolk and thought, one of these people did it.

"Hi." A girl in a cornflower-blue dress had walked up on us. "Do you remember me?"

Selena. Blondina's daughter. We met at the cafe."

"Oh, yes. I remember. How are you?"

"Well, you were right about that snake Larry. I just wanted to let you know." She held out her hand, and I shook it. Selena looked confused. "Is that how you do a reading?"

"Reading?"

"Yeah, a psychic reading like they do at the carnivals. Only, better cause it's real."

She leaned closer. "What'd you see?"

"It doesn't work that way, I'm afraid. I can't control my visions."

"Aww, come on. Try again." She thrust her hand out again.

Babel chuckled softly next to me. Bastard.

I sighed. "Okay, I'll try." I took her hand. "I want you to think about something you really want to know about. Try to concentrate hard on only that."

She squeezed her eyes shut, completely immersed in the process. I fought off a chuckle of my own. I closed my eyes and focused in on Selena. Every once in a while, my visions would work with my friends back in California, but it was rare.

Suddenly, I had the image of Selena in a cream-colored wedding gown standing next to a young guy in a tux. Deputy Connelly? Holy cow, a squirrel and a bear—talk about an odd couple. I let go of her hand. Her eyes popped open. "Well?" I pointed to the lanky deputy.

"No," she said with wide-eyed delight. "Serious?"

"Totally."

"Oh my goodness," she blurted out. "Thank you, Sunny." She turned toward Connelly. "Oh, Michael..." And off she went to get her man.

The next thing I knew, people were lining up to get their palms read. It became a series of short answers.

"You're going to have a healthy baby girl."

"The company is going to call and offer you the job."

"It would be cheaper just to replace it."

"Your wedding ring is in the corner vent of your bedroom. And I'd take it off the next time before you...you know."

"You can find your remote under the third cushion on the couch tucked way down in the crease." (A man wanted that answer.)

And so on and so forth. I'd never worked so hard for my supper in all my life. Someone shouted, "Do the mayor!" Neville declined with a good-natured laugh and shake of his head. But then they started egging him on more.

"It's okay," I said. "Not everyone's comfortable with stuff like this. Don't harangue the man."

But the crowd of townsfolk was not having it. They wanted their mayor to join in the fun. "Mayor. Mayor," they chanted until finally it got to a point where he couldn't say no.

Like sticking his hand in a snake pit, Neville gave me his palm.

"Think about something you want."

Oh, God. I gasped when I saw him with his wife. She was gaunt with illness. Neville pulled his hand away. His eyes filled with caution. I took his hand again. *She'd lost all her hair with the treatments she'd been on.*

"Neville," she told him. *"I can't handle anymore. Please.*

Our savings is next to nothing now, and the insurance won't pay for it. I'm at peace. It's time to let it go."

He put his arm around her. "I'll figure it out. I'll get the money, Mags. I don't want you worrying over this nonsense. Just concentrate on getting better," he'd told her. "Just get better."

The vision broke when Neville yanked his hand from mine. His eyes were haunted and filled with horror, grief, and something I couldn't put my finger on.

"What'd you see?" someone asked.

I stared at Neville as he took another step back.

"Mayor Lutjen is going to win the next election," I said loud enough for all to hear. The partygoers cheered. I wasn't about to share with all of them that the thing Neville most desired was to have his wife back.

Neville gave a startled smile, but his expression clearly said he knew that wasn't what I saw. He played along. "I guess if Sunny says so, it's in the bag." Then he turned around to his constituents. "But don't forget to vote."

A warm hand slipped into mine, and I felt Babel bristle beside me. I looked up. Billy Bob Beautiful had arrived.

"Do me," he said.

"All right." I gulped. "Think about something you'd like to know for yourself."

"I'm thinking." His gray eyes stared at me with full concentration.

When the vision came to me, Billy Bob was standing near a lake…kissing someone but I couldn't make out who. And it certainly wasn't for medicinal purposes.

I pulled my hand back.

"What did you see?" Billy Bob asked.

"Some things are better if you just let them unfold." I couldn't tell who the woman was in the vision, but she was tall. Much taller than me. It made me happy knowing Billy Bob would find someone.

I breathed a heavy sigh of relief when the antique furniture guy called Billy Bob over. Mostly because Babe had taken my other hand and was squeezing it hard enough to make my fingers numb. He relaxed after Billy Bob was out of earshot. I was proud of him for keeping his cool. I guess that meant he could sit at the adult table tonight.

The sheriff arrived when the party began to wind down. Fashionably late, or rather, unfashionably. He was still in his uniform. He made a beeline directly to Babel and me. He had a tear sheet in his hands, and he was panting like he'd run all the way over to Ruth's.

"Sunny, I think you were right."

"About which part?"

He handed me the paper. It was a missing person hot sheet with the names: James Trainer, Robert Nance, and George Herald. The dates they were reported missing were 07/12/04, 07/18/05, and 07/06/06.

My hand began to shake. I was right about July as well. "But I thought you said there weren't any other people in town with those initials who had disappeared?"

"They weren't from the town. On a hunch, *your*

hunch, I went up to the Lake Ozarks police station and used their computers. I got a list of names of all missing persons in the surrounding areas for those months and years. These ones fit. All three of them are integrators."

"Oh shit."

"Exactly."

Those poor men. I felt sick for James, Robert, and George. The only woman had been Rose Ann, and we had to find Chav. I couldn't have her be the second.

Sheriff Taylor looked as sick as I felt. "Is there anything else you can think of?"

"Yes, actually." I told him about Rose Ann, and how Judah's disappearance tied in with her and the other victims.

The sheriff took notes diligently. My opinion of him changed rapidly as I watched him work his job. "Okay, tomorrow I'll make some calls."

"Thanks, Sheriff Taylor." I smiled. "I'm going to grab the bathroom if it's open." After Elbert's stink bomb, I'd forgotten I needed to pee, and my bladder was giving me a painful reminder.

He raised his eyebrow at me. "I don't think you should be left alone until this gets solved. Your ability puts you in a lot of danger."

"It's the bathroom," I told him.

"That's not what I mean, Ms. Haddock."

"I'll be fine," I told him. Famous last words.

The minute I came out of the bathroom to the deserted hallway, I heard a clicking noise.

A flash of my attacker tapping his fingernails

together struck me suddenly. I knew who he was. Fuck. I thought I might even know why.

Before I could really think it out, I felt a sting on my butt, like a bee sting but worse.

I was out before I hit the ground.

CHAPTER TWENTY-TWO

I AWOKE DISORIENTED. I saw bars and straw. Was I having another vision?

Then I remembered. Someone hit me. Again! Now, why hadn't I seen that coming? The back of my head hurt like a bitch. I looked around, trying to figure out where the hell I was.

"No, no, no," I repeated when it dawned on me I was at the hunters' place, caged like an animal. Now that I was actually here, I found I was in one of those Morton buildings.

The ones that were like really big garages people stored stuff in.

I guess I was now "stuff."

I drew my knees to my chest. My silk dress had a tear up the side, my pantyhose was ruined, and one of my shoes had made it into the cage with me, but my other was missing. "This can't be happening."

I crawled to the edge of the cage and shook the door. It had a thick padlock on the outside. I gave it a jerk. Nothing happened. Why would it? How in the world had I gotten myself into this mess?

I'd been stupid and let my guard down, that's how. But how could I possibly know that having to pee would be my downfall?

"Who's there?" I heard someone whisper.

I turned toward the voice and saw another cage about ten feet away. The woman wore jeans and a red blouse; it was hard to see what she looked like otherwise since she was lying on her side with her back turned.

"Hello," I called. "Are you all right?"

"Sunny?" She knew me. When she turned over, I saw I knew her as well.

"Sheila?"

"Oh, God," she groaned.

"Are you hurt?" I certainly didn't like the woman, but it didn't mean I had to be unkind. Besides, we were both in the same boat without a paddle.

"No. I'm not hurt."

"Sunny?" I heard another voice ask. "Is that really you?"

I had to gather myself before I could talk. I couldn't see her, but I was overcome with elation at hearing her voice. She really was alive! Not a gut feeling, not a crazy vision. She was alive and within shouting distance. I hadn't realized how locked down my emotions had been since I'd gotten her text. Now that I knew Chav was okay, or at least not dead, I choked back a sob. "Chav! Oh, God, Chav. You're alive. Are you hurt?"

"Yes." Her voice was shaky. "But not terrible. My arm is broken, and I'm pretty sure my left leg is as well."

There was more she wasn't telling me, I could hear it in her voice, but I didn't press. We had to figure a way out of this mess before dealing with the trauma of it.

"Could we cut the reunion short," Sheila snapped. "We need to figure out how to get out of here before we are all dead meat."

Bitch. "Are the hunters here?"

"No." Sheila sniffled. "The keepers. Five of them. The hunters won't be back until the week of the full moon."

That was over two weeks away. What did they have planned for us until then? Did I really want to know? If Chav was any indication, I didn't want to know. It dawned on me that Sheila seemed to know an awful lot about what was going on here. How long had she been caged? I'd just seen her two days ago so it couldn't have been longer than that. "Do you know where we are?"

"Goddamn you ask a lot of questions," she grumbled.

She *did* know where we were. "You're honey."

"You're nuts."

Great, nice to know even when faced with imminent death, Sheila would be a bitch to the end. "No. Honey. As in, 'how do you want your eggs, honey'? You had the red ledger with the three previous hunts, before Judah's that is."

"I don't have a clue what you're talking about."

Liar! "You've been taking money to give these hunters a few cheap thrills at the expense of your own people."

Sheila moaned. "Someone kill me now and put me out of my misery."

"All in favor of that idea, say aye," Chavvah said.

I raised my hand. "Aye." I moved around the cage, trying to get to a place where I could see her. No luck. Judah growled at the cage door. I guess he was attached to me and not the town. It comforted me to have him near, though it would have been more comforting if he was solid, and on two legs, with a pair of opposable thumbs. Because, then not only would his presence be a comfort, it would also be helpful. Helpful would have been real good. What would have been really helpful was if he could have brought Babe with him. He would be frantic right now.

The double doors of the building slid open. Two guys walked in wearing coveralls and carrying rifles slung over their shoulders. Sheila had been right; they weren't the hunters from my vision.

"Three for the price of one," the first guy said. He had a thick mustache growing down over his top lip.

The other guy had a big scar on his right cheek. He looked the meaner of the two. "I think our bonus just got bigger," Scarface added.

"I'm not an animal!" I screamed. They needed to stop talking like we didn't exist.

Like Sheila, Chavvah, and I weren't real.

Mustache guy laughed. "Like we haven't heard that one before."

Great, they thought I was a therian. Boy, were they going to be surprised when the full moon came around and I remained upright. They threw chunks of raw meat into our cages along with bottled water. I would have pondered the mixed message there if I hadn't been trying to hold down the vomit rising in the back of my throat.

I yelled at the top of my lungs, "You bastards!"

They laughed, then Scarface pulled out a pistol. It reminded me of Ruth's gun, but the barrel was longer. Oh, how I wished I had that gun now.

Abruptly, he aimed the pistol at me and pulled the trigger. It made a slight whooshing noise, and I felt a sting. The same kind of sting that I'd felt in my ass before I'd been kidnapped.

I looked down and saw a feathered dart hanging from my shoulder. He'd done it so quickly, I hadn't even had time to react. Within a few seconds, I'd passed out.

I woke up some time later. I had no clue how long I'd been out. The lights were still on in the building, which told me absolutely nothing. My body felt off—sluggish and violated.

I slurred my words. "They shot me with a tranquilizer gun."

"No shit, Sherlock," Sheila said. "Why do you think I'm keeping my mouth shut?

Because I like it here?"

"How long have I been out?"

"Nearly a day and a half," Chav said. "Jesus, Sunny. You had me really upset."

"Weak-ass human," Sheila muttered.

A day and a half? So, I'd been gone from town at least two days. Babel would be out of his mind. "Do you have to be so unpleasant?"

She snorted derisively. "I really do."

Bi-otch to the tenth degree! "Are those guys coming back?"

"Do I look like a crystal ball to you?" She turned her back to me. "Just leave me be, will you?"

"Sunny, just quit talking to her." Ah, practical Chav.

We'd gotten ourselves into a fix. Even with the information I'd given the sheriff, I didn't think there was any way for them to find me. Well, screw this. I'd be damned if I was going to wait around for Tweedle-Dangerous and Tweedle-Deranged to come back and shoot me again. I was a Cali girl. I had mad skills.

Oh, who was I kidding? I was in a cage with a bottle of water, some yucky raw meat, a torn dress, and one shoe. Looking around, I couldn't see anything helpful or potentially deadly to use as a weapon. Judah stood near a post about five feet from my cage. He barked. So not helpful.

"Would you consider going back to town and just dragging everyone's ass here for a rescue? That'd be really great."

He growled. Awesome, the spirit was getting pissy with me.

"What?"

"Who are you talking to, Haddock?" Sheila asked. I ignored her.

I watched Judah jump up on the post, and I moved over and craned my neck to see what he was getting excited about. There was a hook sticking out of the backside.

On it were some keys.

I reached through the bars; my arms were short the hook by three feet. Sheila's cage was even farther from the pole than mine was, and considering Chav was injured and out of sight, I didn't think she would have a chance at getting to the keys. Quickly, I started formulating a plan. Not a very good one, mind you, but at it was better than waiting for an untimely death.

With purpose, I stripped off my torn pantyhose and started stretching them.

"What are you doing?" Sheila asked.

Oh, so now she wanted to talk? I ignored her.

Picking up one two-inch black pump, I pounded the heel against the ground. It loosened. I worked it back and forth with my hands.

"You're going to get yourself tranqed again," Sheila said.

"If you can't be constructive," I told her, wiggling the heel as the nail in it slowly gave. "Then just shut the hell up. I don't need a critique from the peanut gallery."

"Shut up, Sheila!" Chav yelled.

Sheila screeched her frustration but finally stopped talking.

I tied one end of the pantyhose around the space between the sole and the spike. I swung it around, and the shoe stayed attached to the hose. Woot! One small step for womankind. If MacGyver could blow up a bridge with chewing gum and aluminum foil, I could get a nail off a post only a short distance away.

I stuck my arm through the bars again, this time with hose and shoe in tow. I swung them out and fell short of the pole and nowhere near the hook and keys.

Shoot! Where was the chewing gum and foil when you needed it? I tried again.

The shoe hit metal with a *thunk*.

At least I hit the pole that time. Encouraging.

"What are you doing?" Sheila asked again.

I screwed my lips into the right position to throw again. It always worked when I played darts. It was all about getting the mouth set just right. I swung the pantyhose wide, and the shoe careened around the pole about a foot beneath the keys. "Shit."

"Sunny!"

"There's a set of keys over there, for shit's sake. I'm trying to get them."

"What can I do to help?"

Oh sure, *now* she wanted to help.

I swung the shoe higher and harder, then let it go. It flew up and caught on the hook. "Yes!" I gave the pantyhose a slight tug. The shoe was stuck on the hook. "Damn it."

I tugged again. A slight tearing sound made my heart beat harder and louder. The damn shoe was stuck, and the nylons were ripping.

Fuck!

I yanked again, harder this time, putting all my strength into the pull.

The shoe flew off the hook, sending the keys to the ground and me to my ass.

"You almost had it," Sheila said with enthusiasm.

Sure, *now* she was all about the Sunny-lovin'.

I reeled in the makeshift grappling hook. If I could get the shoe to the other side of the keys, I might be able to drag them in.

The bay doors slid open again.

"Sunny," Chavvah hissed.

Sheila dropped to the floor and balled herself in the corner of her cage.

I didn't need the warning. I stuffed the shoe and hose under my dress and sat down. They didn't know I was awake yet. So, I leaned against the bars and pretended to be unconscious. I didn't want to take a chance they'd shoot me again.

Next, I silently prayed they wouldn't notice the keys were no longer where they were supposed to be.

No such luck.

"How'd these get on the ground?" one of the guys asked. I didn't peek to see which one.

Insert inward groan. Ugh. I could hear the shuffle of feet getting closer to the cage.

"This one's still out? Damn, usually it don't affect them but a couple of hours."

"She still alive?"

"I don't know. Check her."

"You check her."

Great, they were fighting over who was going to

check my pulse. A few seconds later, I felt an arm brush against me when one of our captors reached through the bars. My pulse raced and I could feel the sweat running down my back as his fingers touched my neck.

Fight or flight, Sunny!

Since there was nowhere to go, I chose fight. I opened my eyes, grabbed his wrist with both hands, and yanked him with everything I had head-first into the metal bars.

He yelped as he dropped down to his knees.

I kept a hold of his arm and pushed it sideways until I could hear the snap, then swiveled on my ass and kicked him in the ribs. His body hunched over. It was Scarface. The guy who'd shot me. I wrapped the pantyhose around his neck before he could get his bearings, then pulled him, smashing his face into the bars again. I saw the butt of his pistol in the side holster at his waist. Thank heavens for adrenaline!

"Hey!" Mustache Man shouted. He was trying to grab Scarface's feet and get him away from me.

Sheila had shifted into full-on therian, tall, large, hairy, long tail, and boobs. She roared her frustration while pounding at her bars of her cage.

I screamed as loud as I could, which stopped all activity. I leveled my gaze at the uninjured guard. "I will snap his fucking neck. I am stronger, faster, and will not hesitate. I will go all furry on his ass and eat his heart. Then after I will eat yours. Do you understand me?" Total bluff. But it got him to pause long enough for me to reach the tranquilizer gun.

I said a silent thanks to Ruth, as I pushed the slide

forward, took the safety off, and shot him in the stomach. Not exactly where I'd been aiming, but it worked just the same. Mustache went down.

A flash of Scarface around the dinner table with a wife and two kids made me sick. "You should be ashamed of yourself, Bob. How can you even face your family when you go home at night?"

A bellow to rival any berserker resounded off the metal walls of the Morton building. At the entrance stood my blue-eyed Adonis. My coyote, my lover, my hero. "Babe!" My heart sang. He'd found me. I'd been impossible to find, but he'd found me.

Babel shifted, the fur on his body bristling out as his bones and muscles formed and reformed, causing his jeans and shirt to rip at the seams. My incredible hunk.

His nose transformed to take on coyote-like length. He was broad, even taller than he usually was, and God, he was savagely beautiful.

I let go of the pantyhose and pistol. He howled an angry roar as he swooped down on my broken captor and threw him like a rag doll against the metal pole.

Quickly he descended on the cage door, beating at the lock with his fists trying to get to me.

"The keys are over there." My voice sounded small even in my own ears. "Over there." I pointed to the floor where they'd dropped.

When I was free of my prison, I threw my arms around him and cried. I'd been brave for as long as I could stand it, and now I just wanted to be held. "Oh, Babe. I can't believe you're here. I can't believe it."

I ran my fingers through the warm thickness of his

fur. His body changed and shifted again under my touch until he turned back to human form. "You had me so scared," he whispered.

"Uh, hellooo?" Sheila said. "I hate to interrupt this beautiful moment, but could someone get me out of this fucking cage?"

"Chavvah's here," I whispered with a ragged breath. "I haven't seen her yet, but she's alive."

CHAPTER TWENTY-THREE

*A*PPARENTLY, WE'D BEEN held in some kind of private hunting compound. Outside the
Morton building laid a vast expanse of wooded area with a road leading up a hill to the right. I wanted to know how Babel had found me, but the explanation could wait until we were safely out of there.

Chav looked godawful. She had bruises and cuts all over her face, and her left eye was swollen shut and damned near black in color. Her right arm was a mangled mess, confirming they'd broken it, and it was already setting wrong. The same with her legs and foot. They were twisted and bent at unnatural angles. *What else had they done to her?* Her chestnut-brown hair fell over her good eye, and I could see it was going to be a question for later. Much, much later.

Eager to leave, I searched for Babel's truck.

"It's up at the house." He gestured towards the road.

"I'm out of here," Sheila muttered and started off up the drive.

"You're not going anywhere, bitch." Chavvah, who was in Babe's arms, pointed at Sheila. "She's responsible for Judah dying."

Sheila began to back up, but I pointed the dart gun at her. "Don't even think about it."

Babel growled. "The sheriff's up at the big house," he told Chav then focused on me. "We took out the men on the road and cabin, and I didn't wait for the sheriff to find you."

"How?"

"I followed your scent from the house." He leaned over, a feat with Chav in his arms, and nuzzled my neck. "I'd know it anywhere."

"No, I mean, how did you find me? And where the hell are we?"

"The sheriff figured it out. Those names you gave him, he cross-referenced names in the hunting license database and found out that this place was owned by three businessmen who vacation down here, almost always in July. A John Weatherly, Carl Perkins, and Samuel Wheeldon. They'd been in trouble with the Department of Conservation in the past, and we took a chance." His expression grew fierce. "I'd have torn up the entire state to find you if that's what it took. When you didn't come back to the party…God,

Sunny. Don't do that ever again."

I melted, inside and out. "Never again. I swear."

"Uh, what the hell?" Chav asked. "Am I missing something here?"

Yikes. Best friend's baby bro. I forgot about that hurdle. "We'll talk about it later."

"Damn skippy." She leaned her hand on Babel's shoulder. "Sheila isn't the mastermind, by the way."

"I know," I said. I'd remembered the nails clicking. "It's Neville Lutjen."

"How'd you know?" Chav ignored the look of surprise on her brother's face.

"When he attacked me in his shifted form, he clicked his claws together in a distinct beat. He had drummed the same staccato beat with his fingernails on his desk when I'd gone to his office. I've noticed it at other times, but it didn't click until right before he shot me with the dart. Add in that his wife needed expensive treatments, and the man became the number one suspect on my list." I looked at Babe and Chav. "I can't believe I didn't see it sooner." I really was a bad psychic.

The sound of barking averted my attention, and I saw Judah up on the road. His body seemed to glow as he paced back and forth. I patted Babel's back "Judah's trying to get our attention. I think he wants to lead us somewhere."

"Wait, what?" Sheila asked. "Judah's dead. How's he going to lead you anywhere?" Chav buried her head in Babel's chest.

"I know," Babe said, patting her gently. "But in a way, he's still here. Sunny can see him."

"Sunny," Chav said. She turned her bruised and swollen face to look at me. Her red-eyed gaze gutted me.

"It's true. Billy Bob told me what you suspected

about me, and you were right." She nodded and put her head back on Babe's chest.

His gaze met mine. "Where?"

"I don't know." I pointed up the road with my free hand and jabbed Sheila in the ribs with the gun to keep her from getting any funny ideas about escaping. One thing I didn't understand—well, more than one thing, but this one was bothering me. "Why did Neville put you in the cage? If you were his partner? I don't get it."

Sheila barked a sharp, high noise. "The fucker killed Judah. That wasn't part of our deal. It was never part of the deal!"

Lordy. She really was cray-cray. What the hell had she *thought* happened to Judah? He'd gone off to the live in the land of lollipops and fairy dust? I'd never thought of Sheila as dumb, but she had me reevaluating my assessment.

I prodded her along while we followed the ghost coyote and headed up the road as it unfolded to the large house. It looked like a freaking country club. Backwoods chic, if I had to give it a name. The place was completely cedar-sided, three stories with party decks and full-on landscaping.

The distraction of its grandeur was all Sheila needed. She pushed me backward. I shouted, "No, stop her!" But it was too late; she was already shifting into coyote form as she bounded into the nearby woods.

"Let her go, Sunny." Babel said. "She won't get far. I promise." He squeezed my hand.

I nodded and reluctantly focused my attention back to the house. The sheriff's vehicle, Babel's truck, and two other patrol cars were parked out front, along with two dark Suburban SUVs. Like the one that had run Jo Jo and me off the road. Tyler Thompson stood beside one of the patrol cars. The front door was open, and the dome light illuminated the interior. Three men, I assumed the other "keepers" were handcuffed in the backseat. Billy Bob, his dreads pulled back from his face, ran down to meet us and took Chav from Babel.

"Doc," she said, her voice weak and tired.

"Shh," he told her. "I'm going to get you fixed up. Don't you worry."

I felt a rush of relief. I knew Billy Bob wasn't Babe's favorite person, but I was glad to have him here. Chav needed more help than we could give her, and we couldn't keep her safe if something happened.

At the front steps of the big house, Judah ran up them and through the door. I took Babel's hand, a sense of dread taking hold of me. "We have to go inside."

Oh man, I didn't want to go inside. I had a feeling whatever was inside would not be pleasant.

Babel put both his hands around mine. "We cleared the place. It's safe."

I wasn't worried about the bad guys. There was something else in here. Something I knew—because I could feel it—would change the way everyone who entered looked at the world for the rest of their lives.

Judah waited in the foyer for Babel and me. There was a large staircase leading to the upstairs, like what you'd see in a fancy plantation house in Georgia. Judah's green eyes stared up at me before he turned and loped behind the stairs.

Completely nerve-wracked, I began to shake. My legs were like puddles of warm Jell-O, refusing to cooperate. Babel slid his arm across my shoulder, and his strength firmed my resolve.

We walked around the stairs to a set of French doors with wildlife scenes etched into the glass. I turned the knob and pulled the left side open.

The trophy room.

I dropped to my knees retching.

Near the doorway, a mountain lion had been stuffed and mounted on a rock, as if lying in wait for its prey. I put my hand over my mouth. Rose Ann.

And not just her. Animal heads lined the walls above a high cedar wainscoting. Moose, elk, lion, rhinoceros, then coyote, coyote, deer, coyote, bear, coyote, and...

Oh, God. Tears fell from my eyes as I held my breath. I saw each of the therians as they were hunted. Images of slaughter after slaughter flooded my mind. My chest tightened. Too much. It was too much.

"No!" I heard Babel's hoarse cry.

Helplessly, I watched as he stumbled forward to the trophy on the end.

Judah.

Not only had these therians been caged and hunted like animals, but they'd also been decapitated for decorations. Their murderers had sat in large leather chairs, admiring their kills while they'd sipped whiskey and smoked cigars.

Sheriff Sid Taylor came around the corner at that moment. He dropped the notebook he carried and turned deathly pale. "How could this happen?" he asked, staggering back.

"This can't happen."

"Sheriff?" I heard Connelly's voice from out in the foyer.

I let go of the breath I'd been holding. "Don't let him see this, Sheriff. No one should have to see this."

"I have to get some air," Sheriff Taylor whispered, his voice barely audible.

Babel was methodically unhooking the heads and placing them on the floor, his grief finding purpose. If I had been a stronger woman, I'd have stayed to help. But I wasn't. I needed to get out of the claustrophobic room before I hyperventilated.

I ran from the house, falling once again to my knees as my feet touched the soil in the yard. Every nerve ending in my body was alight with sensation. Eldin Farraday put his hand on my shoulder.

"Don't touch me!" I screamed. His palm alone made my skin feel like a thousand needles were puncturing my flesh. "Just stay back." I heaved a breath, trying to gain some control, but my body wasn't so obliging.

Farraday walked away, leaving me to my choking grief.

While I was still on my knees, Judah started whining and pacing around me. I glanced up too late as a blur of a shape sailed through the air at me and landed on my chest. The brown eyes of the beast glared down at me as it snarled and snapped.

Fucking Sheila!

I threw my left hand up, and she latched on with her

teeth. Sheila jumped sideways, then tried to twist over me to get a better hold. She wanted control, but she was out of luck. I kicked her vulnerable midsection as she jumped over me again, and with my right hand, I grabbed out for anything close. My fingers closed around a rock.

I cracked her in the head with all the strength I could muster, stunning her for a second. She roared back and brought both her hands together into a collective fist to pummel me. I braced myself for the blow, but before she could strike, a loud blast shook the night air. Sheila looked down at me, shock and disbelief written on her face. Blood trickled from her nose. I shoved her, and she fell over, her hand clutching her chest.

She'd been shot. She collapsed on top of me, and I was too exhausted to do anything about it. Someone pulled her off me. When I looked up, Tyler Thompson stood over us, one hand holding a pistol, the other he held out to me. I took it, and he pulled me up.

Seeing Sheila's dead body made a part of me feel sick and disgusted, but the bigger part of me wanted to dance on her grave. Tyler gave me a nod. I returned it. We wouldn't be best friends, but in that moment, we'd come to an understanding. He'd saved my life, and I would be grateful enough to forgive him for being a jerk.

Once again, the air became thick and heavy with energy. Judah began pacing. Soon he was joined by other ghosts, those of the other fallen therians. All of them, except the mountain lion. There was pressure in my chest and head. I felt surrounded. Suffocated.

A soft breeze fluttered against my cheek. "Excuse me, do you know where I'm supposed to be?" a gentle voice breathed into my ear.

Looking up through hot tears, I saw an apparition of grace. For a moment I thought she was an angel, until I recognized the pretty blonde ghost as Rose Ann Corman. "Rose Ann," I said.

"Who?" She dipped her hand against the black bear's face when he stopped in front of her. "It's okay," she said to him.

I reached out and touched Rose Ann's arm. The woman's eyes widened and there was an electric snap in my finger.

"Oh, my. Oh, no." The serene quality of the spirit disappeared. "My son, my husband."

"They're safe," I told her. Though they weren't well. I left that part out.

She looked around at the other ghosts. "You have to help them," she said with a new kind of determination.

"What can I do? It's too late. I'm too late." Like nine years too late.

Judah rubbed against me. There was a slight pressure, not exactly solid, more like the sensation of a warm breath on my skin. How was that possible? Something had changed in me, something tangible. I didn't understand it, but I knew it had purpose. "Tell me what to do."

Rose Ann beckoned me to my feet. All three deputies, the sheriff, and Babel were outside now, staring at me. "I have to help them," I said, sounding absent even to myself.

The ghost of Jo Jo's mother led me out into the woods. We walked along, passing wildflowers like the ones I'd seen in my vision of Judah's death. I don't know how long it took us, but I didn't even feel tired as we stepped into a small open patch of land.

Before I could think about what I was doing, I was down on the ground digging in the dirt and grass with my bare hands. Babel dropped beside me and began tearing at the ground with partially formed claws. Then the sheriff and the deputies were there as well. All of us, even Tyler Thompson, dug at the hard dirt, pulling at clumps of weeds and grass, our hands sheering on sharp flint rock as we dug below the surface.

"I found a bone," Farraday called out.

This place, this serene patch of land—it was a graveyard.

The spirit coyotes began to howl, the bears roared, the deer even joined in with cries of anger. "What do they need?" I asked Rose Ann.

Then it hit me—her body and head had been kept intact. It's why she appeared in human form.

"Their heads," I said to the men who were working even harder at unearthing their fallen from the ground. "They need to be with their bodies."

CHAPTER TWENTY-FOUR

MILLIONS OF ANTS crawled along my skin, swarming my entire flesh. At least it felt that way. The pressure inside mounted and built until I felt like the energy the spirits were passing to me would rip my body apart.

It needed an outlet. It had to go somewhere—somewhere other than me. Connelly and Thompson had brought the heads from the house. Babel whispered soothing words and kept his hand on my back. His touch helped me stay calm and focused. The energy had weight. A burden I had to carry, but with Babel next to me, I didn't have to carry it alone.

I picked up the bear's head first. His ghost directed me to the right bones. When I sat it on the ground where he'd indicated, his ghost transformed into that of a man.

Kind eyes lit his face. He smoothed a hand up his

arm. "Robert Nance," he said before his spirit turned to light then faded. He was gone, finally at peace.

My burden eased.

Next, a coyote head. The spirit led me again. When he transformed, he was a redheaded, fair-skinned man. "Joshua Landon." Again, the spirit faded.

With each ghost crossing, my flesh felt better, like the force inside me eased out with every soul set to peace. I'd saved Judah for last. I wanted to give him peace, but I'd grown accustomed to him. I would miss him.

When Babe picked up Judah's head, my knees almost collapsed beneath me. I reached my shaking hand out to take it, but I couldn't.

The ghost coyote tilted his chin to meet my watery eyes. He trotted to a spot nearly twenty feet away and sat on his haunches, waiting.

I took a deep breath and held it for a second. I didn't have a right to act like such a baby. I nodded and held my hands out. "Okay," I said. "Give him to me."

Babel shuffled his feet. "I'll carry him. Just show me where."

When the coyote's head was laid over his bones, Judah transformed. He was so handsome—so much like his brother.

Judah leaned forward and touched his ghostly forehead to mine. "Now that we can speak, I need to tell you, Sheila was blackmailing Neville," he said. "I found things at her house, and she confessed to having some sort of scheme going on with him. She even tried to get me in on it." He scratched his chin. Could a ghost itch? "I turned her down. I guess that's why I ended up here."

Judah took my hand then and kissed my cheek. "Thank you, Sunny. Thank you." He sadly turned to his brother and sister. "Tell Babe...Tell him to live, *really* live. It doesn't matter where he is, only that he's happy." He stared at me. "I think we both know where he's happiest. Tell him to tell Mom and Dad that I forgive them for being angry with me, but I don't regret leaving. It was the right thing to do, even considering the circumstances. Also, tell Chavvah that I love her. She's really turned into a wonderful woman." He looked back at me. "And she has great taste in friends."

I blushed. "I'll tell her."

"Oh." He grinned sheepishly. "Tell Tyler I'm sorry about kissing his mom. But, come on now, Ruth is hot. I'd have had to be blind and stupid not to try."

I stifled a laugh. Sooo not the occasion. But Judah really had been a man-whore. "I'll tell him the sorry part."

"Fair enough." He put his hand under my chin. "Take care of yourself, Sunny Haddock. Take care of Peculiar. And take care of Babe and Chavvie. I think you are exactly what they need, and vice versa."

He stepped back, his body turning to light. "Bye." He flared brightly for a moment, then faded.

All the ghosts were gone now. I wiped at a tear trickling down my cheek as Babel put his arms around me. He and Chavvah had both lost Judah two years ago, but now, he was really gone. I wept for both of them, for the loss, I couldn't share but understood. I loved them both, and their pain was mine. I wrapped my arms around Babe and squeezed him tight.

He pursed his lips as tears spilled down his cheeks. "Thank you," he mouthed.

I nodded and wiped my fingers across my face. The sheriff wanted my attention next, and for good reason. The men I'd crossed over needed their loved ones notified. As I gave the sheriff the names of the unknown men, I heard a low whistle. "Wow," Deputy Connelly stammered. "That was freaky-deeky."

No doubt. But how did Connelly know? "Uh, did you see the ghosts?"

"I saw a light each time you did the thingy with their body parts. There it was, then gone."

"Me too," Babel said.

"Same here." Farraday.

"Yep," agreed Tyler.

The sheriff simply nodded.

We had a consensus. They'd all seen the light.

"Sunny," Rose Ann said.

Her voice startled me because she'd disappeared as soon as I'd started crossing the others over to wherever therians go in the great beyond. I thought she'd gone as well.

"Why are you still here? You have your whole body in one piece."

"I have some unfinished business I'd like you to help me with."

What was I? The ghost whisperer? Well, more like the were-animal whisperer.

"I'll help you if I can," I said.

But first, there was Neville to deal with. We would not let this man get away with what he'd done to all of the shifters he'd betrayed. He'd managed to fool an entire town of therianthropes for nearly a decade until a bad psychic from Southern California moved into town. Now he'd never fool anyone ever again if I had my way. I wanted his payment in full for what he'd done to the people I cared about.

A few hours later, the sheriff and his deputies made a beeline for the mayor's residence and pulled up with full sirens blaring. This was like being on an episode of *Cops*! Very exciting. I only hoped the bad guy was still home to get his due. I hummed the theme song *Bad Boys* as I watched them, along with Babel, efficiently break down the front door, guns drawn Barney Fife style as they entered.

I was filled with anticipation as I waited to see if they would come out of the house with Neville in tow. As one of his victims, I had a right to face him. To accuse his ass of these heinous crimes and watch him squirm. With determination, I ran to the door, but Farraday stopped me. He shook his head. "Wait."

Neville was standing near the doorway of his bedroom (I assumed, because I could see a bed inside). Just standing there. Why weren't they taking him down?

"You." I pointed an accusing finger.

Neville blinked, but he didn't say anything.

"Sunny," Babe said, coming out of the bedroom. "You should wait outside."

"Why aren't you arresting him? Or beating him to a bloody pulp? Or something equally warranted?"

"It's too late," Farraday told me. "He's gone."

"But he's not." I looked at Neville.

The mayor shrugged. "I'm sorry," he said. "I never meant for any of this to happen. I just wanted to help my wife."

"Shut up!" He had taken a beautiful love and turned it into a horror show. "Your wife will hate what you've become. She'll never forgive you." The words were fiercer than a fist strike.

"Sunny, who are you talking to?" Farraday asked.

Babe walked up behind me and wrapped his arms around my waist. I sank into his embrace. "Neville." I pointed again. He was in a different place in the room.

"He's dead," Farraday said. "A bullet to the head."

I snuggled deeper into Babel's warm arms. "I know." At least about the dead part.

Billy Bob put Chav into a medically induced coma so he could reset all her injuries, and they were extensive and terrible. She'd been reluctant to tell me everything they'd done to her, and I worried it would be a while before the emotional and psychological scars would heal. In the meantime, I'd promised Rose Ann Corman I'd help her with one last thing, and that last thing pertained to her son and husband.

While Babel wasn't real happy about me spending more time with the good shaman-doc, though he had zero reason to lose sleep over the doc now, he agreed to play nice and keep his mouth shut while we were there. Jo Jo was still in the clinic bed. He'd had internal injuries from the accident, and they were taking their time healing. I felt bad. If it hadn't been for me, he'd have never gotten hurt in the first place. After interrogating the "keepers", we'd found out that Neville had arranged for that SUV to do more than scare us. It was one of the compound Suburbans, and Sheila had been the driver. Jo Jo and I were lucky to have survived.

I'd called Billy Bob from Babel's house, where I'd stayed the night before, and told him about Sheila, Neville, and Rose Ann. I wanted him to ease the way for me with her family.

Billy Bob Smith was in full shaman mode. He wore his leather pants, his face and body painted like when I'd first seen him. And now that I knew he wasn't some really old guy, it was kind of hot. Babel stayed with me when I went inside to Jo Jo's room. I needed his support. I didn't think I could make it through the next couple of minutes without him.

Brady Corman looked sober and miserable; his hands were shaking as he sat next to his son's bed. Since Brady didn't verbally or physically attack me when I entered the room, I figured even if he didn't believe, Billy Bob at least had calmed him enough to keep him civil.

"He's trying," Billy Bob said. "It's not been easy. I've given him some herbs to stave off his thirst for alcohol, but it doesn't really help with the detoxification process much."

Jo Jo looked almost frightened, but the idea of your ghost mom coming to call would be enough to unnerve even the strongest kid.

Rose Ann stood by me and looked on at her broken family, so much grief and love in her expression.

Billy Bob lit a rolled-up thing that looked like a big marijuana joint. A contact high certainly couldn't hurt at this point. When it started burning, though, I realized it was sage, a whole different kind of weed.

He took it around to the corners of the room, chanting quietly while he waved the smoke with his free hand. When he was finished, he told me to begin.

I looked at Rose Ann. "Okay, you're on."

She walked to Jo Jo's bedside and touched the gold heart necklace he was wearing. The teenager's eyes widened, and his hand went to his chest.

"Tell Jo Jo, I'm so proud of the man he's turning into."

"Your mom's proud of you," I said. "She thinks you're turning into a fine man."

"Also, I like his haircut and the dyed spots. He really pulls it off."

I smiled. "She likes your hair," I said when he raised a questioning brow.

"I've missed you so much. If there had been any way I could have come back to you, to both of you," she said to her boys, "I would have."

Tears welled in my eyes, and I didn't know if I'd get through this whole process. I didn't know how Melinda Gordon had managed it every week and into syndication. "Rose Ann's sorry she's missed so much of your lives. She wants you to know she'd have been here if it had been within her ability to do so."

Brady Corman choked back a sob, and damned if I wasn't going to follow suit.

"Tell Brady..." She touched his face with her fingers.

"Tell him he's the only man I ever loved, and the only man who could take my breath. I want him to be the man I fell for all those years ago. The man he needs to be for our son."

I didn't even want to try paraphrasing her words on that one, so I repeated it back to Brady verbatim. His whole shell collapsed then as he wept openly.

"It must have been terrible what you went through. I should have been there. I should have saved you." I could see the shame of his years without her hitting him square between the eyes.

"You couldn't have done anything to save her, Brady. Rose Ann doesn't want you to blame yourself. She wants you to be happy."

"I miss you, Rose Ann." His voice cracked. "I miss you so bad."

I was turning into a big puddle of mush, and when Jo Jo took his father's hand in comfort, Babel took mine, and I let the tears fall.

She kissed them both and turned to me. "I'm ready now."

I nodded. "Rose Ann has to go."

Father and son grieved together as they released the anger they felt towards the world, themselves, and each other.

Rose Ann turned to light. Then she was gone.

Babel and I left Jo Jo and Brady to grieve their loss. At least this time, they had closure, but I wasn't sure how much of a consolation it really was. When we walked outside, the scent of pine and fresh cut grass in the air, Babel wrapped his arms around me from behind and nuzzled my ear. "What's on your mind?"

How could I tell him that now the mystery of Judah disappearance had been solved, and now that Chavvah was safe, I was scared about the future—a future without him. It seemed ridiculous and petty in the wake of what I'd witness with the Corman family.

"Babe, what will you do next?"

He turned me in his arms and stared down at me. "Next when?"

"After Peculiar. I know this isn't the life you want. You have things you want to do, dreams you want to pursue, that don't include staying here."

His gaze grew increasingly intense. "You're a fool of a woman, Sunny Haddock." He dipped his head and pressed his lips to mine as he pulled my body into his chest. My feet dangled as he kissed me good and thoroughly. He cupped my face. "Dreams change.

Happiness happens. And the only thing I want to be doing in the future is you."

I turned my head and kissed the palm of his hand. "You're such a romantic."

He brushed my hair back from my face. "Damn it, woman. Don't you know by now that I love you? If you don't, then let me say it again. I love you." My breath caught in my throat. My heart fluttered.

"Are you going to pass out again?"

"Not this time."

"Then what's wrong. You look pale."

I took a deep breath and laughed. "You love me."

"Yes," he said. A smile replaced his worry. "I surely do."

"Good." I kissed him, enjoying the way his arms felt around me. "I love you too."

CHAPTER TWENTY-FIVE

*I*T HAD BEEN a little over a month since Chav's rescue, when we put out our "open for business" sign just in time for Labor Day Weekend. We'd turned the restaurant into a vegetarian deli with a side of palm reading. I wiped the counters and made sure the place looked perfect. Chavvah had healed physically thanks to Billy Bob, though she still woke at night screaming sometimes.

Several people from town helped us to really pull the place together with painting, plumbing, refinishing the floor, and decorating the small bathroom. Even Ruth's son Tyler. He was totally warming up to me. And watching her son Taylor—who was a little thinner and a lot more pleasant than his twin—with Eldin Farraday, I was pretty sure why he hadn't settled down with a woman.

Soon, the whole town, on this holiday weekend, would be traipsing in and out for our very first potluck hosting. I still couldn't believe we'd volunteered. Talk about pressure!

Neville's crimes had rocked the small community, and we would all need time to heal. They voted to bury his head away from his body, along with Sheila, as an eternal punishment. Way harsh, but poetic. Rest in pieces, Neville Lutjen.

The sheriff, through some legwork, found out where the hunters were located. The *Kansas City Star* reported that three businessmen, John Weatherly, Carl Perkins, and Samuel Wheeldon died in a fire at a private property in Lake Ozarks in early July. Shifter justice had been swift in their case.

Brady Corman checked himself into a rehab center finally. He's getting the help he needs now, and even better, I think he really wants it. Jo Jo's staying with me and Chav at her cabin until Brady comes back home. We manage without getting in each other's way too much. Besides, it's short-term, and I spend most of my nights and mornings at the apartment over the restaurant with Babe.

The bodies, what was left of them, were returned to their families for proper burials or ritual pyres. I tried to attend all the local funerals as a courtesy, but as my psychic ability develops, strong emotions like those nearly put me on my knees.

But today, I told myself, I am going to think happy thoughts. The memorial for the twelve victims is being revealed on the courthouse lawn. It is going to be an event to both celebrate the lives of the hunted therianthropes and mourn their passing. A way for them to always be remembered. Billy Bob had blessed the groundbreaking.

The memorial, called Twelve Wandering Souls, is beautiful garden set off to the side of the courthouse in a large clearing. It has flower and herb beds surrounded by short marble walls, each dedicated to one of the dead. Jo Jo, Chavvah, Babe, and I all helped with the planting.

The interim mayor, Babel Trimmel, is going to officiate the ceremony. Since he has a college education and a degree in public relations, he was perfect for the job, even if it still bothered me that he might be happier somewhere else.

I felt his presence even before he reached his arms around me and kissed my ear.

"You okay?"

"Now I am," I said, stroking his arms with my fingers.

"Gah!" Chav shouted from the kitchen area. "Get a room, you two." She'd been happy for Babel and me, but it didn't mean she wanted our hanky-panky thrown in her face.

He just tightened his hold on me and said, "I love you, Sunny Haddock."

And finally, I believed in a happy ending just for me. "Oh, Babe," I whispered against his neck. "I love you, too."

"Jeezus!" Chavvah shouted, throwing a wet kitchen towel at us and turning on the open sign. "Don't make me break out the hose."

Babel and I smiled at her. My heart wanted to burst

from my chest. I was in love with a man who loved me. Only me. I held out my hand to his sister, my best friend, and she took it.

"Okay, girl. Let's get this party started."

The End

MY FURRY VALENTINE (BOOK 2 - IN BETWEEN)

By Renee George

Weeks away from having her first baby, human psychic Sunny Haddock wants to marry the father and love of her life, coyote shifter Babel Trimmel, on Valentine's Day.

Then disaster strikes.

And keeps striking.

Between the personal maintenance disasters and the theft of their weddings bands, it appears Sunny and Babel's nuptials are doomed. Until their friends in the shifter community of Peculiar, Missouri come to the rescue, determined to give Sunny and Babel a happily-ever-after.

Chapter One

February 13th

Normally, I am not a defeatist. You'll never hear anyone who knows me say, "Boy, that Sunny Haddock sure is a quitter." On the contrary, I am an optimist by nature. However, as I lay on the cold concrete floor of Peculiar Paw-On, my wedding dress ripped and stained red, and my stomach cramping so hard I can barely breathe, I am truly ready to cry "uncle."

At least now I know it is a *who* behind the sabotage of my Valentine's Day nuptials, not a *what*. It doesn't matter, though. As of now, the wedding is off.

Two weeks earlier - 14 days until the wedding...

"Oh. My. God." Chavvah Trimmel, my business partner and my soon to be sister-in-law, gasped. Her dark brown hair, long and thick, spilled over her shoulders as she shook her head, her blue eyes wide with horror. "Oh, Sunny! Did you stick your head in the oven?"

"That would've turned out better." I put my hands in front of my face to hide the ravaged skin. "Don't look at me." The tears stung as they rolled down my raw cheeks. "Ow." I rubbed my swollen pregnant belly and hiccupped. I was five months along, which in the therian world was practically full term. Shifter babies only needed six months to cook, unlike their human counterparts who took a full nine. Even though I wasn't a shifter, my baby certainly was.

Chavvah took my arm and led me to a chair in my small but wonderful kitchen. Babel had painted it a sage green with accents of gold and chocolate brown. On the wall above the coppery back splash, he'd stenciled the words, *Above all else. Love.*

Chav patted my thigh. "Tell me why you took a sandblaster to yourself."

Despite my embarrassment, I managed a laugh. "Well, you know those miracle sponges? The ones that take stains off the wall?"

"You didn't!"

I nodded, cringing at the look of pure disbelief in her eyes. "I'm getting married on Valentine's Day. That's in two weeks, Chav." I held up my index and middle fingers. "Two! And this Missouri winter is killing my complexion. It's bad enough I'm going to be fat in my pictures—"

"Pregnant."

"Whatever! I want dewy skin, damn it." I knew I was being cranky, but junior was putting a lot of pressure on the inside of my ribs, I had constant heartburn, and I couldn't walk three feet without farting. It felt like every part of my body was rebelling against me.

"Sunny." She put her arm around my shoulder. "You are—um, were—beautiful."

I wailed. "I look like I've been kissing the sun's ass."

I saw her mouth twitch and her eyes crinkle at the corners.

"Don't you dare laugh at me, Chavvah Trimmel!"

Chav made an obvious effort to swallow her giggles. She walked to the counter to grab the tissue box, her limp noticeable. I worked at hiding my sympathy. There was nothing she hated more than people feeling sorry for her. Her uneven gait was a result of being kidnapped and tortured by monsters—the human variety—and even though she was a therianthrope, or for simplification, an animal shifter, she would always carry the scars of what those men did to her.

I still felt guilty sometimes. You see, I'm a psychic. Obviously not a very good one, considering I didn't foresee the miracle sponge ripping my face off, but when my ability works, it's wicked accurate. I'd left San Diego, California and moved to Peculiar, Missouri in June, shortly after Chavvah had gone missing. My ability showed me nightmare images and clues to her whereabouts, but it still took several weeks to find and rescue her.

She handed me the tissue box. I pulled out several sheets and carefully dotted the tears from my face. It freaking hurt. "I can't let Babe see me like this."

My unsympathetic baby pummeled me right in the

bladder. Even my own child thought I was a doofus. The little darling kicked again, this time even harder.

"Oof," I said, holding my stomach and crossing my legs.

"Are you okay?"

I shook my head and felt my lower lip jut. "My face looks like a piece of aged steak, I can't tell my ankles from my calves, and I'm pretty sure I just peed my stretchy, unflattering maternity pants. I am far from okay."

"It'll be all right, Sunny." Chav hit a button on her phone and put it to her ear. After a short pause, she said, "Hey doc. No, I'm fine. Yes, the therapy is going well. Yes, I'm taking my meds. No, I'm not overdoing it. Yes, I'm doing my stretches. Jesus, Billy Bob, I'm good." She paused again. "I called because Sunny needs you."

Chav disliked Doctor Billy Bob Smith almost as much as she hated people feeling sorry for her. The aversion to all things Billy Bob seemed to run in the Trimmel family. Babel couldn't stand him either. I think it had something to do with the doc being a lycanthrope, or a werewolf, and not a therian. Or maybe it had to do with Billy Bob being a shaman as well as an M.D. The Trimmels had been raised Christian, and mysticism was a hard pill for them to swallow. I didn't get it. He was a nice man, a competent doctor, and super easy on the eyes.

When Chav disconnected the call, she said, "He's on his way over."

"Wow, he must be having a slow day."

"It's *you*, Sunny." Obviously irritated, Chav went to the sink and filled a glass of water. "So, yeah, he'll come running."

"Are you mad at me?" More tears welled in my eyes, threatening to scorch my burning cheeks. Damn pregnancy hormones.

Chav's gaze softened. "Of course not."

"Oh, good. Will you make me lunch? I have yummy sweet potato gnudi in the fridge. Easy to reheat. Oh, and I'd like some spicy pickled beets on the side. Top shelf on the left," I directed.

She shook her head, grinning as she opened the refrigerator.

"Thank you, Auntie Chav," I sang. I kicked my legs like a happy toddler. "This niece or nephew of yours is hungry." Thanks to my psychic powers, I knew the sex, but Babe wanted to be surprised, so I hadn't told anyone that I'd had a vision of him throwing a football around with our daughter. She would be a hella-tomboy. I smiled, absently rubbing my stomach. She would be strong and fierce, just like Chavvah, and this knowledge pleased me to no end.

By the time the gnudi was hot and on a plate in front of me, the juice from the beets adding a vibrant shade of burgundy to the brown butter sauce, Billy Bob arrived.

When I'd first met him, he had waist-length dreadlocks, but in the past month he'd had his hair cut to his shoulders, and his thick, silvery hair framed his face in a tangle of lush curls. I sighed. A man shouldn't be that beautiful.

His skin was a light shade of mocha, his eyes were a pale shade of gray, and his body... *Oof.* I grabbed my stomach as Baby Trimmel gave me another good kick.

Chavvah cast me a slightly judge-y gaze, and if my face hadn't already been on fire, I'm sure I would have felt the heat rush to my cheeks.

"Hey, Billy Bob," I said, trying to cut through the now awkward tension in the room.

He held a small tub in his right hand. He smiled, and his eyes lit up with humor. "I heard you decided to perform dermabrasion without a medical license."

Chav snorted. "That's one way to put it."

"I've made you a mixture of salves and herbs, along with something to help with the pain." He handed me the container.

I unscrewed the lid and sniffed. It smelled like sweet clover and honey. "Nice. How long will it take to heal my face?"

"A couple of days." He must have seen my disappointment because he winked, and added, "I could always kiss it better."

I didn't even try to fight the grin. Lycanthropes had healing properties in their saliva, and once, after I'd had my jaw dislocated, Billy Bob had definitely kissed it better. Which is the exact moment I knew I'd fallen in love with Babel. The kiss had been all kinds of awesome, but all I could think about was Babe. Babe hadn't appreciated the doc's treatment protocol at the time and had made me promise to forgo healing by kissing in the future. "Nope." I tapped the lid. "Better to heal up the old fashioned way."

Billy Bob laughed. It was rich and melodious. "No worries, Sunny. I added some kisses to the ointment."

Oh thank Heavens! It meant my face really would get better quickly. Slow healing was one of the many drawbacks of being human. "You're the best."

He walked over, tucked his finger under my chin and gave my face a once over. "You really did a thorough job." He placed a brotherly kiss on the top of my head. "But nothing that can't be fixed."

"Thanks," I said with genuine gratitude.

"Glad I could be of service."

"I'll bet you are," Chav mumbled.

Billy Bob gave her a wry glance, but before he could rebut, my front door flew open, and Ruth Thompson rushed inside.

"Sunny!" she shouted.

I stood up, alarmed at her urgency. "What's happened? Babe? Is he hurt?" Ruth had been helping Babel settle into his official job as mayor of Peculiar. He needed an assistant and she needed a break from Doe Run Automotive, the business owned by her husband, Ed.

"Jesus," she whispered, her doe eyes (and I do mean doe) widened. "What happened to you? Did you fall into the fireplace?'

"Focus, Ruth." The baby kicked again, and I leaned on the table. "Just tell me the news before I go into premature labor."

Ruth inhaled deeply to slow her breathing. "Your almost in-laws are driving up here. They'll be here this evening."

"Mom and Dad are coming tonight?" Chavvah said. "They weren't supposed to arrive until the tenth. Where they hell are they going to stay?"

Heart pounding, gut wrenching panic welled inside me. Bile burned my throat. I couldn't entertain Babe's folks for fourteen days, I was barely holding on to my sanity as it was. Besides, they'd already voiced their unhappiness about Babel marrying a human. I found those protests somewhat hypocritical because the Trimmels were integrators—therians who didn't believe in isolating themselves in shifter-only communities. They believed the only way to survive in the modern world was to stay immersed in human culture. Ironically, they blamed me for their children's choices. In their minds, it was my fault that Babel and Chavvah had decided to live in a shifter community.

"I am so screwed," I whispered.

Billy Bob patted my shoulders. "Keep your chin up and your face greased."

"What?"

"You have to layer the ointment on thick and leave it on your skin until it's healed. The formula will make you look like you smeared on bacon fat, but it'll be worth it."

Crap! Panic twisted inside me. "Can't you just lick it better?"

"Sunny!" Chav protested.

Billy Bob grinned. "Not unless I want to get into a dogfight with a coyote."

"Fine," I said grumpily. I opened the tub and

grabbed a handful of the salve. Ruined face. Peed pants. Fat ankles.

What else could go wrong?

Get My Furry Valentine at your favorite eTailer!
www.peculiarmysteries.com

ABOUT THE AUTHOR

I am a USA Today Bestselling author who writes paranormal mysteries and romances because I love all things whodunit, Otherworldly, and weird. Also, I wish my pittie, the adorable Kona Princess Warrior, and my beagle, Josie the Incontinent Princess, could talk. Or at least be more like Scooby-Doo and help me unmask villains at the haunted house up the street.

When I'm not writing about mystery-solving werecougars or the adventures of a hapless psychic living among shapeshifters, I am preyed upon by stray kittens who end up living in my house because I can't say no to those sweet, furry faces. (Someone stop telling them where I live!)

I live in Mid-Missouri with my family and I spend my non-writing time doing really cool stuff...like watching TV and cleaning up dog poop

Follow Renee!
Bookbub
Renee's Rebel Readers FB Group
Newsletter

MORE BOOKS BY RENEE GEORGE

Peculiar Mysteries
www.peculiarmysteries.com
You've Got Tail (Book 1) (FREE)
My Furry Valentine (Book 2)
Thank You For Not Shifting (Book 3)
My Hairy Halloween (Book 4)
In the Midnight Howl (Book 5)
My Peculiar Road Trip (Magic & Mayhem)
Furred Lines (Book 6)

Barkside of the Moon Mysteries
www.barksideofthemoonmysteries.com
Pit Perfect Murder (Book 1)
Murder & The Money Pit (Book 2)
The Pit List Murders (Book 3)

Madder Than Hell

MORE BOOKS BY RENEE GEORGE

www.madder-than-hell.com
Gone With The Minion (Book 1)
Devil On A Hot Tin Roof (Book 2)
A Street Car Named Demonic (Book 3)

Made in the USA
Columbia, SC
14 August 2019